RACHAV

RACHAV

SANDI K. WILSON

Dedication

To my heavenly Abba,

From you and to you, all things flow.
I love you.

Sandi.

Contents

Characters and Places

Helel - satan 'the shining one'
Bo'az - Hebrew for 'quickness'
Ziva - Hebrew for 'splendour'
Rut - Ruth means 'friendship'
Sarah - Sarah means 'princess'
Rivka - Rebecca means 'to bind'
Yitz'chak - Issac means 'he laughs'
Avraham - Abraham means 'father of a multitude
Messiach – Messiah means 'the chosen one or the anointed one'
Noach – Noah means to rest or repose
Shlomo – Solomon is a variant of 'shalom – peace'
Savta – Hebrew for 'grandmother'
Saba – Hebrew for 'grandfather'
Abba - Father (God)

Place Names
Kena'an – Canaan
Isra'el – Israel
Beit-Lechem – Bethlehem
Yarden River – Jordan River
Y'hudah - Judah
Yericho – Jericho
Sh'khem - Shechem
Hevron - Hebron
Mount 'Evial - Mount Ebal
Mount G'rizim - Mount Gerizim
Be'er-Sheva – Beersheba
Gilgal – Gilgal means 'rolling'

Sheetim - Shittim
Bharat – India
Suione – Sweden
Anatolia – Turkey
Charan - Mesopotamia
Kushan – Afghanistan
Gilgal – means 'rolling'
Yam Suph – Sea of Reeds, the Red Sea
Yam HaMelach – Sea of Salt, the Dead Sea

Miscellaneous words
Shalom – peace
Talmidim – a group of students
Cohanim – priests
Cohen - priest
Terroir - the aggregate characteristics of the environment in which a food or wine is produced, including regional and local climate, soil, and topography
Torah - the first five books of the Old Testament
L'vi'im - a Levite
Shofar - rams horn trumpets
L'Chaim - to life
Kodesh - holy
Kittel – robe
B'resheet – Genesis
Sh'mot - Exodus
Vayikra – Leviticus
B'midbar – Numbers
D'varim - Deuteronomy

Prologue

The Meeting

The room was bathed in a soft glow as mist drifted through the open window, curling gently through the air like silver ribbons. It moved with purpose, wrapping itself around every corner of the room.

Standing beside Alexandria's bed was Ruah.

Her presence filled the room with peace. Light seemed to radiate from within her, warm and gentle, like the first rays of dawn touching the sea.

With a smile, Ruah extended her hand.

"Awake, dear one."

Alexandria stirred and opened her eyes.

A grin spread across her face immediately.

"Ruah."

"There is much for us to see together."

Alex sat upright and glanced down at herself.

"At least tell me I'm properly dressed this time."

Ruah laughed softly.

"You are."

Alex looked down and found herself clothed in a flowing gown.

"Well, that's convenient."

Ruah's eyes sparkled.

"Come. Someone has been waiting a very long time to meet you."

Alex followed her gaze.

Near the loveseat stood a woman unlike any she had ever seen.

Long dark hair cascaded over her shoulders. Her skin carried the warmth of the Levant sun, and her rich burgundy gown shimmered softly in the moonlight. Yet it was her eyes that captured Alex's attention. They held both great sorrow and great joy, as though this woman had known the depths of grief and the heights of redemption.

The stranger smiled.

"Alexandria."

Something stirred deep within Alex's spirit.

"Rachav?"

The woman nodded.

"You may know me as Rahab."

Alex found herself speechless.

The woman before her was no longer simply a name from Scripture. She was real. Living. Warm. Beautiful.

And somehow, familiar.

"Oh, Alexandria," Rachav said softly. "What a pleasure it is to finally meet you."

The two women embraced.

Alex felt tears unexpectedly fill her eyes.

There was such tenderness in Rachav's presence, and yet beneath it lay something deeper. A longing. A burden carried for a very long time.

When they sat together, Rachav gently took Alex's hand.

"Daughter, I have desired this meeting for many years."

Alex looked at her curiously.

"Why?"

Rachav smiled sadly.

"For centuries, others have told my story."

Her gaze drifted into the distance.

"Some have judged me. Some have pitied me. Some have reduced my entire life to a single word."

Alex knew exactly which word she meant.

Harlot.

Rachav's eyes returned to hers.

"Yet very few have ever asked who I truly was."

The room grew quiet.

"I was a daughter."

A pause.

"A wife."

Another pause.

"A businesswoman."

A soft smile.

"A traveller."

Then her expression deepened.

"A woman searching for truth in a world filled with darkness."

Alex listened intently.

"I lived among the Canaanites. I witnessed things most people would struggle to imagine. I loved deeply. I lost deeply. I made mistakes. I carried wounds. I believed lies. And yet through it all, Adonai never stopped pursuing me."

Tears shimmered in Rachav's eyes.

"My story is not really about a harlot."

Alex felt her heart tighten.

"It is the story of redemption."

Silence settled between them.

Finally, Alex nodded.

"I would be honoured to hear it."

Rachav smiled.

"Then come."

The room around them faded.

Mist swirled once more.

When it cleared, Alexandria found herself standing beneath a brilliant blue sky beside ancient ruins weathered by time.

Rachav stood beside her, gazing across the landscape.

Emotion flooded her features.

"This was my home."

Alex looked around.

"Jericho?"

Rachav nodded.

"Yericho."

A gentle breeze stirred her hair.

"This is where my story begins."

PART ONE

The Harlot's Heart

1

Rachav's Voice

My culture is something of a mystery to many people, its roots stretching back through the Phoenician and Mesopotamian worlds.

Women were honoured and entrusted with positions of influence within our society. Some were teachers, some were leaders, some devoted themselves to raising families. As for me, my path was destined for another purpose entirely.

My name is Rachav—you know me as Rahab.

History has called me many things: harlot, temple prostitute, sacred prostitute, innkeeper. Some of those titles contain fragments of truth; others reveal more about those who wrote them than they do about me.

I was born an only child to loving parents who did all they could to protect me. Yet even the love of devoted parents cannot shield a young woman from the darker desires of men or from a world that often takes what it has no right to claim.

Very early in life, I decided I would become a business-woman. I would build something of my own. I would rely upon my own mind, my own determination, and my own hard work. I had little interest in the romantic tales and expectations that surrounded me. While others dreamed of marriage and family, I dreamed of success, independence, and the freedom to shape my own future.

Many women resented me for my beauty, though it was never something I sought. It simply was.

I was strong-willed, ambitious, and not particularly impressed by the endless demands of the gods and goddesses that governed our culture. I questioned much of what others accepted without thought. Perhaps that was my greatest strength—or perhaps my greatest flaw.

What I could not have known was that Adonai was already weaving a story far greater than any I could imagine.

I would travel beyond the walls of Yericho. I would meet people from distant lands and cultures. I would experience great joy and profound sorrow. I would witness both the darkness of mankind and the astonishing mercy of the One True God.

Most importantly, I would learn that the labels placed upon us rarely tell the whole story.

Before we continue, there is something you should understand.

Adonai allowed me to live within two very different worlds: the world of the Canaanites and the world of the Israelites. Those worlds often stood opposed to one another, yet each shaped the woman I became.

The story you are about to read is not the account preserved by historians, priests, scholars, or storytellers.

It is mine.

It is the story of a woman who sought her own way, only to discover she had been seen, known, and pursued by Adonai all along.

This is how I lived much of my life—separated from the Almighty God.

But that is not how my story ends.

2

Baba

Baba strode confidently into the Inn. As a man of the Upper Classes, he wore a bright-coloured close-fitting tunic that showed off his large muscular physique, along with tan sandals and several pieces of jewellery. He was a Canaanite, but his tribe had mingled with the Amorites. They were sworn enemies of this foreign god the Israelites always talked about. This could be why he was so tall and why he was so strong, physically.

Today, his long flaxen locks were pulled back in a ponytail, and his skin shimmered bronze from working in the sun. Baba's iridescent blue eyes gazed in the direction of the beautiful Inn Keeper, Rachav, with lust and longing welling up within himself. He didn't know how to ask, so he decided it was best to come straight out and make her an offer.

Her long dark hair had been piled high on her head, using two pins to keep it in place, with long tendrils falling loose, framing her perfectly formed divine face. She wore a simple shift, long sleeves and full length in the body, but in a deep claret colour, making her even more beautiful in Baba's eyes.

Baba had a pouch of gold coins in his possession, and he went and placed them on the bar in front of her. She looked up from her work and smiled at this gorgeous-looking man.

"Baba, how are you on this beautiful fine day?"

He gulped at the sound of her divine gracious voice. "Oh, Rachav, I am very well."

"How can I help you today?"

He looked around and asked if they could talk privately.

"Yes, of course," she replied. Taking him to her private rooms, much to his shock, Baba continued.

"Rachav, I am a man of means. You know I work as a mercantile and travel to many different places for my work." He blushed, then carried on. "I would like to make a transaction with you, please?"

"What kind of transaction, Baba?" Rachav glowed, knowing what he was going to say.

"I will pay you handsomely if you allow me time with you, please?" Baba blushed immediately.

Rachav smiled. He was an expansive brute of force and might, and she had felt lustfully towards him for a while, so she thought this might be an excellent and convenient idea.

"Baba, what are your terms?"

He felt giddy, not thinking that should would actually say yes!

"My terms are when I'm back from my travels, and I come here, we can quietly slip away, and you can give me a few minutes of your time. I will leave a pouch of gold coins for you in exchange."

Rachav felt excited yet remained calm and aloof. "I agree." She extended her hand to shake his in agreement.

She then led him to her bedroom, where they completed their first transaction. There was something disarming about him and his vast manhood. He had more stamina and energy than any man she had ever encountered. Rachav liked this very much, to her utter bewilderment.

They straightened up; she kissed him on the cheek, and he left hurriedly.

In all his dreams of his beloved Rachav, he never considered this the pinnacle of their desire. He had waited for quite some time to lose his virginity, and unbeknownst to Rachav, today had been the day. Battling within his mind, between having entered into an agreement with her and wanting to run back and tell her how much he was in love with her, Baba berated himself.

Rachav returned to work, feeling somewhat odd. Baba was gorgeous. But love was foolish and not needed in her ordered world. Still, she couldn't help wondering about him.

The next time he entered the Inn, Rachav smiled. After ordering a large bowl of stew and some beautiful new wine that had just been delivered, Baba whispered to Rachav. The Inn Keeper motioned to her barmaid Abiah to run the place and took Baba to her rooms.

Baba wanted to talk. He wanted to tell her. He wanted all of her. He wanted to kiss her beautiful full mouth and remove her shift, ravishing the seductive body he knew she possessed underneath. But he didn't dare ruin this agreement.

After months of Baba visiting her, Rachav suggested they have a wine together before their transaction and chat with one another. Baba was elated once more!

She then went to where he was sitting, and with the look of a smouldering seductress, she sat astride him. This time, whilst they didn't kiss, she allowed them time so she could arise. She held her emotions in check with all her might, fighting the desire to passionately kiss him, rip off her shift and roll everywhere with him! While trying to remain stoic in her presence, Baba was internally ecstatic at this progression.

Their pattern emerged, and both of them left their encounters somewhat richer and more at ease. They learned the art of conversation, and Rachav was intrigued and amused at the tales from Baba's travels and encounters across the world.

A friendship developed between them, and they grew to look forward to their time together.

Oftentimes, Baba would just sit in the room with Rachav and converse without any physical touch. He just wanted to be around her. During those times, she would refuse the pouch of coins. Baba would then take them home and put them away, knowing that one day, when she was ready, he would take her far away from here and treat her as the princess he knew she really was.

During one of their encounters, Baba almost confessed his ardent passion and love for her. It was getting so difficult to hold it all in. He wanted to shower her in all this world's goodness, but there wasn't that breaking down of her walls, yet.

3

The Oldest City In The World

Rachav and Alexandria were standing near a dilapidated wall. Scanning her surroundings, Alex surmised they were in the Levant, though she wasn't entirely sure where. Looking to Rachav for answers, the elder of the two seemed overcome with emotion.

"This was my home. Right here, in this very section of the wall, my inn once stood."

"You mean we're in modern-day Jericho, Rachav?"

"Yes, my friend, we are. We wanted to show you the context in which you'll be writing. To truly understand, you needed to visit Yericho." Rachav wiped her tears and smiled gently.

"This place holds so many memories—some precious, others painful. But yes, this was my home in the first part of my life. The part where I lived with a 'harlot's heart.'"

Something in that phrase reached deep into Alexandria's soul and touched her. It was a truth she had lived as well. Those who have lived without the presence of Papa know the aching void all too well.

Rachav began her narration. "Yericho is said to be the oldest continuously inhabited city in the world, with settlers originally living here as far back as 12,000 years ago. It also holds the distinction of being the lowest city on Earth, sitting more than 250 metres below sea level.

"The earliest homes were rounded adobe structures, but over time, they evolved into rectangular dwellings, often two-storeyed—with work areas below and living quarters above. Many had courtyards where cooking took place, keeping smoke out of the home.

"Yericho was known for its flocks and abundant crops. Its water systems were fed by the nearby Yarden River and the Ayn Al-Sultan spring, which still bubbles to the east of the city. The Kena'anites developed a remarkable irrigation system that kept the land lush and fruitful.

"Ibex, deer, sheep, cattle, and donkeys roamed the region. With the ability to store food surpluses, many residents moved beyond farming and took up trades—artisans, priests, merchants, and warriors. Crops were often cultivated outside the city walls in secured enclaves.

"As the city expanded, new quarters were built beyond the original walls. These walls were impressive—three metres thick and four metres high, providing protection from marauders and nomads.

"My inn was in one of these newer districts, right up against the massive city wall. In time, I would come to see how perfectly placed it was."

They strolled along the ruins, Alexandria taking in the silence of the stones.

"We Kena'anites reintroduced urban life. Excavations uncovered our homes and furniture, often buried with the dead for use in the afterlife. These findings give insight into the culture that the Israelites encountered—and largely absorbed."

Alex tilted her head. "I thought the Israelites remained faithful to Adonai after entering the land?"

Rachav gave a sad smile. "Not for long. They soon adopted the customs they were meant to destroy. Papa knew their hearts. He warned them what would happen if they didn't drive us out completely."

She continued, "Herod the Great even built a winter palace here and died in Yericho in 4 BCE. Excavations in the 1950s uncovered a grand facade near the Wadi Al-Qilṭ—likely part of Herod's palace. His Roman-style buildings dotted this region, turning it into a centre of New Testament Yericho.

"Later, during the Crusades, Yericho moved again—a mile east. Eventually, the modern town took root there."

Alex folded her arms thoughtfully. "Herod seemed to build on a whim. Why so many palaces he barely stayed in?"

Rachav giggled. "Pride, dear one. He built because he could."

"The Old Testament Yericho corresponds to Tall Al-Sultan, near the Ayn Al-Sulṭān spring. British archaeologist Kathleen Kenyon led excavations there in the 1950s, hoping to date the city's fall to the Israelites. Most of the walls had eroded, but traces remained. It's believed the city fell in the late 14th century BCE, though precision is elusive. The site was then abandoned until the Iron Age.

"By the 7th century BCE, a new settlement had grown, only to be devastated during the Babylonian exile. Eventually, the site was deserted, and Yericho shifted locations yet again.

"One Umayyad-era marvel still survives—Khirbat al-Mafjar, an 8th-century palace-mosque-bathhouse complex just north of Yericho. Though unfinished due to earthquake damage, its mosaics are exquisite. Historians debate whether Caliph Hisham or al-Walid built it."

"In Ottoman times, Yericho was just a small village," she added. "But under British rule in the 1920s, it became a winter resort. Then came major expansion after it was incorporated into Jordan in 1949."

"You certainly know your history, Rachav!" exclaimed Alex.

Rachav offered a small smile, then looked over the crumbled ruins. Turning toward a narrow path, she motioned Alexandria to follow.

"What is that, Rachav?"

"You'll see, dear one. You'll see."

4

Temple Worship

The drumbeats grew louder with every passing minute. Everyone in the city knew what that meant.

It was time to bring your offerings to the Temple to offer to Astarte and Ba'al. They demanded loyalty and offerings, including food, drink, firstborn animals, and children – specifically babies.

It was this part of their culture that Rachav abhorred. She utterly refused to join in the procession to the great Temple and be a part of this macabre demonic tradition. This was the very reason that she would not have a child. The gods insisted that your firstborn be sacrificed and then placed as the cornerstone of your house if you had a new dwelling. Rachav thought this to be a most debased and disgusting custom.

She went outside and watched all the devotees and worshippers walk up in time to the beat. She knew she would need to keep her emotions in check, but she wanted to scream at these people for being so dumb, blind and ignorant. Men and women danced the rhythmic beat, swaying their hips and whipping themselves into a frenzy. Tambourines were being played, and chants were going up to the chief Goddess and God. Once inside the vast open temple, it was all on – or off if you liked. Astarte demanded sexual activity all the time, with whomever and wherever, the better. Rachav hated this with a passion. Alongside this, the population sort Astarte into performing magic and enchantments in their lives. She was the Goddess of spells, involving rituals, the use of objects, apples, pomegranates, weaving cords into knots – all-out witchcraft to inflame a person's sexual desire or romantic affection.

Looking out over the crowd from where she stood, Rachav noticed the big burly physique of Baba. "*My god, he is perfect in every way,*" she thought. She took a breath and looked back in his direction, watching his every move. She drank him in from afar. She thought lustfully, "*What a god he would be if I let him have his way with me completely and utterly.*"

Rachav let out a slight groan, and then he turned in her direction and locked eyes with her. Holding her gaze intently, he strode over to her before murmuring, "Is the Inn closed?" He burned for her, as she burned for him.

"Yes, but please come in." She walked in, turned and locked the door, grabbed his hand, and virtually ran to her rooms. Whilst she wouldn't allow him to disrobe or kiss her, they rode the waves of pleasure and shuddered in delight several times. Sitting there both spent, Baba holding the bed and holding her back, he rested his head upon her ample bosom. "Woman, you almost wear me out!"

"You better not be complaining, Baba." She looked down into his eyes. Seeing his love radiating towards her, she quietly got off the big brute and offered him a cloth.

"I'm sorry, Rachav, I hadn't planned to come here today and haven't bought a pouch."

"No, Baba, this was different." She turned from him.

"Can we talk about it, please?" He stood in front of her, imploring her.

"No!" she exclaimed a bit too rudely. "You know the rules."

"Argh, woman, you and your bloody rules! What about your heart? What about mine?" He pleaded with her.

"Baba, I think you should go. Maybe you should stay away for a while until we both calm down and get back to thinking properly and honouring our agreement." "Maybe, I should stay away and find a woman who wants to love me completely and doesn't play games!" he bellowed.

"I have never played games with you, Baba! I have never promised or given anything other than the terms of our agreement and friendship! Stop demanding from me what I cannot give!" This time Rachav yelled loudly and intently.

"Well then, I shall go. Goodbye, Rachav. It's been wonderful. I wish you well."

With that, Baba stormed off. Rachav figured she wouldn't see him again, well, not for a long time. She chastised herself accordingly.

"My god, that man is infuriating. I was clear and concise. I never committed to marrying the giant brute! Why couldn't he just be like other men and keep to the terms? And why the hell couldn't I just keep it to a few minutes without all the niceties? And why do I long for

him so! He's a patron, an incredibly gorgeous hulking one, but still a patron. Get a grip on yourself, Rachav!"

Rachav hammered herself in doubt and confusion. She wanted life to go back to before this day. This god-awful Temple offering day, where everyone was out of sorts, out of their minds and lust-drunk on Ba'al and Astarte.

She pulled herself together and opened the Inn, knowing that drink and stew would be plentiful tonight to celebrate their gods and goddesses. Also, being a full moon, it would be quite the chaotic night she dreaded. However, she also knew that this would financially be an exceptionally lucrative night.

True to her predictions, the Inn was noisy and crowded, with men and women climbing all over each other, groping body parts and causing quite the fuss. Drink was being spilt, food was on the floor, and furniture was being ransacked. Suddenly, a booming voice was heard above the noise and cheer of the frantic crowd.

"Citizens! This is a prestigious establishment, and it would behove you to settle down, take your seats and wait your turn. Rachav and Abiah are doing their best to meet your demands, so you either behave, or I will personally pick you up by the scruff of your neck and throw you out of here. Do you understand?" The big burly brute had returned, and with remorse written all over his face, a silent apology went to and fro between Rachav and Baba. Immediately the patrons settled back into a more manageable mood.

Baba made his way over to Rachav and offered to serve the patrons, for which she was grateful. Then, before she knew it, the last patron had left, and it was just Abiah, Baba, and

Rachav left. Pouring them a large drink and serving a large bowl each, the three sat laughing and enjoying each other's company. Abiah decided to leave, so it was just the two of them left.

"I won't come back to the room, Rachav. I would like to apologise for pushing you. I can't help the way I feel for you, but I will leave it there for now. My work is taking me away for a time, so I will be back to resume our agreement at the beginning of the next new moon."

"Baba, you are the last person I ever want to argue with. Please travel safe, and I look forward to your return." She winked at him. "Thank you for saving us this evening. It really did get out of hand!"

"The Temple festivals seemed to have taken on a life of their own now, have they not? People seem to have gone bat crazy!" He blushed and hugged her, swatted her on the bottom, and strode out the door before turning back to wave and smile at her with that glint in his eye.

Rachav thanked the gods that all had not been lost between them.

Just the thought of him, made her quiver.

5

Rachav

Sitting in front of the mirrored bronze, Rachav gently brushed her long brunette locks. Picking up a small vial of oil with hints of sandalwood and vanilla, she gently applied some to her neck, temple and clavicle. Thoughts wandered to some stories one of her visitors had told her. Great miracles performed by a god more extraordinary than those she had worshipped growing up piqued her interest immensely. Tales of seas parting, food appearing out of thin air, and water gushing from a rock! This was either utter blasphemy, or there was more to it than they realised.

After securing her gleaming locks in a loose bun at the nape of her neck, Rachav stood and walked to her dressing room. Something of a rarity amongst the townsfolk of the day, she had been greatly rewarded for her services to the few menfolk who had visited the vast city of Yericho. Beautiful foreign fabrics had been stitched into divine clothing, fit for a queen – yet Rachav knew internally that she was the least among the women who dwelt within these city walls – despite what appearances suggested. Rachav took a gown that, whilst modest, had the hint of allure required.

From humble beginnings to living with the abuse that women didn't mention, the young Rachav had turned her humble abode into a thriving inn. Combining several rooms for travellers and visitors to use, alongside her infamous cooking, Rachav employed others to help with the running of the establishment. Never one to shy away from hard work, Rachav could often be found in the fields, alongside others, ploughing, planting and harvesting her crops.

Rachav knew she was one of the lucky ones, living within a culture that allowed women to choose their own way of life and have their own voice. She knew that some cultures treated their women as nothing more than baby carriers, having little to no option for any life other than what they were told to do. Rachav knew that could never be her. She may not go off spouting her ideas and philosophy, but she knew her own mind and drew her own conclusions on matters. No man would take that ability away from her - ever again.

Many were taken with her divine beauty, and she saw an opportunity arise. She fed her patrons her tasty stews filled with savoury meats, herbaceous herbs and earthy vegetables, and she also served exquisite wines flavoured with juniper berries, mint, honey and cinnamon. A master winemaker had been among her patrons, and their brief liaison had opened up a lucrative deal for the best wine in the city, straight from the palace, to her bustling Inn.

Not one to give herself away so freely to any old patron, Rachav selected and allowed only men of prestige and ability for a fee. This was, after all, a business transaction, not a 'come one, come all' affair!

Somehow, this night was different. Rachav looked out her window at the bright new moon and breathed a sigh of relief. Spring seemed to be coming on, and hope arose within her heart. Sensing change, Rachav looked around her patrons and wondered, *"Will he be here this evening?"* She chided herself for swooning like a foolish virgin!

Heading out to the Inn, Rachav and Abiah seemed inundated with visitors again. Checking them in and ensuring there was enough food and drink for them and their animals, made for a busy night. After the noise died down, Rachav heard someone booming behind her.

"Ah, Rachav, you have outdone yourself tonight! You are looking more stunning than usual!"

"He is here," she noted with glee. The exceptionally handsome and somewhat merry patron, Baba, had come up behind her and wrapped his big burly arms around her waist. Feeling a strange pang within her belly, she whirled around with a steely look and, ever so cleverly, removed his hands from her body whilst smiling into his eyes disarmingly. Quivering inside at his touch, Rachav knew she must keep up the appearance of being in control, then spoke to the great hulking man. "Baba, come sit. Let me bring you some delicious stew. You must be so hungry after your long trip back from your travels?"

"Rachav, my love, you certainly know how to care for me, don't you?" The merriment gleaming in his eyes masked the sorrow he was feeling at that moment, knowing that he would never have Rachav fully to himself. His love for this well-adored Inn Keeper had left the silent pocket of his heart and spilt out for all to see.

He banged his fist on the table in anger and embarrassment. "Bring me my stew, Rachav!" he bellowed, trying to hide his apparent shame.

She smiled at Baba, raising an eyebrow at his behaviour, then turned to the bar to retrieve his bowl of stew. She again glimpsed at this man, someone she had been intimate with many times, yet tonight he seemed so different. Suddenly, she found herself gazing at his well-muscled physique and catching herself going flush in the face!

"Settle down, woman, keep your cool; he's just a patron and no more," she spoke internally. Taking a breath, she took the bowl and set it down in front of him. She whispered into his ear with a quiet boldness that shocked herself, "Once you have eaten, come to me." He smiled gleefully at her, knowing what she meant.

Baba was a man not to be messed around. Working as a merchant in the timber trade, he was responsible for locating the finest timbers for his high-end clients. His travels were all through the Near East and the Levant. Baba's tactics were known throughout the land, and Rachav knew not to mess with this giant of a man. Rumours had abounded that he was a descendant of a tribe of giants, but these things were of nothing to Rachav.

Baba made his entrance known, bursting through the door with a slight wobble. Rachav made sure she secured the door so they would not be disturbed. She took his hand tremblingly, led him to the bedroom, and seated him on the bed. She went about removing her gown ever so slowly. In times past, this was something she had never done. Business dictated that their transaction would be mere minutes; therefore, intimacy and enticement weren't necessary. She stood and then took the pin out of her hair that held her hair in a bun and let her beautiful locks fall, covering her bare breasts, willing Baba to take her ravenously. Baba looked at her, surprised and wantingly, surveying her glorious nakedness, then approached her and covered her mouth with his. He picked her up and lay her on the bed, then, with the prowess of a lion, leapt on top of her. Rachav giggled, and there they devoured one another lustfully.

Rachav sat up, sipping on some water. Baba lay utterly spent from the drink and his desire for Rachav, snoring as he slept. She looked over and saw the money pouch he had slammed on the nightstand and the coins that spilt from within. Confusion enveloped the woman immensely. Rachav made a mental note to return the pouch. This had not been a business transaction – rather an admission.

The longing in her heart was unbearable at this moment, having thought she had mastered the art of ignoring and crushing those feelings completely, rendering them silent. Longing led to loneliness, desire, neediness and eventually love – something she couldn't afford. There was no time to fall in love. That was something that fools did. She chastised herself for allowing her feelings to arise and spill out the way they had and couldn't believe she had allowed his lips to touch hers! What the hell was she doing?

She swung her legs over the bed, went to her dressing room, removed the traces of their lustful encounter, and refreshed herself. Rachav would not admit she utterly adored Baba or that she knew it was mutual. What they enjoyed when they could was going to have to be enough. She slipped on her gown and was getting ready to do more work for the Inn when she heard the man awaken. Rachav looked in at Baba and smiled.

Baba sat up in the bed and looked rather comfortable. There was an awkward silence.

"Are you not dashing out the door as you have done in the past?" quipped Rachav. He shook his head no. She felt a little miffed. *This* wasn't part of the plan. *This* wasn't how they did things!

The hulking male could sense her anguish and just stared at her wantingly.

"Come back to bed, Rachav. I have something special for you," Baba grinned mischievously while patting her side of the bed.

"I can't. We shouldn't. I think you should go, Baba. This isn't how we do things." He wouldn't move. Instead, he sat there with his arms folded, watching Rachav pace up and down the floor, arguing with herself.

Rachav looked at Baba longingly but fought with every ounce of strength she possessed. "Are you going to leave or not?" she almost yelled at him.

"No. I want you to come here and sit down. You're making me tired watching you pace up and down the floor!" Baba smirked.

"This is NOT funny, Baba! How can you sit there in MY bed and act so casually like this is the most normal thing in the world?"

"Because it is, Rachav. This is the flame that you and I have been stoking for years, and yet neither one of us had the audacity to approach it. Now, come here, please – or I will jump out of this bed, pick you up and bring you over here myself!" Baba and his demands made Rachav smile and obey for the moment.

"The time for talking is over, woman." Then Baba kissed her again, disarming her and making her head swoon in chaotic delight.

"Oh, Baba, you spoil me so!!" They both burst into laughter and tumbled around the bed. Baba undid Rachev's gown and enjoyed her again. Groans and shudders escaped from her body – she had never experienced this feeling before, and whilst her heart and mind argued, her body delighted in utter ecstasy.

Feeling the full weight of passion overcome her, she managed to flip the giant man over and rode the rapturous waves like never before. They both felt rigid, and explosions went off inside them. Collapsing on the bed, they both panted for breath.

"Baba!" exclaimed the breathless Rachav. "We've never been like this before." He looked deep into her eyes and drank her beauty into his soul. "We've never allowed this passion to rise before. My love for you, Rachav, is no secret, but why do you fight it?" He implored her with his vulnerability.

"I never wanted to fall in love with anyone. Love equals pain, but I'm getting too old to fight it, or you, anymore."

"Old? My darling, you are but in your prime! You've just proven that!!" He tickled her, and she giggled in response. "But Baba, you know what I am and what I do. It's too late for me to change."

He sighed. "The gods have been kind to us, Rachav. Let's, for tonight, be kind to one another. Tonight, you are mine alone. Is that alright with you?" He stroked her hair off her face, tucking the strands behind her ears. "Yes, Baba. Tonight I am yours alone."

As the morning sun rose, a sleepy and exhausted Rachav opened her eyes. She looked and saw the giant handsome Baba sleeping soundly. She traced the curve of his back, the definition of his arm muscles, and lightly kissed his masculine neck. His flaxen hair spread over the pillow. Oh, how they had poured themselves out as an offering to each other the night before, but Rachav was worried about how things would be today.

She slipped out of bed and bathed herself quietly in her dressing room. Knowing she would receive new patrons at the Inn this morning, she wanted to be prepared. She dared not wake Baba, for he would want a repeat of the night before, and whilst her body ached for all of him, business came first.

Baba woke to find Rachav missing from the bed. "Rachav, where are you?" he bellowed.

"Right here, getting ready for the day. Why are you bellowing at me, Baba?"

"Come here, Rachav; we have unfinished business."

"Am I at your every whim and desire, you big brutish man?" she retorted smartly.

With that, Baba jumped out of bed and, picking up his beloved, kissed her good morning, breathing his morning breath all over her. "Wow, you need some mouthwash, you brute! And put me down!" They giggled and kissed, and then he finally put Rachav down, reaching for his clothing strewn in a heap near where he lay.

"I have business to take care of for the next few days that will take me to Lebanon. I will see you when I return."

With that, he kissed her on the forehead and left.

The aching in her heart was unbearable. It had only been a few days, and she felt she was going crazy. Never had she spent so much time thinking about a man, let alone Baba! *This* was the very thing she had spent all her formative years and beyond trying to eradicate. Love equals pain. Pain needed to be exorcised with pleasure – any kind of pleasure, yet the one who could give that to her was the very person causing her pain! Rachav was a mess internally, so she took herself off for the morning and visited her beloved mother, Yaffah.

"Rachav, my darling girl, it has been a while. How are you?" Her mother instinctively knew when things were out of sorts for her daughter but allowed Rachav to speak her mind.

"Eema, I have done the unthinkable." Tears welled in her eyes. Her mother put her hand on Rachav's arm, allaying her fears. "Whatever it is, daughter, you can tell me."

"Oh Eema, I have fallen in love! Rachav, the great business-woman, has succumbed to the affections of a big brutish giant of a man who says he loves me!"

Rachav's mother smiled. "Darling, it's about time! Your father and I thought you'd be on your own forever; such is your stubborn streak!"

"Eema, you're not helping!" Rachav smiled a tiny smile amongst her tears. "This feels awful. I can't cope with the longing. The questions. The uncertainty. Argh, love does make fools of us, doesn't it?" She and her mother laughed and held hands.

"My beautiful, independent, stubborn daughter. Is this man Baba?"

"Yes, how did you know?"

"Darling, he has loved you since he was a young man. He only ever wanted you. And I would say the gods have heard his myriads of prayers. Everyone in this city knows who Baba loves. And now, you love Baba. How utterly wonderful!" Her mother looked a little concerned.

"But you know he descends from the tribe of giants, don't you, Rachav?"

"I've heard that rumour. What does that mean to me, though?"

"My darling, it means that certain traits run into his family line. I know Baba to be kind and loving, but also, he can have a violent, brutal side that may surprise you."

"Yes, I know of this. It doesn't worry me in the slightest. However, what concerns me is that I didn't even know he's loved me all these years. Am I blind or stupid, Eema?"

"No, Rachav, nothing could be further from the truth. I would surmise that part of your heart shut down when that other dreadful creature hurt you as a child. And that, my darling, would account for your chosen 'activities' that your Abba and I have frowned upon."

"So you know then, huh? You never said anything, Eema."

"Rachav, you have been gifted by the gods with an almost divine beauty that has been evident since you could walk. This wasn't meant for you to use for financial gain, but that is not my business. What is my business is that you open your heart fully to the possibility of being with a man who worships and adores only you and that you treat him well. I want a son-in-law, Rachav!"

Yaffah and Rachav laughed heartily and then walked to the local market together, arm in arm. Whilst mulling around and looking at the latest wares from places throughout the Levant, Rachav noticed some new fabrics that she cast her eye over. Picking up a dark purple heavy brocade with gold weaved throughout the background, Rachav moved towards the vendor to make her purchase. She organised to have some gowns made for her mother and herself and then chose something for her lovely barmaid, Abiah. Whilst deciding which one would suit her, she noticed out of the corner of her eye some beautiful guilded-looking sandals. Trying them on, she gasped at their comfort and their high price. Still, she decided that this purchase was necessary, then found her mother, and they started back towards Rachav's Inn.

"Thank you, Eema. You have been such a tremendous help to me." The two women embraced, and then Rachav's mother returned home.

Rachav spent days serving patrons, cooking her delicious meals for the Inn, making up the rooms and sorting through her paperwork. That wasn't the most fun thing in the world, but it was necessary. Down in the field, she would harvest her crops alongside the other workers and use the fresh produce for her meals.

Almost like telepathy, Rachav knew when Baba arrived back in the city. She felt her stomach thump.

Summoning Abiah, she told the barmaid of her leaving for the evening, then donning her hooded cape, venturing out towards the home of Baba. She had brought the pouch of coins along too, to return them.

Steadying her heart and wiping her clammy palms on her cape, Rachav did something she had never done – she knocked on a man's door.

Baba was sitting at his beautifully hand-crafted but humble table that he had made himself, going over his mercantile orders, having just returned from Lebanon. He startled at the knock; receiving a visitor after dark was unusual.

He went and opened the door and gasped at the beautiful face looking at him. Immediately he picked up Rachav and kissed her deeply, not wanting to put her down. After greeting so passionately, he closed the door and turned to look at his beloved.

"Darling Rachav, I was coming to you shortly. I've just returned and was going through the financials and the plans. Boring as they are, they indeed are a necessity." He looked at her enquiringly.

"Baba, I need to tell you something, and please forgive me; this is so hard." She took off her cape and then removed the pouch of coins, which she handed to him. He put the coins on the table and motioned for her to sit down.

"I cannot keep them. You gave them to me the night when things changed, but I can't accept them. Baba, I am used to money changing over a business exchange, but this wasn't. This was an admission – of our love for one another." Baba raised his eyebrows and started to smile. Seeing that Rachav was desperate to keep going, he stayed quiet.

"Baba, I love you. I want you. I want to be with you, always. These past few days without you have been horrendous. Never have I felt the pang of love and desire so strongly! Please say you still feel that way too?" Rachav felt flushed, utterly embarrassed and worried that she had said too much at once.

"Rachav. I love you. There is no one else, not anywhere else in this world, that I love and adore, such as you. There are no other women I visit. It is you. It has always been *only* you. And it will always be, only you." Rachav gasped, then put her hand to her mouth. "Really, Baba – you've only known me?" She blushed.

"Yes, my darling. Only ever you." He reached across the table for her hand. "My love, trust me. Trust us. Thank the gods, they have shined down on us and brought us together for such a time as this." He smiled and laughed. "About time, really!" he exclaimed. "I know what you do in your business, but I fell in love with you knowing what you do and that you are an outstanding businesswoman. But this isn't who you are – who you are is a woman of great worth and honour in my eyes. I only pray that the day will come when you see yourself that way. Now, be at peace, my love." Baba stood and took Rachav's hand in his, and then she stood before him, looking up into his face, taking in every part of him and breathing a sigh of relief. Smiling at one another, Baba exclaimed, "Woman, I need some of your magical stew. Can we go now?"

Rachav laughed, and they left Baba's abode to head towards the Inn.

She admired Baba having a merry time with some other patrons whilst seated at the Inn. She walked over and smiled at them all. Baba patted her rear and demanded his large bowl of stew. Rachav bought him his meal and then disappeared into her abode.

Readying herself for her lover, she sat in her bronzed mirror, brushing her hair and applying her oils. Baba walked in, but this evening but didn't reek of wine or stumble in the doorway. He secured the door. He wanted no interruptions.

Walking over to where Rachav was seated in front of the mirror, Baba lightly touched the nape of her neck, then leaned down and kissed it. He ran his fingers ever so gently over her shoulders, pushing the sleeves of her dress off of them. "You won't need this tonight," he murmured as he removed her gown. Sweeping her into his arms, he again thanked the gods for this woman's love. He looked deeply into her eyes, noticing the flecks of gold shimmering against the warm brown tones. He'd never seen that before, yet now he wanted to notice everything about his beloved. He laid her down on the bed and held her gently while stroking her hair and contemplating their love. "Baba, you seem so quiet and gentle this evening?" It was more a statement than a question.

"Yes, my love, I was just pondering all that has transpired between us and thanking the gods they heard my silent prayers. I have dreamt of this for so long, and now we are here together; I want to savour every moment. I look into your eyes, and for the first time, I see the gold flecks against the warm brown of your irises. I see the contour of your neck and how regal your gait is. I touch the softness of your hair, and stroking it makes me feel like a child again. Ah, Rachav, you have turned this hardened fool into a soft man! What shall I do now? My reputation will be ruined!" He laughed so heartily, knowing he was being silly, but Rachav, whilst giggling too, knew their entire worlds had changed.

"So, time for sleep then, huh?" Rachav giggled and squirmed as Baba exclaimed, "Woman! Brace yourself!" She laughed and suddenly felt very excited. This evening was different for both of them; this evening, they consummated their newfound love.

Waking in the morning, Baba hadn't needed to arise as his work was done for now. Rachav kissed him gently and watched as he reacted to her touch. Rolling over, he embraced her and looked sleepily into her eyes.

"I love you, my darling Rachav. Thank you for such a beautiful night." He kissed her nose, then she too spoke, "I love you, my beloved Baba. I am still giddy from our lovemaking!" She giggled nervously.

"Hmmm, my love, I shall be giddy from the taste of you, every part of you, for the rest of my days!" Then they kissed again.

After supping on a hearty breakfast, Baba left, promising to return later that day.

Rachav swooned as she watched this hulking man walk up the rampart. *"My god, he is beautiful,"* she said under her breath. His profile in the sunlight seemed to shine and appear like a Greek Adonis. And he was hers – all hers. She sighed, then closed the door and went to her chair to have a refreshing drink, and spend some time thinking. This was all so new, so foreign, so scary. Yet somehow, so beautiful in its infancy.

Abiah knocked softly on the adjoining door to the Inn.

"Come in, Abiah. How are you?"

"It seems I'm much more present than you! Long night, Rachav?" Abiah grinned and pushed for information. Sitting with her Madam, she smiled in utter delight seeing this woman she cared for, so in love and passionate about someone, and no longer just about her business.

"May I have the night off, please, Rachav? I need to tend to matters, and I would appreciate a clear head to do so?"
"Of course, dear Abiah. You have been so kind to me, keeping everything running over beautifully whilst I have been in dreamland!" The women laughed together. "Is there anything I can help you with?"

"I should be fine, but for now, an evening away from here and some calm to sort out things will be great. Thank you, Rachav, you are so good to me."

"Ah, Abiah, we are good to each other. Women helping women, that's always been my motto."

"And what of Baba now being on the scene?"

"Well, we will have to work that out now, won't we?" Again, they both smiled.

Rachav could see a lot going on for Abiah but knew she would confide in her when the time was right. For now, Abiah needed solace, and quite frankly, Rachav herself could do with some normality – and physical rest. That man was outstanding in his love for her but exhausting!

Noticing several new patrons within the Inn, Rachav inquired whether any were actually staying. Abiah laughed!

"Rachav, all the rooms are booked and have been for several weeks now. You've been somewhat preoccupied, but I've handled everything fine."

Rachav felt a tinge of pain and regret that she'd been so self-absorbed. Yet she was so grateful that she had such loyalty in Abiah.

Rachav readied the Inn, prepared the meals, and ensured the current patrons had all they needed. She went out to the barn, saw plenty of animals using the facility, and noted new hay and water should be replenished as soon as possible.

Rachav could feel herself getting rather tired and grumpy as the nighttime wore on. No one was to blame, but she did need to rest, and if Baba were going to stay, he would need to understand that.

As he entered the Inn, he went up and placed his arms around Rachav. Unlike previous times when he'd tried to be affectionate in public, she enjoyed his presence immensely. Patrons noted the loved-up couple and started to whistle at them. Baba waved his hand and laughed. Rachav smiled at her beloved. He was the best thing to have ever happened to her, and she would make sure she reminded him of it.

Life together proceeded for Rachav and Baba at a beautiful rate. Their love grew and nourished the parts of each other's souls that had been so empty and starving. Taking in the beauty of their surroundings, they walked atop the walls surrounding their large city and strode inland towards some lush, dense forest. It had been the longest time since Rachav had visited here, and she delighted in its quietness and calm outside the bustle of their typical day.

Having found the waterfall Baba mentioned before, they found themselves alone and stripped down to enter the pool at the base. Feeling the cool water over her skin was pure heaven for Rachav as she dove under the clear water and felt her way around. A little distance from her was Baba watching whilst paddling around. He swam over to her, and they drank each other in to their delight and melted on the pool's edge afterwards. Finding a secluded and private place in the sun, they lay down and enjoyed their time in nature. They clothed themselves once the sun had waned and started walking back to the Inn. They hurried on because the gate to the city was always locked, just at dark. Once inside the gate, they made their way back to the Inn and helped themselves to some stew, having been utterly famished from their physical exertion.

Abiah approached Rachav and handed her a goblet of wine, which the Madam was grateful for since she was parched from their time outside the city. The barmaid couldn't help noticing her Madam was mesmerised by the large gentleman Baba and smiled to herself. She'd never seen Rachav like this and wondered when he would ask her 'the' question.

6

Astarte The Chameleon

Here stands the Queen of Heaven. This lustful, passionate deity who demanded worship, sexual exploits and blood-lust at all times.

To the Israelites, she was Ashtoreth.

To the Kena'anites, she was Astarte, Queen of Heaven and consort to Ba'al.

To Sumerians, she was Inanna.

To the Assyrians, Babylonians and Mesopotamians, she was Ishtar.

To the Greeks, she was Aphrodite.

And to the Romans, she was Venus.

She is the Goddess. The Transgressor. The Enchantress. The Seductress. A goddess of magic and spells, specialising in love magic, altering one's affections and behaviour. She seized upon and completely possessed her worshippers, moving throughout her priests and prostitutes, who served as her vessels. Her worship was engrossed with carnal pleasure, sensual delights, and sexuality.

Every woman within the land was expected to perform acts of prostitution at least once in her life, charging for the pleasure to satisfy this goddess.

Astarte was infamous for her ability to flout the convention of the day and break rules when and where it suited her.

Her perverse will and desires led to the Queen's unbridled passions. There was no thought of not getting her way, and she would eliminate all who tried to stop her. Her bloodlust for war was infamous also; she was the original Warrior Woman.

Even though she was consort to Ba'al, Astarte hated marriage and anything that got in the way of her pleasure. She would think nothing of tossing her husband aside for another lover and push the taboos of culture if it served her. She had no interest or knowledge that her actions had dire consequences. She lived as she pleased at all times.

Adding to the allure she portrayed to the average citizen were the intoxicating potions she blended that would make any man or woman putty in her hands. She was the Patron of the Inn; therefore, those businesses were usually the most lucrative and hedonistic. Adding to the consumption of the typical beer and the not-so-common wine, were herbs that had been blended to give the illusion of relaxation. She knew how to send men and women into a psychedelic spell when it suited her. Of course, these became a lucrative trade in her empire, too.

Astarte was also known as the morning and evening star. Her duality meant she would be at the polar ends of both the planetary and gender spectrum.

On the one hand, being the Queen of Heaven, the goddess of love, the goddess of beauty and sexuality, were also tempered with her ferocity, aggressive behaviour and fascination with war. She had the unusual ability to turn from being a woman into a man. It was her nature to bend and transform to her own will and desires.

Not being known for her compassionate or maternal side, Astarte was more known for her sexual pleasures and her more masculine characteristics. She was courageous and fierce and fought in wars with other men, frequently appearing as the winner.

"Her androgyny is attested to in her cultic personnel, which included eunuchs and transvestites and during her festivals, young men carried hoops, a feminine symbol, while young women carried swords." *

Alongside her androgyny, Astarte promoted homosexuality with her priests and priestesses. Nothing was off limits to her, and she would often have the priesthood walking around with clothing and makeup of the opposite sex.

"Astarte's consort Ba'al was an entirely different God. His worshippers prayed to him to make fertile soil and cause their crops to grow. He was the God who rode the clouds and was Lord of the storms. He was the one who hurled down bolts of lightning on the earth. He was a warrior, most known and notorious amongst the Israelites. He was the chief God of the Kena'anite pantheon."*

And he had no control over his Queen Consort, Astarte.

Ba'al was very much entwined in the Israelite culture. He aimed to derail Yahweh as their One True God, and therefore he promised the Israelites fertility, fruitfulness, increase, gain and prosperity, in turn for their complete worship and adoration. Ba'al so infiltrated the Israelite culture that he was directly affiliated with their falling away from Yahweh and its subsequent destruction. So great was Ba'al's thirst for Israelite worship; he went after the next generation by implementing child sacrifice to the god Molech. The smell of the blood and human flesh frequently blew over to distant shores, causing others to shudder at this demonic god and his hideous demands.

7

Questions

As a Timber Merchant and Mercantile, Baba had been taught the ways of timber, its uses, and importation for many different utilisations.

Having a high-end clientele afforded Baba much travel, and the ability to be introduced to new ways of improving his expertise, with new materials to take samples off to present to his clients.

Within the Levant, the plentiful timbers were cypress, oak, ash, sycamore and olive, alongside the lesser quality woods of poplar, willow, plane, tamarisk, elm, beech and acacia. Travelling to Lebanon, whilst expensive, was the beautiful cedar tree, that was in high demand amongst Baba's clients.

The giant of a man had learnt to keep his carpenter's tools well-oiled and ready. He never knew when he would be called upon to replace a carpentry worker or want to make his own creations, when he was inspired. Keeping the saw, mallet, adze, plummet and line, chisel, rule stick, plane and squares in tip-top condition was imperative. He also occasionally used a bow-lathe, although a more primitive tool, but being a skilled woodworker, Baba and others could produce decorative spindles and bowls at will. These were very popular within hospitality and in homes.

Baba was particularly fond of Lebanon for reasons he couldn't quite explain. Famous for the purple dye they sold, the people of Lebanon were recognised for their fishing communities, open, friendly hospitality and well-forested hinterland.

Baba returned from one of his trips away and was received with pleasure and delight by his beloved. Laying early one morning in their bed, Rachav asked the question she had been dying to get to the bottom of. "Baba, what do you know about your family lineage? Is it true that you descend from the race of Giants?"

Baba rubbed his face and thought for a moment. "I guess I am, but I don't know what that means. I've always been just 'me' and left it at that. Does this bother you, my love?"

"Not at all, but it's something my mother mentioned some time ago when I confided in her about my feelings towards you."

"You spoke to Yaffah about me? I like your mother. She's always been so affable towards me and made me feel very welcome. What did she say?"

"About the giant story, only that you may have certain traits, and I assured her I didn't care!" She tickled Baba, and he laughed.

"Oh, you mean my brute strength and ability to pleasure you for hours, darling Rachav?" He teased her.

"You must be a god, Baba. I swear, you have superhuman strength in the bedroom!" She laughed as he tickled her now. "Are you trying to distract me while I'm trying to have a serious conversation with you, Baba?" She feigned annoyance at him.

"My darling, I don't need to distract you – you willingly take all you desire of me!"

"Mmmmm, yes, I do!" She slapped him lightly on the hand. "Stop that; I want to keep talking, darling!"

"Okay, Madam, ask away," he smirked at her.

"What are some of these other traits you may have?"

"I guess that violence seems natural to our family. I wouldn't say I like it, and I do my best not to allow those feelings to stir. But I assure you, my darling Rachav, you will never have a thing to worry about. I would never hurt you in any way."

"I assured my mother of that already. This I know about you, my beloved Baba." She kissed him lightly on the temple.

"So, now I have a question for you, Rachav?"

"Anything, my love."

"What happened to you, that you kept yourself so focused on business, instead of marrying and having children?"

Rachav leaned on her arm and looked at Baba.

"I was a young girl, and some men whom my parents knew seemed to be besotted with my looks, even back then. When I was out playing with other children, one of them swooped down and picked me up roughly, took me behind the city walls, and did things to my body. The thing is, whilst they were nasty for a child, they actually felt nice, and I spent a lot of time feeling conflicted about sexuality after that incident. I made a mental note that beauty could be used to gain what I wanted, so then, as you well know, I entered into a few business transactions along the way." Her eyes grew a bit misty, and Baba wiped them gently.

"You don't have to say anymore, my love. It is enough that you are willing to be honest with me." Baba embraced his beloved, then kissed her gently.

Breaking away, Rachav looked at him with a sly look. "You're the only patron I had who paid in coins. The rest were all transactions where I acquired 'things'. You want to know why?"

Baba was intrigued.

"Even in my hardness, you Baba, were the object of my desire. I knew I could not afford to fall in love with you back then, but I sure did lust after you for quite some time!"

"My goodness, Rachav, you hid that well until the night you whispered in my ear to come to you."

"Were you surprised when I undressed in front of you and took out my hair?"

"Darling, that night changed us both forever. I'm so glad you took that chance. But you really were shocking at hiding your feelings from that point – you even allowed me to kiss you for the first time! However, I couldn't rush you, even though I wanted to propose to you at least a dozen times over the years!"

"You what?" Rachav blushed, then tilted her head, staring straight into his eyes.

"Oh, for goodness sake, woman, marry me! I want to be your husband and for you to be my wife, and I want to hang the biggest sign on this Inn that says, 'She's mine alone!'" He laughed and yet looked serious.

Rachav stroked Baba's face, then kissed him gently on the lips.

"Forever, yes!" she whispered.

With that, Baba jumped out of bed, ran to the door stark naked, opened it and yelled, 'Yesss!' then slammed the door shut! He jumped back into bed to his gleeful waiting lover.

"Baba, I have a question for you?"

"You can ask anything, my darling."

"You said on the night I professed my love for you, that I was your 'only' one, had been your 'only' one. Is that correct?"

"Yes. Not all of us men are sexual animals, Rachav." He looked at her thoughtfully. "Do you remember when I approached you about our business transaction?" Rachav smiled and nodded. "Well, darling, that was my first time. With you, on this bed - my god, it was a letdown, nothing at all like my fantasies!" Baba baulked, then laughed.

"Hmmm, the first time usually is, unless you're prepared," Rachav responded. "I know not all men are sexual animals, darling. But I am curious where you learned the things you and I do when neither of us had done them before? And believe me, you are absolutely perfect!"

"Of course I am!" He strutted around, puffing up his already large chest. "Ah, unfortunately, growing up, we were taken to the Temple and saw the Temple Prostitutes doing their occultic and sexual worship rituals, you know? A 'rite of passage' for a growing young man. I made a couple of mental notes, but then I saw you – all those years ago, and that was it for me."

"See Baba, I don't like all that Temple stuff. I don't believe in all those gods; I think they're horrible. Imagine having a beautiful baby, only to give it as an offering when you build your first dwelling. And people wonder why I never wanted children. I did, or I do, but not to offer up to some blood-thirsty god who never seems satisfied!" She blurted out. Knowing she may have offended her lover, she tried to backtrack. "Sorry, Baba, but they demand so much, yet we gain so little. But if you believe in them, that's okay."

"Oh, Rachav, I prayed to all the gods I could think of so that you would notice me. But yes, what I saw at the Temple put me off. In my travels, I've heard of this other god who seemed to perform some outlandish miracles, but I'm not sure I believe any of that is true."

"Well, I believe in us, in our love. I have faith in our love. And you are a perfect lover, Baba. I'm just glad you never tire of me," she giggled underneath her blushing cheeks.

They embraced, then got dressed again. This time, they readied themselves and went out to the Inn to relieve Abiah of her post for the evening.

8

Marriage

The day of the marriage arrived, a day of union and celebration as two families became one. Rachav prepared for the festivities by washing her body with water and soap, applying body creams, herbs, and perfumes, and adorning herself with ornaments of gold. She was dressed in the brightest pink, gold, and silver garments, shining like a jewel in Baba's eyes. Baba, too, was dressed in his finest attire, a long tunic of silver with his hair falling past his shoulders and a ceremonial hat upon his head.

Despite initial concerns, conversations were held, and the two lovers stood before a High Priest, with Rachav veiled and standing proudly beside her father. The ceremony began with the signing of the marriage contract, a solemn agreement that solidified the union.

As the ceremony progressed, Rachav received several gifts from Baba's friends, a gesture of support and blessing since his family was no longer alive. Her father, Ever, also presented her with a lovely gift, a token of his love and best wishes for her future.

Baba stood at the altar, his heart full of love and anticipation, holding several gifts for his bride that he had purchased with care. Family members held these gifts as he poured perfume over Rachav, a symbolic gesture declaring, "She is my wife!" Their fingers were then tied together with leather, symbolizing their union and commitment to each other.

Rituals were performed, and more gifts were exchanged, including rings that symbolized their eternal love and commitment. Vows were made, sealing their promises to each other, and numerous contracts were signed, outlining the responsibilities and rights of both parties.

After the ceremony, the couple and their guests returned to the Inn, where Baba had arranged a sumptuous dinner to celebrate their union.

As the night progressed, Baba and Rachav removed their hats and veils and danced in each other's arms, the music of the musicians filling the air with lively, entertaining melodies. Rachav's parents, Ever and Yaffah, toasted the couple, with Ever making a sweet speech to the crowd, expressing his joy and blessing for the newlyweds. "My esteemed guests, gathered here today under the watchful gaze of our gods, I stand before you with a heart filled with joy and gratitude. Today, we celebrate the union of two souls, Rachav and Baba, whose love has brought them together in this marvellous land of Kena'an.

Rachav, my daughter, your journey to this moment has been marked by your independent spirit and business acumen. You have shown strength and determination in all that you do, and

I am proud to see you standing here today, ready to embark on this new chapter of your life.

Baba, son of strength, your presence here today is a testament to your love for Rachav and your commitment to our family. Your brutish strength is matched only by your kindness and generosity, and I welcome you into our family with open arms.

As you stand here, surrounded by friends and family, I offer you both my blessings. May the gods smile upon your union and grant you prosperity and happiness in your life together. May your love be as enduring as the mountains and as bountiful as the fields of Kena'an.

Rachav, Baba, as you begin this journey together, remember to honour the gods and each other. May your home be a place of peace and happiness, where love and understanding reign supreme.

To Rachav and Baba, may your union be blessed by the gods and celebrated by all. Raise your glasses, my friends, and let us toast to love, to happiness, and to the future that lies ahead. Salammu!"

The night was filled with joy and feasting as friends, parents, families, colleagues, and dignitaries from the surrounding regions came together to celebrate the union. After the festivities ended, the couple retired to Baba's abode for a night of passion and glory, the beginning of their journey together as husband and wife.

9

Honeymoon

Rachav had never ventured too far from Yericho, so the two set off for a honeymoon to a faraway land with Abiah and an assistant minding the Inn and all of Baba's contracts fulfilled for the season. They rode by camel to a boat, then found themselves in a beautiful suite whilst floating down the river. Rachav had secretly dreamed of going to Egypt, having heard so much from visitors at the Inn, and she squealed in delight at the boat they would be staying on and realised that she would be holidaying on the River Nile.

The sights and sounds were not entirely foreign to either of them but, in their context, were more fantastic.

The days were for docking at sites and discovering all the mystery and wonder that Egypt had to offer, and the nights were for mysteries, wonders and pleasure within their suite. They were the only guests aboard this particular boat, along with the captain, the cook and the housemaid. They felt so wonderfully spoiled.

53

Imagine their amazement at seeing the large white pyramids completed only a few years before. On top of the large monuments sat caps of gold. Rachav found it hard to believe these were just monuments for the Pharaoh, so Baba explained that he felt they were energy sources, electricity if you will, that ran in conjunction with the Nile. Back then, the Nile was only a few hundred feet from the Great Pyramids of Giza.

Next along the trip was seeing the prominent temples that were still in use. They were more awestruck at the size of the statues and wondered how such an architectural feat had been accomplished?

Egypt was enjoying a period of unprecedented prosperity and splendour during the reign of Pharaoh Amenhotep III – aka Amenhotep the Magnificent. During this Pharaoh's long reign, the nation reached the peak of its artistic and international power.

Known for his mighty prowess, the ruler was said to have killed at least one hundred lions in his first ten years of reigning over Egypt.

Baba and Rachav had arrived during the Sed Festival, to celebrate Amenhotep III's thirty-year reign. The festival was held primarily to rejuvenate the pharaoh's strength and stamina while still sitting on the throne, marking the continued success of the pharaoh.

The couple witnessed the king's dual coronation, where he would be crowned separately for Upper and Lower Egypt. The festival had already been going on for several weeks, and Rachav couldn't help noticing that many new buildings had been erected along the infamous Nile. New shrines had been built, and the relevant statues of Deities had been placed within them.

Within the Sed Festival, of which the couple wanted to be a part of for curiosity's sake, were elaborate temple rituals, offerings, processions and acts of religious devotion. The Pharoah had to run a fixed course to prove his fitness was intact. The Pharoah had run four times with a young Apis Bull as the Ruler of Upper Egypt and four times as the Ruler of Lower Egypt. He would then go on to fire four arrows toward the four cardinal directions to symbolise his power over Egypt and his ability to bring other nations under Egypt's influence whilst increasing Egypt's wealth and prowess.

The end of the Festival was marked by Pharoah appearing in public with his family after reclaiming his throne. The public was encouraged to celebrate, feast and rejoice with different regions celebrating their own way. As with the great festivals, the state provided people with food and beer for the entire event.

After all the celebrations, Rachav and Baba enjoyed the festivities and retired to their boat. As the night wore on, their peace and solitude was occasionally marred by revellers and those who had misguided ideas of celebrating.

During the entire trip, Baba and Rachav were absolutely mesmerised by one another. After years of being together, being newlyweds seemed a funny thing to them both! They were already one in their hearts, minds and bodies, but this 'contract' had brought about a feeling of unity they hadn't experienced before.

Symbolic of having their fingers tied together during the ceremony, they employed a jeweller to make them matching simple gold rings, which they chose to wear on their fourth fingers on their left hand. It didn't matter to anyone else, but it mattered to them.

Knowing that Abiah and her family were taking care of the Inn and Baba would be tending to business as they travelled along the Levant, made Rachav even more relaxed than usual.

She had acquired some more fabrics and dresses and found ways of enticing Baba all the more. She lived for their pleasure and was incredibly excited about this trip. Rachav loved being married to Baba; he loved calling her his 'wife'. They loved being alone, just the two of them, with no responsibilities and no hassles from anyone.

The ship's owner had installed a new contraption that looked like a pipe with a flowerhead, and if you switched on a tap, it had water flowing from it. Baba and Rachav were fascinated with this and figured it must be for cleaning their bodies, so they would get into this large receptacle and together splash the water over one another while soaping each other up.

Another fantastic contraption was a small receptacle not unlike Rachav's women's facility for her sanitary needs, but this had a seat upon it. They had figured this would be a toilet and so laughed when they pushed a pedal near the base, and all the contents would go down under the boat! They felt very spoilt indeed. This was a top-of-the-line luxury that most folk wouldn't have ever seen, let alone used.

On one of their excursions to the shore, the newlyweds took themselves off to visit one of the numerous prominent temples that dotted the coastline.

Watching priests, in their short skirts, with shaved heads, heavily kohled eyes and smelling of a musky aroma that smelt like incense, they seemed to be in some kind of trance.

The priests met with the King and Queen, watched as the royal couple stripped off their clothing, and walked into a large pool filled with a milk-like substance.

As drums beat and worshippers bowed down, torches flickered within the darkened room as the priest donned the royal couple with crowns upon their heads, and then the couple proceeded to copulate in front of everyone, in this pool. It seemed too cold and mechanical, but apparently, this was their custom. Not something that the newlyweds were particularly keen to watch, yet Baba appeared overcome by the spirit of it all.

He looked intently at his wife whilst she watched his eyes turn dark. It frightened her, but she remained silent.

They turned, held hands and started walking out of the temple. Baba stopped and breathed in a gulp of fresh air.

"What did you see in me that you looked so fearful, darling wife?"

"Husband, your eyes turned dark. What was that?" She shuddered at the thought.

"This may have something to do with my ancient lineage. I'm not sure, my love. But please know, I would never hurt you, not ever!" He became deeply emotional, and Rachav reached up and embraced him.

"Let's go. We have a wonderful adventure ahead of us."

At a preappointed time, they met with a camel rider who was employed to take them out to an oasis so that they could camp overnight. Along with the rider were a cook, a tent worker and a guard. Several thieves were on the lookout for wealthy tourists to rob and plunder, so it was of some comfort knowing that all the men had swords and scythes upon their person.

When they eventually arrived at the oasis, the men went about setting up the tent, and the cook made some beautiful cuisine for the couple to indulge in. They had bought along some wine they had acquired at a merchant's shop back in the city centre, so their evening promised to be pleasurable.

After dinner, the men disappeared, leaving the couple alone in their beautiful abode. A lovely bed of fleeces had been made up for them, and lamps decked with bronze slits created a romantic atmosphere within the tent.

Laying snuggled into the fleeces, Baba kissed his wife tenderly, and then sleep fell upon them.

They both awakened in the middle of the night to the sounds of yelling and fighting. Peering out quietly, Baba saw several men trying to steal all the goods they had bought with them to the oasis; then, he decided it was time to take matters into his own hands. He didn't like violence, but these men were out of order.

Baba donned his tunic, headed out into the night and took a swing at the nearest man to him. Realising that it was the camel rider, he apologised, then asked which men were the robbers and thieves, as it was dark. He returned and grabbed a lantern to guide him, found the men, and then punched them to the ground. They got up eventually and took off into the night.

The men who had come with the couple slapped Baba on the back in congratulation and offered him some pipe, which he kindly dismissed. He wanted to make sure his wife was alright – of which she was, albeit somewhat amused.

After a beautiful sleep within the fleeces and in each other's arms, the couple rose to find a lovely breakfast waiting for them. Exquisite fresh dates, hot thick coffee, a crepe-like dish with dried raisins, and a smattering of honey. Delicious.

Next, it was back on the camels and back to the city centre.

From there, they went onto the boat again and were able to freshen up and rest before their next expedition.

The large pyramids of Giza stood out on the skyline, beaming white, with their caps of gold glinting in the sky. Monuments to the dead kings, as they were known, were the Pyramid of Menkaure, the Pyramid of Khafre and the Great Pyramid of Khufu. As utterly breathtaking as they were, something within Rachav felt strange about these pyramids. A sense she couldn't yet quantify.

<h1 style="text-align:center">10</h1>

Travels

Baba and Rachav immensely enjoyed their love, life, and passion. They were the epitome of Managers at the Inn and relished in their businesses turning a very healthy profit. They were afforded the luxury of a lot of time off, having spent years training a few trusted individuals to step in when they needed or wanted the spare time. Rachav had spent most of her early youth developing, building, furnishing and expanding her Inn. Several rooms now had more than just a single bed in there. There were rooms for families now; such was the great demand. She had single-handedly furnished every room to reflect a different part of their culture and those she had visited with Baba abroad. When he wasn't travelling, he assisted in expanding their now huge Inn. They were very satisfied with their lot, and their reputations were decidedly favourable.

Frequently, Rachav travelled with Baba on his business trips, which he absolutely delighted in. He was the best travelling partner, making their time abroad much fun. He often would find the most exquisite little Inns to stay in, and they would go on buying trips, emulating what they had happened upon. They travelled to several different countries and marvelled at the similarities and differences in their cultures. It was something to behold, watching Rachav being taught how to dance with veils, wiggle her tummy and wearing a veil whilst shimmering her bust in a provocative dance. She loved the feel of the drumbeat and felt quite intoxicated with the rhythm. Baba couldn't help getting excited, as his wife danced privately for him too – they learnt quickly to stay quiet.

In some places they travelled, Rachav was expected to remain silent, culturally speaking. Whilst she was indeed the owner and chief businesswoman of her own Inn, some cultures wouldn't deal with a woman, and Baba had to speak up on her behalf. She almost sulked but then learned to turn even that into a positive.

Rachav was quite enamoured watching Baba and his negotiation skills, and having to learn to speak about Inn matters on her behalf was a challenge for him – one that he willingly stepped up to. He loved his wife so dearly and passionately; there was nothing he wouldn't do for her.

Rachav and Baba had spoken about children while away in one of these foreign countries. They realised they were heading into their late thirties. Neither one had bought it up before, aside from Rachav's confession of not wanting a child due to the cultural expectations of offerings back in their homeland. Even though the thought of children was alluring to a degree, neither one wanted to give up their current lifestyle. They didn't feel they needed a child to express their love for one another; they could do that easily in spades. Besides, they loved each other so dearly, so jealously, that neither wanted to devote any time from the other more than they had to. They were settled on this matter in their hearts.

Drifting on a boat one balmy evening somewhere in the Levant, Baba awoke from a puzzling dream. He seemed deeply troubled, then decided to do something that wasn't the norm for him anymore – he bowed his head and prayed. All he ever wanted or needed was lying asleep next to him on this beautiful vessel, and he dared not ask for anything more. Peace settled upon him again, and he succumbed to sleep. Rachav awoke early the next morning and gazed at her beloved husband. Flaxen hair fanned all over the pillow, his iridescent blue eyes closed. She marvelled at his strong gait, even as he rested on this beautiful boat, and she silently gave thanks to whoever was listening for the love of this beautiful man. Beautiful soul, deep, beautiful heart. Ah, Baba, she worshipped him and delighted in him, openly and freely.

After another wonderful day exploring a new city and meeting business acquaintances, Baba and Rachav returned to their boat. Dining under the stars, feasting on local cuisine, and standing together looking up at the canopy of glittering orbs piercing the dark night, they kissed one another. All the staff had retired to their rooms, so they felt the freedom to express their love on the deck amongst the pillows, on this balmy evening. As Baba embraced his wife, they groaned quietly in each other's ears, feeling the familiar rhythmic dance of their bodies in unison, staring deep into each other's faces, reaching and feeling that familiar rise.

As was their custom now, they awoke early. They could hear the hustle and bustle of the staff above them but were in no hurry to arise today. They lay in each other's arms, stroking, kissing, whispering sweet nothings, and chatting in their own world.

They felt the boat jolt and jumped out of bed to have a look. They could see a massive hippopotamus from their window and hear the staff working overtime to move the boat onwards. The hippo seemed to stay behind, the crisis was over, and two very naked people thought they'd better jump back in bed so as not to be seen by others through the window! Giggling amongst themselves, Rachav started kissing Baba's earlobe and telling him her secret desires; now he was alive! Laying there in their afterglow, they both whispered, *"I love you."* After taking in some water to nourish them, they promptly fell asleep.

Waking at midday, there was a knock on the door, "Lunch is ready, sir and madam." Baba put on his tunic and took the lunch from the waiter, thanking him kindly. He then closed the door and went to wake up Rachav. "Darling, our lunch is here. Time to wake up and eat. We've worked up quite the appetite, my love."

Rachav awoke, kissed her Baba, then excused herself for the bathroom. After refreshing herself, she returned to some hot coffee and wonderful delicacies. Baba took himself off and re-freshed, then returned to the bedroom. He eyed up his lover. She was so beautiful. He adored this woman, every single piece of her. She caught him staring at her and felt coy. She took a part of the bedding and wrapped herself in it, blushing as she did so. "Darling, a piece of fabric won't keep me from you. Why are you blushing so?"

"Sometimes, I feel like a silly young girl, that's all. And darling, you can rip anything off me; I would never say no to you. You should know that by now!"

11

Gone Fishing

The couple disembarked on the shores of this great sea and then readied themselves for another camel ride to their next destination. Several cases of new items for their home and the Inn had been sent on beforehand. Rachav had not been too keen on this new leg of their trip, but not to disappoint her husband; she decided not to say anything.

They had come to Lebanon, where many occupants seemed as tall as Baba and physically active. Lebanon had been the centre of trade for Baba's mercantile business for a long time. He was familiar with the area and longed to show his beloved some of his favourite places in the region.

The trees of Lebanon, particularly the cedars, were very much in demand and were a constant source of revenue for the man.

One of the places that Baba wanted to take Rachav was a caving system up near the border of Tyre. Rachav was not very confident in the water, hence her hesitation, but she knew she would be fine alongside Baba. The seas were astoundingly blue, deep and teeming with fish. Baba wanted to catch some to cook on the shore when they came back in. Rachav thought this was a great idea. Not living too near the sea, this was a rare treat.

They both stripped down and headed into the water. Rachav was used to swimming at the waterfall naked, but here she was unsure. There didn't seem to be anyone around, so consented to follow Baba's lead. The waters were rather rough on this day, but Baba held his wife, and they kept near the edge. When he spotted some fish that were ripe for the taking, he lifted Rachav upon a rock near the entrance to some caves, then dived down to catch some fish with his bare hands. He came back to the surface and impressed his wife with his skills. He then told her to turn her head and crushed the fish's heads so that they could swim back to shore and eat them.

After this experience, Rachav had an even deeper love and respect for her multi-talented husband. Gosh, super lover, super businessman, and now keen fisherman – was there anything this man couldn't do?

They redressed and then cooked the fish, which Rachav ate in utter delight. "We need to add this to our menu somehow, Baba," she exclaimed.

Once finished, they returned to the small Inn where they were staying. It had a beautiful outlook towards the beach, and they could hear the sound of the water lapping up on the seashore from their bedroom. She was glad she had come to Lebanon after all. She kissed her beloved and immediately fell asleep.

Baba kissed his wife passionately upon their early morning waking, then rolled over and stared at the ceiling.

"Darling, what troubles you?" she inquired.

"I keep having this reoccurring dream that we lose each other and that I end up in a fire somewhere. It really is bothersome, to the point that I even prayed when we were on the boat."

"Baba, you yourself have said to me that the gods have been kind to us, so I suggest we make a prayer, an offering, and see if they will continue to shine down on us. All I ever want is right here with you. Although it's lovely, not the Inn or the travel – you are all I want and need." She snuggled into him and tried to reassure him the only way she knew how.

They bumped into some travellers who had been around this Israelite tribe. More stories of supernatural events came up. They were curious. Maybe this god was real, after all?

Upon returning to the little place they were holidaying, Baba nourished himself in Rachav. He hurriedly removed her clothing and threw her on the bed, ravishing her roughly. He groaned and then went silent. Again, staring up at the ceiling, Rachav knew she had to take things into her own hands. She sat up and urged him to do so as well. "Baba. This has to stop. Nothing, and I mean nothing, will separate us. Even when we do eventually die, we will always be together. You and I are one soul, one heart in two separate bodies. Do you understand?"

He looked at her delightedly and shook his head. "I'm sorry, my love, I was rough on you then."

"No, I can handle you. But you're allowing dreams, albeit a few, to affect us. That's not on. Now, if you please, let's take this back to a pleasurable tone."

Baba looked at his wife and knew she was right. He had to stop this, and determined he would.

They returned home to Yericho, where Rachav had some surprises in store for her petulant brute.

12

The Dress

Rachav had gone to Baba's abode to surprise him again. After being in the Levant with him, she had purchased several pieces of Egyptian-style clothing that she knew Baba would appreciate in private.

She placed herself in a chair so he would notice her sitting there seductively when he walked in.

Baba opened the door and smiled. "Rachav, please stand. Let me look at you?!"

He was mesmerised by her beautiful white gossimer dress, with an exquisite gold and turquoise necklace, which also acted as the top of the gown. Coupled with that, Rachav had placed kohl makeup on her eyes and a deep red stain on her lips.

Kneeling in front of her, Baba looked at his wife in total pleasure. She had dressed herself up, made herself up, all for him. He bent down and lifted her up in his strong arms, then laid her on the bed, slowly unfastening the clasps and removing her gown.

"I want to see this gown on you again, please." He demanded. He then removed her jewellery and put it on the nightstand. He then joined her on the bed, and they lay there kissing, touching one another, for the longest time.

He leaned on one elbow and stroked her tummy whilst she queried, "How was your trip, my darling?"

"It wasn't the same without you. Nights away from you with no pleasure have made travelling boring." He sulked.

"Sweetheart, I will be with you next time if you like? Just this past trip, I had to relieve Abiah so she could have time away. I think her lover has wonderful things in store for her." Rachav smiled. "It will mean that we may need to train someone so that we can safely take off on our own if Abiah needs more leave. I want to be prepared. And darling, nothing would make me happier than always being at your side. You are the best travelling partner, my supernatural lover, and my eternal husband – how could I not want to be with you always?!"

"I've come across a new place to visit. It may be a little strange for us, but I think we should go. This place has millions of gods, though; how utterly confusing. But I hear they have temples that are dedicated to the art of love, which sounds rather intriguing.

Immediately Rachav was interested. She was always willing to try new things with Baba, not because she was bored but because she wanted to keep Baba on his toes, so to speak.

"I will go, of course, but it does sound very curious." She giggled and blushed a little, thinking she wouldn't want anyone else to guide their bedroom positioning.

Their love was total and complete. They showed it through their physical bodies – it was all they knew and wanted.

Baba's strength was so entire; he stood nearly seven feet tall, and whilst Rachav stood almost six feet tall, she looked tiny next to her hulking lover. But oh, how she didn't care. She loved that he could pick her up like a doll and carry her around. She loved every inch of him, but oh, how she loved his heart. He was demanding at times and gruff, but his heart was so pure and beautiful; why would she ever withhold herself from him? To that end, Rachav was beautiful and kind to her lover husband. Baba never tired of her in any way. She was always finding ways to tease him, please him and surprise him. She was an utter delight to take away on his travels, and she had a wide-eyed wanderlust about life. She was so excited about seeing the world; taking her away was an absolute pleasure.

Baba began to plan this latest trip. It would take quite a long time, so he enquired of her parents if they would like to help run the Inn, for a reasonable wage, of course. They were delighted to do so, and plans fell into place at an alarmingly fast rate for Rachav.

13

The Vacation

Baba had arranged another beautiful boat for their vacation. They sailed down many different waterways, rivers and oceans before happening upon the start of the Far East region. Baba delighted in conversing with the captain and learning more about sailing as the days and weeks wore on. Upon their many stops, the crew decided to take themselves off for a break on a particular day, mainly so they could present offerings to their gods. Baba and Rachav had opted to stay on board and make an offering to their own personal gods – each other.

As Baba ensured the boat was secure, allowing no visitors could board unannounced, Rachav prepared herself below deck. Living in close quarters with others had not dampened their desire; instead, it made their love very quiet.

They both walked up onto the deck and realised it was time for the midday meal. Wafts of spices and aromatic herbs assaulted their senses as they sat on the deck, sipping some wine and eating some bread they found on their breakfast tray. They surveyed the shoreline and saw there were many boats, but theirs being quite a bit larger, had been moored a little back from the rest.

She queried her lover from her chair, and Baba responded by telling her a story about a forebear he had.

"One of the original fathers who came down from heaven was Azazyel. He taught many different things to the occupants of earth, including beautifying the eyelids as the Egyptians do; making bracelets and ornaments to wear, as all our cultures do: all kinds of weapons made from the metals of the earth; and all kinds of sexual pleasure, positions and such, as you see within our culture and those around us. You see, my darling, we are sexual creatures. We need this to be whole; therefore, you and I are keeping the gods' commands. My beloved, you need not fear; you are actually being obedient."

Rachav and Baba spent a wonderful evening above deck, eating foreign delicacies once again, drinking local wines, and enjoying their exotic surroundings. As they retired for the evening, the heavens opened, and it poured down in a deluge. Baba had been warned of this weather; it was called the monsoon rains.

In their cabin, drying themselves, they retired to their bed. Rachav sat up and leaned against the headboard, and Baba lay against her breast. Two lovers. Two best friends. Husband and wife. They were so happy.

Rachav got up and blew out all the oil lamps except one beside her bed. She wanted to look at her beloved. Her source of joy, her god, her everything.

She blew out the lamp and fell asleep.

Baba awoke early the next morning, got up, relieved himself, and then looked out the window to see it was still raining. He sat on the bed and watched Rachav sleeping. She had changed her whole world for him. She embraced everything he wanted and went even further – embracing elements of his lineage that would otherwise scare most people. She wasn't afraid, although he knew at times she struggled internally, but together they rode the highest heights and encouraged one another to go further.

He had never realised that in falling in love with Rachav and their eventual marriage, they would be where they are today. He would have been satisfied to keep his job, raise a family and have an everyday life, but that wasn't what the gods had in store for them. Theirs was a love that traversed the heavens and aroused the passions of the very gods they were supposed to be worshipping. Theirs was a love that transcended time and space and would be written about in the stars. Theirs was a love so rare, encapsulating, and consuming that mere mortals could very rarely contain it. Baba was so enraptured by his lover that he wept.

Rachav woke to find Baba staring at her and weeping quietly.

"My darling, what is the matter?" she asked her husband.

"Oh, sweetheart, just your husband being thankful and turning into a blubbering mess because of all the joy and passion you bring to me." He felt a little silly but didn't excuse his emotion.

"Come here, darling, please." Rachav requested.

Baba hopped back into bed, and the two embraced while quietly kissing and adoring one another.

"We are lucky, Baba, so very lucky." She kissed him again, sighing and quietly giving thanks.

The knock at their door let them know it was breakfast time, so as was Baba's routine, he put on his tunic, then took the breakfast from the waiter whilst Rachav remained in bed. Usually, they ate breakfast in the stateroom, but today Baba brought it into the bedroom. "It's raining outside, so I think most of our day will be in here, darling."

"Rachav sat there ogling her husband and responded, with a seductive smile, "Hmmm, that will be nice, for a change," then giggled naughtily.

"Woman, go relieve yourself, then come back and have some breakfast; that's an order!" He slapped her bottom lightly as she ran off to the bathroom.

14

Anatolia

The shoreline of Anatolia was divine – the beautiful deep azure blue of the Mediterranean Sea that they had become accustomed to, met them upon their arrival at the port. Several men with various donkeys in tow were awaiting them to take them on this expedition to the Place of the Gods.

After refreshments and heading to an Inn that housed both man and beast, Rachav and Baba were guided around the city of Hattusa by one of the locals, Usman.

Hattusa was the capital of Anatolia, a Hittite Kingdom, within the great loop of the Kizilirmak River. Rolling lush landscapes surrounded the city, including rich agricultural fields and hill lands for pasture, and surrounded by extensive woods. Crops of barley, wheat, lentils and flax could be seen as far as the eye could see, alongside dozens of fields of sheep. Sheep wool was the primary source of fabric for clothing and was in plentiful amounts.

Merchants from nearby Assyria had established a trading post in the area, which had grown to a sizeable population. To that end, they had set up their own quarter within the city walls. Bringing with them a vast amount of business knowledge, the Assyrians taught the Anatolians writing in the form of cuneiform. It revolutionised Hattusa and, eventually, all of Anatolia.

This area had become a melting pot of various cultures and ethnicities and a significant trading post where East meets West. Within the city centre were large bazaars which sold international materials, clothing, spices, animals, fish, meat and produce. Also being sold were the local vegetables, fruit, nuts and seeds. Rachav was in heaven – what to sample and taste next? Baba and Rachav took great delight in being introduced to the local coffee, thick and strong tasting. It sure did make their eyebrows raise!

As they were returning to the Inn for the evening, Rachav couldn't help noticing their sphynxes installed at the city gates. Flashes of their Egyptian adventure flooded her mind. With that, she smiled and held Baba's hand.

Early the next day, after once more tasting the delicious local coffee and sampling some sweet cakes for breakfast, they headed out on their trek, which would take them close to the Assyrian border.

Baba could see the tremendous worship site in the distance as dusk neared. All over the fields adjacent to the temples were myriads of tents and a large crowd of people. The small group could smell aromas of spices and delicacies, prompting a response of grumbling stomachs.

A humming sound grew louder and louder, much to the dismay of Rachav. Sitting astride her smokey-coloured donkey, the woman had a sense of foreboding about her. She did not know this place besides what patrons at the Inn had shared, so there was no way of knowing what she and Baba would find upon their arrival.

Rachav found the humming noise incredibly jarring to her ears and physical body. It was as if the humming penetrated through the ground and moved up from her feet throughout her entire body. It was not a sensation that she liked or wanted.

Baba could see her discomfort and asked their guides if there was another more fitting place for them to stay. Unfortunately, this is what they had signed up for, and as soon as they knew it, the attendants had erected a tent for them and were making their meal preparations.

Baba took some wine he had brought from Yericho and poured some into cups for himself and Rachav. With each sip, she calmed down a little but still found herself on edge. What was this noise? What happened here at this site? Why were all these people here, and furthermore, what were she and Baba doing here? The questions piled up in her mind until she felt she would explode.

"Baba, darling. What are we doing here? This place is horrendous?" Rachav's exasperation slipped out her mouth rather loudly.

"Darling woman, we were curious by the adventures some of our patrons shared with us, and thus, here we are," motioned Baba with his arms widely outstretched.

"Doesn't the noise bother you, darling?"

"Not as much as it annoys you, obviously. But I am curious about what goes on here, so I shall find this adventure rather intriguing, I should think." Baba had that look in his eyes, which Rachav couldn't help but melt at.

She walked up to her husband and embraced him. Feeling safe at last, she let out a big sigh. He truly was her rock and protection. Her lover, best friend and husband, all rolled into one perfect god-like being. She smiled at her good fortune.

In the distance, as night drew, bonfires were lit, and deep earthy drumbeats were heard. Men and women wearing cloaks of bright colours along with brightly painted faces were beckoning the crowd to draw closer.

Baba and Rachav walked closer on the tail-end of the crowd and watched the night's festivities begin.

The drums grew louder, producing a trance-like state in the most ardent of worshippers. As Baba and Rachav arrived at the worship site, they noticed the large supplicatory structures with elaborate engravings depicting rather lewd scenes. Baba was the first to notice some structures shaped as prominent phallic symbols across from equally enormous V-shaped structures. One didn't have to guess too hard to decipher what this particular temple was for.

Rachav looked up at Baba, exclaiming, "We came all this way for something that we see every year in our own city. What a waste!"

Baba started laughing and stroked his wife's hair. She too, giggled at their inquisitive foolishness.

They turned around and walked back to their tent, where they found a sumptuous dinner cooked for them, by their guides. There had also been an attendant who made up their bed and hung curtains to give some privacy to the couple, for which they thanked him profusely.

After supping on delicious food and wine, they made their way to bed, somewhat exhausted from days on a donkey, climbing up into this mountainous terrain.

Just before shutting her eyes to sleep, Rachav looked at her beloved. She reached over and kissed him, not expecting him to respond, as she thought he was asleep already. He wrapped her in his arms, and to the melodic sounds of the drumbeat, the two made love.

Waking early the following day, Rachav went to the adjoining tent to refresh herself. She was surprised to see a lot of people up already. Noting that it was sunrise, she then deduced that many were up worshipping their gods and goddesses.

The drumbeats had ceased, and Rachav was relieved not to have that vibration reverberating through her body. Baba was relaxed and at ease, lying on the cushions in the front of their tent.

"Something about this site seems familiar to me, Rachav. Do you have that sense too?"

"Yes, I do, darling, but I can't put my finger on it. I should think things will become clearer today as we watch the ceremonies and chat with some of the crowd." Baba agreed.

"Come and eat, woman. This food is delicious!" He motioned for his wife to join him on the cushions.

"What are we eating, Adil? It is the food of the gods!" Baba bellowed in utter delight.

"Ah sir, this is baklava. A sweet pastry with chopped nuts and honey. I see you are quite taken with it, huh?" The man smiled.

"Yes, I would love some more, please. Also, do you have that beautiful thick coffee Anatolia is famous for? I would love some of that."

"Of course, sir. Madam, would you care to try some as well?"

"Ah yes, thank you, Adil," responded Rachav, nearly drooling at the mouth.

After filling their bellies, Rachav and Baba meandered over to the worship site. Seeing it in the daytime had a different effect on the couple, and Rachav was a lot more respondent than she had been previously.

Looking at the temple from their viewpoint, Baba noticed a large stone slab that seemed elevated and directly in front of an altar, where several enormous stone gods had been erected. He knew instinctively what the stone slab was for and found himself staring straight at it as if in a trance. He managed to break his stare and shook his head.

"Rachav, there will be sacrificing something or someone on that altar today; you mark my words. And I, for one, don't want to be here to see it."

Rachav was not alarmed; she too, had the same experience. It was in the air – this unusual electrical energy that would pulsate through your body and cause your thinking to become blinded to the reality of what this place was.

As they were about to turn and walk back to their tent, they couldn't help noticing that many other people were shaking their heads. They tentatively approached some of these strangers and started conversing with them. After some interesting facts had been swapped, Rachav and Baba knew what they were dealing with.

The same people who had initially built Yericho were the ones who built this temple site and several other sites some distance away. There appeared to be an invisible current that ran through and connected them, which was odd to the couple, but at the same time, it explained why this site had that familiar feeling.

Baba instinctively knew that his ancient forefathers were the ones who built all of these sites. He needed to leave here, now!

Returning to their campsite, Baba instructed the men to dismantle the tent and pack everything immediately. He used the excuse that Rachav had become unwell, for fear of looking foolish if he spoke the truth. Within a short time, they were on their way on the back of the donkeys once more.

Baba experienced a deep sense of fear, for perhaps the first time in his life. He just wanted to get home and be back in familiar surroundings - with Rachav and his friends at the Inn. He never wanted to return here, nor did he ever want to feel this way again.

A few hours after leaving the site, Baba had calmed down enough to realise they still had a distance to travel, and new experiences lay on the horizon. He put the bad feelings out of his mind and returned to his usual jolly, adventurous self.

The Kena'anite culture had been merged with Phoenician, Mesopotamian and Egyptian cultures over the centuries. Mesopotamian cities had established trade up and down the

Tigris and Euphrates Rivers into Anatolia. Overland trades went east over the Zagros Mountains into Persia and Kushan. A busy sea route to the Indus Valley in Northern Bharat was established through the Persian Gulf across the Arabian Sea. To that end, Baba and Rachav found themselves sailing into the Far East to a magical land neither of them had ever ventured into. Their excitement and curiosity were at an all-time high.

15

Bharat

Waking up the next day, they discovered they had arrived deep in the Far East, where colours, scents, gods and temples were the norm.

Rachav ensured she was covered correctly, having asked the staff on the boat so as not to offend culturally. Baba couldn't wait to get off this boat and start exploring.

The first thing they would do was ride an elephant. Rachav had never seen such a large creature and was somewhat hesitant. The locals had coloured in the elephant's face, bright colours that she had never known existed. It made her world seem so, beige. They climbed up onto a two-personal saddle and rode all over the city on the giant grey beast. Never in her wildest dreams did Rachav ever think she would be doing this. She was utterly delighted.

They visited many different temples, enquiring of their guide about why and who the gods were and their significance.

There were so many to choose from, and the whole explanation confused the couple even more.

After a full day of exploring, they made their way back to the boat for their evening meal and a night of long, restful sleep. They were eager to wake up the following day and discover the temple that highlighted the act of love.

After refreshing themselves and having a beautiful breakfast on the top deck, their guide took them to a beautiful large temple out in the countryside. The temple seemed to be composed of many rooms with long-coloured gossimer curtains dividing it. After speaking with the Priest that appeared to them, they were taken inside.

They found themselves in a small room covered with long beautiful curtains. Within the space was a large receptacle in which they were encouraged to immerse themselves. This would be a new experience for them both, but there was a warning that this was not about a sexual experience; rather, this would be a profoundly emotional and spiritual experience if they allowed it to be.

An attendant came into the room and asked them to remove their clothing. Then with delicate expertise, they proceeded to rub oil over their bodies whilst they stood, arms outstretched. The scent was like nothing they had ever smelt. The attendant left after indicating they should step into the large receptacle. The water was warm, and flowers were strewn over the surface. Something about the fragrances made them relax. They held one another and just looked into each other's eyes for the longest time. After moving around and feeling the magic of the water, they lay on their backs and closed their eyes. They found each other's hands and held them whilst floating around. As time passed, they resumed sitting up and speaking to one another about things they wouldn't usually talk about. It was such a beautiful experience for them both, totally unexpected but very welcomed within their hearts.

After being transported back to their boat, they were greeted with a sumptuous dinner, under the brilliant stars, with some beautiful deep claret red wine and a dessert covered in tropical flowers.

They were full and completely satisfied. Murmuring sweet nothings to each other across the table whilst holding hands, they decided to call it a night and head back down to their room.

For the first time in a great while, their lovemaking was soothing and deep. Explosions occurred within their hearts, making them all the more breathless and emotional. And for the first time together, they wept for joy.

The next day, they met with other mercantile representatives in the area. Baba knew his timbers but was keen to see if some others hadn't been used from this area to take back to Yericho. His clients were always trying to outdo each other, with the best of this and that, so he knew whatever he would take back would be a good investment long-term.

Whilst Baba was busy with the men talking wood, Rachav had been met with some of the wives and spent some time with them. They showed her some traditional dishes their husbands loved, and then she was shown some beautiful fabrics to make some traditional Sari. The women, who knew her language, were warm and welcoming, and it wasn't long before they were laughing and swapping stories with one another. The women were fascinated with the tall warrior-looking white man, Baba, and asked questions of Rachav about him. Was he a real-life god, was he normal, and did he do things other men did in the bedroom? Rachav blushed but answered their questions as best as she could. It humoured her immensely that they thought Baba was superhuman! She called him that in the bedroom but had never mentioned it to another person. When Rachav mentioned going to a temple and learning some acts of love, the wives giggled and blushed. They all had been there as young maidens before their marriages and had some funny stories to relay. As older married women, they had gone back with their husbands and, by all accounts, had themselves beautiful times. Feeling slightly flushed and heady, Rachav decided to change the subject to the gorgeous traditional foods they were cooking. Even the taste of these beautiful dishes made her feel hot on the inside!

Baba returned with the men to find Rachav and the women having a wonderful time making delicious food. Before long, it was time for them to head back to the boat, so Rachav embraced the women and took her fabrics and spices along with them.

Baba spoke, looking at his wife with a new glint in his eyes. "You seemed to have a wonderful time with these women. What did you talk about, beloved?" Rachav smiled.

"They were very interested in you and whether you are a god or a human. They also wanted to know if you were like a normal man in the bedroom or superhuman!"

"Well, of course, you told them I am a demi-god and worship at the throne of your womanhood night and day, didn't you?" Baba laughed heartedly.

"Not quite, you brute!" Rachav giggled alongside her lover.

"I told them you were normal. What else do I have to compare to, my demi-god?" Rachav winked at her beloved.

"Hmm, very true. Yes, I can see your dilemma. But I do hope you told them I am a demi-god!" Baba chuckled and kissed his beloved on the cheek.

Upon their return, they supped and then proceeded to the bedroom.

"Oh, Rachav, I have a surprise for you!" called out Baba from the bedroom. He was wearing a traditional cotton longsleeved tunic with matching pants. Slippers bejewelled with sequins, beads, and bright colours on his large feet, culminating in a pointy toe. He looked an absolute treat!

Rachav's eyes bulged! "Oh, Baba, I just don't know how I'll keep my hands off you, darling!" She laughed so much that she had tears running down her face. Baba, too, thought this ridiculous outfit was hilarious.

"Well, darling, you did tell me I could surprise you with a new outfit too!"

"I did indeed, Baba. I did indeed." She went up to her husband and kissed him on the cheek.

"Sweetheart, please remove your clothes; I fear I would rip them if I tried!" Rachav kept giggling.

They were on the floor in seconds, and Baba stood utterly naked. "*My god, he is gorgeous*," thought Rachav as her arousal grew hot.

"Darling, what would you like to do tonight?" Rachav asked. She usually set the tone but wanted him to instigate their evening this time.

"I want to blow out these oil lamps, hop into bed, and see what happens." He cocked his eyebrow. "Let's just leave the lamp on the bedstand going." They embraced and kissed slowly. Baba slid his arm under Rachav's neck and held her closer to himself. "Rachav, my goddess, I am so in love with you. Something has changed in my heart since visiting this magical land. It's like seeing you for the first time. You are more beautiful to me than you've ever been. You are my beautiful, magical wife, the Queen of my heart." Rachav's eyes welled with tears. He was so close to her face that she felt every breath and was desperately lost for words to convey her love for Baba. "My King, I am more in love with you than I've ever known. We've been together for so long, yet there isn't a day when you aren't the first thing on my mind. I can't even begin to say in mere words how much you mean to me, darling." He moved closer and kissed her softly, sweetly and lovingly.

Baba swept Rachav's hair off her face and behind her ears in the lamplight. He traced the line of her perfect nose, cheekbones, and lips. He drank in every drop of beauty until he too welled with tears. As they dropped on her, she reached up and kissed them all away—two lovers in perfect harmony. Two lovers were finding a depth of love previously hidden deep within their souls.

With the arrival of dawn, Rachav slipped out of bed, donned a plain shift, caught up her hair, walking upstairs to the upper deck. Watching the last of the sunrise, Rachav felt so grateful to be here now. Travelling with her beloved Baba had given her a new outlook on the world and widened her little narrow life. She was eternally thankful for her big hulking husband and smiled to herself. Indeed, something different had transpired after being in that receptacle together – but instead of overthinking, she just looked out at the view.

Morning rise had ushered in the fishermen who had been out all night catching fish for the local markets. Women were up scrubbing their bodies in the water, washing clothes and bringing floral offerings to the god of the great Gange River.

The outside air was warm and balmy, with the rain having stopped earlier. Rachav loved being up here and being out on the water. Something about the ocean stirred her deeply, and she couldn't help feeling a little sad that her own abode was out in the desert.

Baba woke and, hearing it was silent, figured Rachav was atop the deck. He got up, freshened up, took some food, walked up the stairs and spotted his beloved whilst chewing. She was sitting, just staring out and possibly dreaming. He was in awe of her. In her natural beauty, she stirred him profoundly.

Walking over towards her, he felt somewhat dizzy and promptly fell over. Hearing the thud, Rachav noticed Baba in a heap on the deck.

Running over, she exclaimed, "Baba, Baba, what's wrong?"

He didn't respond. She called the captain and asked if a physician was onboard – fortunately, there was. The man examined Baba, who was breathing but still out cold, and summarised that he had an unusual condition to do with his heart, which was beating rather rapidly. They got him back to their room and placed him on the bed.

Rachav was fraught with worry; she had never known Baba to be anything but his robust and brutish self. She thought the worst, so she did the only thing she knew - she dropped to her knees, besought the one true, merciful God, and pleaded for Baba's life.

Days passed, and Baba stirred in and out of consciousness. The severity of his condition wasn't yet known, but he was given strong broths to drink and several different types of herbs that helped with the healing.

He grew stronger in a matter of days, and Rachav thought it might be because she had prayed to a merciful God. She was profoundly conflicted but knew something had changed.

There were days when they could disembark and look around, but those excursions stayed relatively short so Baba could conserve his energy. Their exuberant lovemaking became non-existent for the first time in their relationship. They were terrified that Baba would die of over-exertion, so they abstained for some time. Whilst this was highly unusual for them, it opened up a new aspect of their relationship that they had never really ventured into – spirituality.

Rachav confessed that she had prayed to the one true, merciful God for his help with Baba. There had been no plea bargaining, just the cry of a woman who wanted her husband well. Baba knew that this was the God he had prayed to when he had those awful dreams on the boat back in Egypt, all those years ago.

The two of them did something on this boat they had never done. They knelt and cried out to the all-merciful one true God to help and heal them. Something then shifted and changed in their relationship, and where there had been a thirst and insatiable lust for one another, now there was a sense of peace. A calm. A knowing that they were safe.

Baba and Rachav spoke about finding others to learn about this God, for they were sure He guided them towards Him.

16

The One True God

Upon returning home, they found the city seemed to be rather glum. With every person they spoke to, there were stories of this tribe that seemed to be systematically going through and plundering, looting and overturning different cities within the Levant. Their God seemed all-powerful and gave them victories bordering on the supernatural.

Both Rachav and Baba listened intently. They had not forgotten that this foreign God healed Baba of his affliction. There was no other explanation they could argue, so they were keen to ask the citizens more questions.

During Baba's work and travels, he would occasionally pluck up the courage to ask someone if they knew about this One True God? Alas, each time, Baba would come up short. Rachav too, would query the occasional patron at the Inn. All their efforts were seemingly brought to nothing.

Neither of them could know the destiny that was about to collide with their present-day reality.

17

Abiah

As life resumed its regular routine, Rachav mesmerised Abiah with her tales of travel, food and hilarity. Explaining what a camel felt like to ride, and then the massive elephant, brought tears rolling down the faces of both the women.

Abiah also had some news for Rachav. Her lover was an up-and-coming Winemaker at the Royal Palace. Novac had great affection for the Barmaid. Abiah was elated but was a little concerned and asked for advice.

Rachav asked what she was after, and Abiah confessed that she was a virgin and needed help not being one anymore – something Rachav knew oh so much about!

"Abiah, my sweet, has your mother not educated you in the matters of sensuality?"

"We spoke; however, she went silent on me and wouldn't divulge much. She only warned me that Temple Prostitution was unacceptable in their eyes and that I should remain chaste for my future husband. That doesn't help with my current situation. I don't want to be chaste, nor do I intend to marry yet. May I ask who taught you, Rachav?"

Rachav grinned, "Of course, sweet Abiah. I know you are trustworthy, so I am happy to share it with you. My life was changed irrevocably when I was a little girl, and one older man took me outside the walls and abused me. I guess because of that trauma, my mother didn't want to overwhelm me as I came into womanhood, so funnily enough, it has been Baba who taught me everything I now know."

"I'm very grateful you trust me to share that, Rachav." Abiah rubbed Rachav's wrist and then held her hand. The younger woman looked at her questioningly. "Would you please teach me what I need to know, Rachav?"

"Of course! Now?"

"If that's okay, that would be wonderful."

"Well, Baba is away for a day or two, so yes, let's get started."

Rachav ensured the Inn was secured, then took a jug of wine and a key to one of the rooms.

"Light some lamps, Abiah. I shall be back shortly." Rachav headed to her room, grabbed a small bottle, sponge, and cloths, and returned to Abiah.

Walking into the room, she placed the items down then locked the door. She motioned for Abiah to sit on the bed. "Alright, my sweet, what do you know? What have you experienced?"

Abiah shook her head and blushed. "I only know how to kiss Novac, and when he kisses me, I do feel tingling down there," she pointed to her womanhood.

"Well, I am glad you feel that," she smiled at Abiah. "Have you done anything else at all?

"No. I have been too worried that I would get it all wrong!" Abiah seemed utterly embarrassed.

After some time, with animated explanations and much giggling, the women sat in the sumptuously decorated room, and Rachav spoke.

"Darling Abiah, there is nothing to worry about. Novac is lucky to have you. You know what to do now, but take your time. Don't be in such a hurry. Love and lovemaking take time, patience and trust. If you have those ingredients, you'll be fine."

Rachav thought some more, then added, "I know that most of our society has been deeply permeated with the over-sexualisation of the gods and goddesses. However, as much as you can, ignore them and trust your instincts. We are not mere rabid animals; we are human beings, created to experience delight and pleasure within a loving relationship."

Abiah nodded, taking in all that Rachav had taught her. "Thank you for being so patient. I would never have trusted anyone else."

The women laughed and hugged, and then Rachav left. She heard the door lock and a wee giggle from the room. She laughed to herself. She had never had the honour to help another woman in this way, so she was deeply humbled at Abiah's trust in her.

Walking back to the room, Baba was sitting waiting for her, a smile on his face.

"Darling, you're home!" She leapt on her lover and kissed him passionately.

"Did you have a productive time away?"

"I certainly did. Now, what have you been doing, my gorgeous wife?"

"You won't believe what I've witnessed, my beloved," she smirked at her hulk of a husband.

"Abiah asked me to help her in the ways of sensuality as her mother would not do that with her. We've been next door, and I have been guiding her. I think she's going to be in there a while – she's got a lover – Novac, that she wants to please, but she herself is a virgin."

Baba's eyes were wide!

"So you're having all the fun without me!" He burst out laughing.

"Oh yes, my supernatural god!" Rachav laughed at Baba's shocked expression.

"I learnt from the best, so I wanted to teach her the best ways of love, lust and sexual prowess. If she has half the fun and satisfaction we do, she will be happy, and dare I say, Novac won't be able to concentrate for a while!" Rachav winked at her husband.

"I must say, she is incredibly beautiful. So perfect in her virginal state – unlike this old girl!" Baba slapped her round bottom and felt her up under her clothing.

"You are my goddess, darling, and you are perfect." Baba kissed her neck and demanded some fabulous stew alongside a large cup of wine.

There was a quiet knock on the door. Baba opened it to see Novac standing there. He looked bewildered. "What can we do for you, Novac," he bellowed.

"I'm looking for Abiah. I thought she'd be here at the Inn, but I can't locate her." Baba smiled. "Wait a few moments; I believe Rachav knows where she is." Baba winked at him."

Rachav went next door, knocking quietly on the door. "Abiah, darling. Novac is looking for you. Would you like me to send him through?"

Abiah answered the door in her shift. "Yes, please! She squealed in delight. "And can we have some bread and wine, please, Rachav? I will pay you in the morning."

Rachav put her hand up. "Sweetheart, no need. I shall bring Novac and some supplies right now. And Abiah, enjoy yourself!"

Rachav sent Novac next door. Rachav gave him the necessary food, wine and other supplies she knew Abiah would need. He looked excited but bewildered!

Knocking on the door, Abiah opened the door. Novac froze as he stared at his lover in all her glory. He put all the items down, locked the door and gulped. He had never seen such beauty, and he wanted that beauty right now.

The two lovers rolled around and found each other in the dim lamplight, taking small breaks to replenish, wipe and reacquaint each other to the heights of ecstasy and pleasure. They lay in the bed, utterly spent and with goofy grins on their faces.

Waking in the morning, they donned their clothing, kissed goodbye, and left for work. Both had a difficult time that day concentrating. They asked Rachav and Baba if they could pay for another evening in the Inn. The couple laughed and insisted they use it as long as they wanted. After all, because of Abiah's business sense, loyalty and friendship, they had been afforded so much time off, alongside travel and adventure overseas.

Abiah and Novac were deeply in love, almost rivalling Rachav and Baba. They, too, had an insatiable lust and love for each other. Abiah with her beautiful tanned skin, blonde locks and buxom bosom, and Novac with his tall, dark and handsome looks, long black hair, big thick lips, and utter worship of his lover.

After Novac had left the previous evening, Baba motioned for his wife to come to bed. Baba was ravenous.

Baba let fly, having spent weeks being cautious and not being too assertive. He ravished his wife, moaning and groaning as he flared inside her. She delighted in her husband and motioned for him to slow down to enjoy themselves.

Rachav arose from the bed, refreshed herself, and then donned another provocative gown, seating herself in the chair. She had missed their lovemaking and teasing and was also ravenous for more of her husband.

Afterwards, they both sat quietly, looking at one another, then Baba lifted his beloved out of the chair and placed her lovingly in their bed. They held each other, looking deeply into each other's eyes, and then slept for a while.

Novac leant on his elbow, looking at Abiah in her beauty, and bent down, kissing her clavicle. He looked at her shimmering body and could hardly contain his good fortune.

"My sweet Abiah. How I wanted you for the longest time. I remember the first time I saw you at the Inn. Oh my goodness, I thought I'd seen an angel sent from Heaven: your long golden locks, your beautiful turquoise eyes. Your beautiful body under that shift," Novac hesitated. "I never thought you would be interested in someone like me."

"Why do you say that, my love?"

"You and your beautiful Suiones ways, seemed so foreign to my own, and I thought you would look for someone from your own land."

"Oh, Novac, no! We moved here when I was such a young girl, and I love being part of this culture. I know I look different, but I truly feel like a citizen of Yericho. And lover to a budding Winemaker of the King's Court!" Abiah giggled.

"Well, my goddess, I think you are an angel. The things you do to me are heavenly!" Abiah slapped Novac, who then tickled her and made her squeal with glee.

"So, the lessons with Rachav paid off, huh?"

"Oh Novac, I was so nervous at first, but I was off after having some warm wine! She left me to it, and I amused myself greatly." Abiah smiled. "Rachav has been my closest friend for so many years. She's raised me in the ways of business and hard work since my early teens. We owe her a big debt, Novac. She is a wonderful woman. Look how they're even allowing us to stay here together as long as we want."

"Yes, my lover, you are correct," Novac spoke.

"Abiah, my darling. I want you to know I am so in love with you. You are all I can think about during the day when I'm working and all I want every evening, every morning." He kissed her deeply and passionately. Gazing into her turquoise eyes, he welled up with emotion. "Please say you love me too, that you think only of me, want only me?"

"Novac, you are my everything. I love you insatiably. You are my lover, best friend, my night and day. I want only you, forever and ever." Abiah wept openly as Novac took her in his arms and held her tightly.

"Then I must ask you something you may be unprepared for?"

Abiah looked at him questioningly. He cleared his throat, then asked, "My darling beautiful Abiah, will you be my wife – now and for eternity?"

Abiah was shocked but elated! "Yes, my darling, a thousand times yes!" They laughed and cried together.

<h1 style="text-align:center">18</h1>

The Strangers

One evening, Rachav noticed two new strangers that sat at the back wall, partially hidden in the darkness. She motioned for her barmaid Abiah to head over to the men with a jug of wine, and barley bread whilst Rachav turned and greeted some familiar faces.

Rachav turned and noted the two men again. Something about them intrigued her, a sense of curiosity. She shook her head and turned to walk out the back of the Inn.

A soft rapping on the door alerted Rachav. Having donned her gown, she went and unlocked the door. Peering out, she saw Abiah, who had shut up the Inn for the evening. Looking at her questioningly, the barmaid spoke, "I'm sorry to disturb you, Rachav, but those two men you had me serve, seemed rather insistent they needed to speak with you. I told them to come back in the morning. I hope that is alright with you?"

"Yes, that's fine, Abiah. Did they say what they wanted?"

"Not a thing. They seemed very secretive."

"Oh, I see. Well, you did the right thing. Thank you."

"You're welcome, Rachav. I'll see you in the morning."

Rachav relatched the door and turned to walk back to her bedroom. She put the men out of her mind, seeing that Baba was now awake and sitting up in bed.

"Rachav, come here, my darling. I want a morning kiss, please." Baba had woken up and was famished for his wife.

"Baba, that is all you're getting out of me this morning. I have to prepare for a visit from two foreigners about some strange business. Don't you dare distract me!" She moved towards the bed and leaned down to kiss her beloved when he picked her up and pinned her down. "Baba!" He started kissing her, morning breath abounding, and her body began to respond.

Just then, a quiet rap was heard from outside the door. "Don't answer it," Baba demanded. "I have more important needs." He giggled, and Rachav pushed the big man off of her. Straightening herself up, she answered the door, only opening it slightly.

"Rachav, these are the two men from last night, Azriel and Salmah," explained Abiah.

Rachav looked outside and, seeing that no one seemed to be looking, quickly ushered them into her abode. She looked around, and thankfully Baba was not in the room, though she could hear him in the bedroom getting dressed.

"Of what assistance can I be to you men?" asked Rachav.

"We have been sent from the land of Sheetim, from Y'hoshua, the son of Nun. We are spies sent to stake out the land. We had been doing surveillance last night and need another night to finish our findings. Do you have a hiding place available, Madam Inn Keeper?"

"If you come back later this evening, I have an area upstairs upon the roof where I dry my flax. You can hide under that. I think you'll be safe there." With that, the men nodded and expressed their appreciation, then left. Abiah then went next door to prepare inside the Inn for the day.

Baba was still in the bedroom and waited for Rachav to return.

"Darling, who were those men?"

"Two spies from Sheetim. They are surveying the land for what purpose I do not know." Rachav shrugged her shoulders. "I have agreed to hide them tonight under the flax drying out on the roof."

"Are they the Israelites, Rachav? The men who know the one true, merciful God?" Baba seemed excited.

"I believe they might be – maybe this God has heard our prayers and sent these men directly to us?"

"Well, we must enquire of them before they leave. There are things we should know." Rachav nodded in agreement.

Evening fell, and with it came another knock on the door. Baba answered the door and let the visitors in.

"Friends, please, come in and allow us to feed you. My wife is famous for her homemade stew, and we have the most exquisite wine. Please come, sup with us."

Rachav served Azriel and Salmah some stew and wine, asking questions about the one true, merciful God.

The two men were delighted that others knew about the exploits of the Israelites and answered their queries as best they could.

Being satisfied with the food and the company, Rachav took them quietly upstairs to the hiding place beneath the flax. She had hoped this would be enough to protect them. Before she left, she asked one further question, "What is the name of this one true, merciful God?"

The spies looked at each other. "His name is Adonai. It means Lord or Sovereign Lord."

"Thank you. This helps me a lot." Then Rachav went back downstairs to Baba.

Not long after hiding them, there was another knock at the door from the court of the King of Yericho.

The King of Yericho sent a message to Rachav, "Bring out the men who came to you and are staying in your Inn because they have come to do reconnaissance with this land."

However, after taking the two men and hiding them, Rachav replied, "Yes, the men did come to me; but I didn't know where they had come from. The men left around the time when they shut the gate, when it was dark. Where they went, I don't know; but if you chase after them quickly, you will overtake them."

The men pursued them all the way to the fords at the Yarden; as soon as the pursuit party had left, the gate was shut.

When she returned to the roof, the two men had not yet lain down and said to them, "I know that Adonai has given you the land. Fear of you has fallen on us; everyone in the city is terrified at the thought of you.

"We've heard how Adonai dried up the water in the Yam Suph ahead of you when you left Egypt and what you did to the two kings of the Emori on the other side of the Yarden, Sichon and 'Og, that you completely destroyed them. As soon as we heard it, our hearts failed us. Because of you, everyone is in a state of depression. For Adonai, your God is God in heaven above and on the earth below.

"So, please, swear to me by Adonai that you will also be kind to my family since I have been kind to you. Give me some evidence of your good faith that you will spare the lives of my husband, father, mother, family and all who are theirs so that we won't be killed."

The men replied to her, "Our lives are certainly worth yours, provided you don't betray our mission. So when Adonai gives us the land, we will treat you kindly and in good faith."

Then she lowered them by a rope through the window; since her house abutted the city wall, indeed, was actually built into it. She told them, "Head for the hills so that the pursuit party won't get their hands on you, and hide yourselves there for three days until the pursuers have returned. After that, you can go on your way."

The men told her, "We will not be guilty of violating the oath you made us swear, provided that when we enter the land, you tie this piece of scarlet cord in the window you let us down from. You must gather your husband, father, mother, family, and entire household. If anyone goes out the doors of your house into the street, he will be responsible for his own blood, and we will be guiltless. But everyone who stays with you in the house — we will be accountable for his blood if anyone lays a hand on him.

"However, if you say a word about our business, then we will be free of your oath that you made us swear."

"According to your words, so be it," she said, sending them away. As they departed, she tied the scarlet cord in the window.

They left, arrived in the hills, and stayed there three days until the pursuers had returned. The pursuers had searched for them all the way but hadn't found them.

The two men returned to their camp. Descending from the hills, they crossed over and came to Y'hoshua, the son of Nun, and reported everything that had happened to them.

"Truly, Adonai has handed over all the land to us," they told Y'hoshua. "Everyone in the land is terrified that we're coming."

The people came up out of the Yarden on the tenth day of the first month and camped at Gilgal, by the eastern boundary of Yericho. Twelve stones which they took out of the Yarden, Y'hoshua piled up at Gilgal.

Then he said to the people of Isra'el, "In the future, when your children ask their fathers what these stones mean, you are to explain it to them by saying, 'Isra'el came over this Yarden on dry land. For Adonai your God dried up the water in the Yarden from before you until you had crossed, just as Adonai your God did to the Yam Suph, which he dried up from in front of us until we had crossed. From this, all the peoples of the earth will know that the hand of Adonai is strong, and you can fear Adonai your God forever.'"

When all the kings of the Emori on the west side of the Yarden and all the kings of the Kena'ani near the sea heard how

Adonai had dried up the Yarden River ahead of the people of Isra'el until they had crossed it, their hearts failed them, and they fell into depression because of the God of Isra'el.

When all the nation had been circumcised, they stayed where they were in camp until they had healed. Adonai said to Y'hoshua, "Today, I have rolled off from you the stigma of Egypt." This is why the place has been called Gilgal [rolling] ever since.

The people of Isra'el camped at Gilgal, and they observed Pesach on the fourteenth day of the month, there on the plains of Yericho. The day after Pesach, they ate what the land produced, matzah and roasted ears of grain that day.

The following day, after they had eaten food produced on the land, the manna ended. From then on, the people of Isra'el no longer had manna; instead, that year, they ate the produce of the land of Kena'an.

One day, when Y'hoshua was there by Yericho, he raised his eyes and looked; in front of him stood a man with his sword drawn. Y'hoshua went over to him and asked him, "Are you on our side or on the side of our enemies?"

"No," he replied, "but I am the commander of Adonai's army; I have come just now."

Y'hoshua fell down with his face to the ground, worshipped him, then asked, "What does my lord have to say to his servant?"

The commander of Adonai's army answered Y'hoshua, "Take your sandals off your feet because the place where you are standing is holy." And Y'hoshua did so.

Yericho had completely barricaded its gates against the people of Isra'el — no one left, and no one entered. Adonai told Y'hoshua, "I have handed Yericho over to you, including its King and his warriors. You will encircle the city with your soldiers and march around it once. Do this for six days. Seven Cohanim are to carry seven shofars in front of the ark. On the seventh day, you will march around the city seven times, and the Cohanim will blow the shofars. Then they are to blow a long blast on the shofar. On hearing the shofar's sound, all the people are to shout as loudly as they can; and the city's wall will fall down flat. Then the people are to go up into the city, each one straight from where he stands."

Y'hoshua, the son of Nun, called the Cohanim and told them, "Take up the ark for the covenant, and have seven Cohanim carry seven shofars ahead of the ark of Adonai."

To the people, he said, "Move on, encircle the city, and have the army march ahead of the ark of Adonai." When Y'hoshua had spoken to the people, the seven Cohanim carrying the seven shofars before Adonai passed on and blew on them, with the ark for the covenant of Adonai following them. The fighting men went ahead of the Cohanim, blowing the shofars, while the rearguard marched after the ark, with incessant blowing on the shofars. Y'hoshua gave this order to the people: "Don't shout, don't let your voice be heard, don't let a single word out of your mouth until the day I tell you to shout; then you will shout."

So he had the ark of Adonai make a circle around the city, going around it once; then, they returned to camp and stayed in the camp. The following day Y'hoshua got up early, and the Cohanim took up the ark of Adonai. The seven Cohanim carrying the seven shofars ahead of the ark of Adonai went on, continually blowing on their shofars, with the fighting men marching ahead of them and the rearguard following after the ark of Adonai; all the while, the blowing on the shofars was incessant. They went around the city once and returned to camp the second day. They did the same for six days.

The citizens of Yericho were getting incredibly nervous. The men were ready for war. The women were prepared to throw anything and everything at these ludicrous Israelites! As the days wore on, the mental anguish grew intolerable. Who the hell but these ingrates would walk around a city blowing their animal trumpets or shofars?! It was outrageous.

But for those who had gathered at the Inn with Rachav and Baba, none of these creatures would be safe. Not even the babies or the animals. Rachav struggled deeply with the brutality that would ensue, but she also knew that Adonai had his reasons for wanting their city levelled. Baba had made his peace with his genealogy and with his Maker.

On this, their final night at the Inn, before utter madness reigned down on them, Baba, Rachav, Abiah, Novac, and Rachav's parents, knelt before the God of Israel, crying out for mercy. As per their instructions, Rachav had put a red cord out the window. The army would see that. She trusted what Azriel and Salmah had said and left that in place.

After prayer, the couples all went to their rooms for their final night before leaving the only place that had been their homes. Their city, with all its wonders and memories, tomorrow would be no more.

Baba embraced his wife, and they went about gathering all the belongings that they could carry on their donkeys. To Rachav's surprise, Baba had a lot of gold, silver and bronze coins in pouches from their days when they didn't fulfil their 'transaction'. She laughed and couldn't believe her eyes. "Baba, you amaze me! Always looking forward and planning, that's my gorgeous beautiful husband." Baba smiled, then looked at her wantingly.

"Once more in this Inn before it goes down to the earth, my beloved goddess?" They gently made love and laughed as they reminisced about their beginnings and their life together. They slept till the early shards of sunlight invaded their rooms.

Abiah and Novac, who hadn't yet married, prepared for their long journey ahead in the next room on the previous night. Having fled the Winery and Abiah having gotten all her belongings from her parent's home, the two of them spent the remaining time soaking up their love and lust for one another. Whatever happened, they had each other, and that would be enough.

On the seventh day, the Israelites got up early, at sunrise, and went around the city, in the same way, seven times. That was the only day they encircled the city seven times. When the cohanim blew on their shofars the seventh time, Y'hoshua said to the people, "Shout! Adonai has given you the city! But the city and everything in it is to be set aside for Adonai and therefore to be obliterated; only Rachav the Inn Keeper is to be spared, she and everyone with her in her house, because she hid the messengers we sent. So you, keep clear of everything reserved for destruction. If you bring a curse on yourselves by taking anything set aside to be destroyed, you will bring a curse on the whole camp of Isra'el and cause great distress there. All the silver and gold and all the brass and iron utensils are to be separated out for Adonai and added to the treasury of Adonai."

So the people shouted, with the shofars blowing. When the people heard the sound of the shofars, they let out a great shout, and the wall fell flat, so the people went up into the city, each one straight ahead of him, and they captured the city. They completely destroyed everything in the city with the sword — men and women, young and old, cattle, sheep and donkeys.

Y'hoshua told the two men who had reconnoitred the land, "Go into the Inn Keeper's house and bring the woman out with all she has, as you swore to her." Salmah and Azriel, the spies, went in and brought out Rachav with her husband, father, mother, Abiah, Novac and all she had and put them safely outside the camp of Isra'el.

Then they burned the city to ashes with everything in it except for the silver, the gold and the brass and iron utensils, which they put in the treasury of the house of Adonai.

Y'hoshua then made the people take this oath: "A curse before Adonai on anyone who rises up and rebuilds this city of Yericho: he will lay its foundation with the loss of his firstborn son and set up its gates with the loss of his youngest son."

So Adonai was with Y'hoshua, and people heard about him throughout the land.

Rachav watched the city of Yericho burn. She was in utter disbelief. Black smoke rose like tendrils kissing the clouds, then dispersed all over the surrounding area like a canopy of doom.

It smelt horrendous. Diabolical. As if the gods had come up from Tartarus itself and smeared their unholy stench all over the atmosphere. Tears flowed down her face as she dropped to her knees in deep wails of guttural mourning. All the years she had spent building her empire, all that she had worked so hard for, was in the city of Yericho – which was now no longer. The only home that most of them had known. The memories of living a beautifully rich and wonderous life were now piled in a heap of dark smoke and hot orange-red ashes. However, she knew that the One True God, Adonai, was just and merciful, and without a fuller understanding of all the complexities yet, recognised why this had to be.

Rachav looked up at her husband, himself shedding tears, and reconciled herself with the knowledge that she wasn't alone in this. Her husband, family, and closest friends – whom she considered family, were with her to start this new phase of life. Looking over at Ever and Yaffah, so desperately in pain with great emotion, she ran over to them and embraced them. Deep shudders shook them as they turned and walked away from all they knew.

Nearby, Novac and Abiah walked in stunned silence, not really understanding the brevity of what they had just witnessed. They stopped and embraced, allowing bittersweet tears to fall down their faces and their clothing, spilling onto the parched desert sand.

Together, they all walked behind the tribe to their new life.

What would become of them now?

<h1 style="text-align:center">19</h1>

Gilgal

As the sun beat down on the tribe, the women, children, and animals grew impatient and frightened. It had been a long time coming over the Yarden River, albeit another incredible miracle of Adonai. Watching the water banked up into the formation of a dam, so they would all walk over on dry land was more than the tribe expected. It was just like Adonai to show up, show off and then let the tribe settle down into some sense of normality.

One man from each tribe had been instructed to carry a stone upon their shoulders in front of the Ark of the Covenant and then place it where they would now dwell permanently. Consequently, Y'hoshua set twelve stones in the middle of the Yarden River, at the spot where the Cohanim carrying the ark of the Covenant were standing – which remains.

Tents went up in the usual fashion – fast and furious! Before the women could even think about it, the tents were being furnished with all their belongings and goods, water gathered for both men and beasts and quail collected for dinner. In amongst the business, holiness and ceremony of the day, Adonai had provided their sustenance too. They were all exhausted yet extremely grateful.

Upon waking the following morning, the orders were clear. It was the time of the flint knife. Each man was to be circumcised and rest until they had fully recovered.

Y'hoshua and Calev made it clear this was not a punishment – this was a physical sign that Adonai had removed the reproach of Egypt once and for all.

A large structure shaped like a foot was erected in stone around the camp. This was to signify Adonai's promise to Avraham - you will possess the land wherever your feet go. Within the structure was an altar that Y'hoshua built, alongside a tabernacle that would house the Ark of the Covenant and all the precious articles that Adonai had instructed Moshe to build, many years before.

For the first time in the years that the tribe had been nomadic, there was a sense of permanence, and an excitement that drifted through the encampment.

Thus, the first Pesach was observed from their new permanent dwelling. That evening, no quail fell, and the following day, no manna was to be found on the ground. The people could now forage around and eat from the land for the first time in decades. Having seized the city of Yericho and tightly shutting up the gates so that no one came in or left, the tribe could help themselves to the crops that lay outside of the city. This then encouraged them to plant crops for themselves and their kinfolk too. Noting that sheep were plentiful among the hills and the plains, they took their fill and learnt to cook meat over the fire. The new inhabitants of the land were somewhat happy with their lot!

After conquering the city, new people were added to the tribe – one, in particular, was rather large and reminded some of the elders of the ancient races of giants that inhabited the land previously.

He would go on to be a mighty warrior for Adonai and a beloved friend to many within the encampment.

20

A New Home

Life living with the Israelites was indeed an extraordinary time for the former residents of Yericho. There was one God. There were rules between males and females. They liked cleanliness most inordinately! And they did bizarre things to the manhood of their tribe – Baba and Novac were not having a bar of that!

Where Baba and Rachav had a life filled with ardent love-making, lust and pleasure, there was much to do within this camp, which had been set up at Gilgal.

They had their own tent, but had to learn to be very quiet and not take off during the middle of the day to tease, taunt and tantalise one another. Many physical things needed to be done, and Baba having such intense brute strength, was required to help a lot. At times, he would come back to their tent utterly exhausted, and at other times, he would bounce in, shed his tunic and chase Rachav around like a naughty child!

One such time, as they were getting used to living in the desert in a tent and using animal fleeces as blankets, Rachav had gone to bed a little earlier than the rest of the people. She grew tired of constantly being around others and needed time alone. Also, she longed for some wild lovemaking with her husband and decided to take matters into her own hands.

Baba went to their tent looking for his wife, which was a little further back from the rest of their family. He opened the flap and saw a soft glow from their inner sanctuary. Rachav had put up curtains around their bed to add some privacy should anyone burst into the tent. She had installed a room divider to the side, offering a private place to refresh and dress. Rachav lay on the fleeces, looking seductively at her beloved; Baba immediately disrobed and pounced on his wife. A lot of noise ensued.

Laying there panting, she looked at her beloved husband. "Darling, I needed that. I am so thankful that Adonai has saved us and given us a new beginning, but privacy is lacking now, isn't it?!" She laughed out loud.

Baba laughed and looked at her, "Don't ever change, my darling. You and your warmth are why I can keep going during the day, knowing that you will feed and nourish me when we come here. I miss our days of laying in bed, frolicking all day, drinking expensive wine and eating your fabulous stew. More than that, I miss our privacy too." Baba was quiet with his thoughts. "We should see if we can get away. I still have a lot of money, as do you; why couldn't we leave and go somewhere for a while?"

Rachav lay there thinking. "I don't think this tribe is like that. I'm sure they don't even know what a holiday or travel for pleasure is. Being nomads, they are of no fixed abode, so how would we know where they are when we return?"

Rachav pondered, "I have to wonder if we ever saw some of these people or their relatives, when we were in Egypt all those times?"

"I hadn't thought of that, Rachav. You are a smart woman," he stated as he kissed her shoulder.

21

The Lovers

A wedding was planned and prepared for Abiah and Novac. It would consist of two parts, one a contract and the second being a large ceremony. The arrangements were being drawn up, and many discussions were held, without the bride but including the bridegroom. Abiah didn't seem to care; she wanted it all to happen yesterday.

The tribe's head man Y'hoshua insisted the two of them abide separately until they were man and wife. That didn't seem right to them. However, with the respect that was due to the head man, they decided to obey – in part. No one discovered they would sneak off for their little triste occasionally. Learning to curb their lust made wedding preparations hurry along all the more.

One evening when the camp was quiet, Novac snuck into Abiah's tent near his. He kissed her awake, then hopped into her bed of fleeces and proceeded to drink her in. Abiah muffled her groans.

The two lovers were deeply in love, for all their sexual escapades and youthful conquests!

Sitting upon a rock, having some time alone, Abiah fantasised about Novac and married life. Rachav approached her and asked if she would like some company. The two women decided to go for a walk and spoke openly to one another.

"Rachav, I miss home. I miss our former life. I still don't fully understand why Adonai had to obliterate our entire city, alongside most kinfolk and animals. I miss having a room," she cried out, exasperated.

"Oh darling Abiah, as do I. Baba and I have been lamenting not having days of love, wine and leisure. I guess we didn't fully comprehend the restrictions of having no permanent abode, did we?"

"I want to be with my lover. There's nothing like going to sleep next to Novac and waking up with him. I'm not too fond of all the sneaking around, but we have to in order to be together. It drives us both crazy."

"Well, it seems in this tribe, the Israelites have more traditional views and roles for the sexes. I'd like to strip off and sunbathe for now." Rachav was serious.

"The problem is, we come from a culture that was so sexually open, and women were treated as equal too and, in some ways, better off than men, but here there are things such as modesty and new ways of doing things. Baba and I are considering going on a holiday, but my thought is that they wouldn't even know what a holiday is." Rachav laughed.

"Rachav, there's no one here. Why don't we strip down for a few minutes and bathe in the sun?" Abiah suggested. Rachav nodded, and the two lay down in all their glory, sunning themselves and marvelling in the absolute quiet.

"Rachav, it is wonderful to be able to talk openly with you and experience all this newness with you too."

"Thank you, Abiah. And thank you for understanding. We are both in the same situation - but one of us must get married immediately."

Upon their arrival at camp, the older women took them aside and chastised them, explaining that many dangers could hurt, maim or kill them. Upon reflection, the women understood.

22

An Israelite Wedding

Next came the wedding.

The Israelite clan were befuddled with Abiah, not being a virgin and proud of it. She couldn't understand being separated from her lover, as they were engaged, but a slight issue with demolishing their city had gotten in the way. Abiah was rather indignant that, as a foreigner who was trying to integrate into this community, she wasn't treated with a little more respect and understanding.

However, after discussions with the elders and the council, it was decided that Abiah and Novac should marry as close to the Israelite custom as possible, with a few exceptions.

Since their parents were no longer with them, there was no mohar needed. As the two of them were genuinely in love, there wasn't a need for formal contracts, but a small ketubah was drawn up instead.

However, Abiah did want a beautiful gown, and she did want to be given away, so it was decided that Rachav's father,

Ever, would do the honours. At any rate, they considered themselves a family, so he was the natural choice.

Rachav's father, Ever, would declare when the wedding would commence, and Rachav's mother, Yaffah, would conduct a fine celebration with the help of her Israeli counterparts.

Rachav had acquired some beautiful silk fabric when she was in Bharat. Several different colours were available for Abiah to choose from. She chose a beautiful light blue colour with silver threaded throughout. Rachav showed her how the women of Bharat had worn the garments, and Abiah agreed this would be lovely in the style of the sari. Rather than wear her long golden tresses loose, Rachav piled them upon Abiah's head, adorning her with a matching veil over much of her face, with just the eyes showing. Around Abiah's eyes, Rachav applied some kohl, in a muted brown colour, along with some light red stain on her lips – not too much, for fear of it getting all over her groom! Rachav and her mother, Yaffah, preened and shaped Abiah, then took a few steps back and looked at her – she was stunning. Her turquoise eyes shone, as did her golden locks, but more importantly, she was calm. Not the petulant girl who was forever trying to break the rules – but a calm woman ready to commit to her one true love.

Rachav motioned that they were ready, and Ever came and took his place next to his adoptive daughter. Abiah looked up at him with tears, knowing that her own parents had been too stubborn to bow their hearts to the One True God, and therefore perished in the burning of Yericho. Yet here was Ever, tall, handsome and regal, ready to walk her to her beloved. She whispered a raspy, "Thank you," to Ever and placed her arm in his.

Abiah arrived under the chuppah, Ever kissing her cheek and placing her hand in Novac's. The prayer of Rivka was spoken, "*Our sister, may you be the mother of millions, and may your descendants possess the cities of those who hate them.*" Abiah then walked around Novac three times, signalling the three virtues of marriage: righteousness, justice and loving-kindness. A cup of wine was then presented to the couple, which drank happily. Novac presented a ring to Abiah, then recited the declaration, "Behold, you are consecrated to me with this ring to the law of Moshe and Isra'el." Abiah then presented a ring to Novac, declaring, "I am my beloved's, and my beloved is mine." Seven blessings came forth from Y'hoshua, Kalev, Baba, Ever, Yallah, Salmah, Rachav and Ever. They all grew misty-eyed as the cup of wine was given to the Novac, who drank, and then to Abiah, who too, drank. The cup was then given to Novac in a cloth, all wrapped up, and he was instructed to place it on the ground and smash it with his foot. It is said the primary reasons for this custom, are the reminder of Moshe breaking the tablets and joy must always be measured.

The couple were then taken to a small tent to relax for a few minutes alone and have a small meal. After a short while, an attendant came to gather the couple and join in the festivities that had broken out.

The couple were escorted to a large tent where there was dancing, singing, eating and drinking. Towards the beginning of the wedding feast, the men and women were separated for a while.

As some of the older guests left, the crowd mixed together and resumed dancing.

Baba was flinging Rachav around and having a very merry time! She glanced over and noticed her parents dancing with the biggest grins on their faces. This brought such delight to Rachav, having very rarely socialised with Ever and Yallah since her teen years.

Baba looked over at Novac and grinned. Novac was being 'spoken to' by some of the older women and looking somewhat flushed in the face! Abiah was giggling away at her new husband's embarrassment!

At the close of the ceremony, Novac and Abiah were treated to a larger tent with full flaps that were closed and had more privacy. An inner sanctuary was within the tent, around the bed, where beautiful fabrics had been hung. On the back of their donkeys, Rachav brought out two chairs from the Inn – one from her room and one from the room that Abiah and Novac used. She placed one in their marital tent, along with some other goodies, much to the newly married couple's glee.

23

The Day After

As a surprise for herself and Baba, Rachav placed their chair in their marital tent and some beautiful fabrics she had acquired in their travels. When Baba returned that night, she was seated in the chair, wearing her white Egyptian dress. Baba nearly fell over.

"My goddess, the chair! The gown!" He whispered as he fell to his knees and buried his head on her lap. "Oh, I thought you had left these beautiful gowns behind. Bless you, darling Rachav, my wanton, lustful Queen!" Baba enjoyed his wife as she sat and enjoyed his desirous worship of her.

Unbeknownst to her husband, Rachav had secured the back of the bed so that there was a headboard to lean against now. Leaning up against it, she encouraged Baba to lean against her. "Darling," she whispered, "strut for me, please," Rachav giggled, knowing that Baba was a proud man and would strut when asked! Sure enough, Baba got up, strutted around, flexing his biceps and then turning and flexing his buttocks! Rachav sat fascinated as he isolated his buttock muscles.

Turning around, Baba pounced on his lover and ravished her.

Afterwards, she admitted her desert encounter with Abiah as they lay there. Baba looked her in the face, "smouldering, and said, "Next time, I demand to be there!"

"Darling, I cannot have you excited about seeing Abiah in all her glory! I'm your Queen, and you should only want to see me!" She pouted.

"Oh, my darling Queen, you've got that all wrong. Next time you want to lay in the desert sun, I demand to be there to participate – that's what I meant. As much as Abiah is lovely, you're my sexual goddess, and I don't care about any other woman!"

Rachav kissed her lover and snuggled into his big burly arms.

"Are you ready for sleep, darling?" enquired Baba.

"What do you have in mind, loverboy?" purred Rachav.

"A secret triste in the desert moonlight."

"Where were you thinking, darling?"

"Just behind the tents are some rocks, and amongst those is a large flat surface, where we can lay down in privacy and look at the stars." Baba looked at her wantingly.

"Let's go, sweetheart."

They donned their tunic and shift, then took a large blanket and quietly snuck out to the rock plateau.

As they lay down, they looked up at the night sky and marvelled at the billions of stars looking down on them.

Laying quietly, Baba touched his wife, and she responded in kind. Together, under the stars, they made love for the first time since being on the boat. They returned to lying quietly when Baba spoke. "After all these years, my beloved, I still don't ever tire of you in any way. I still get as excited as that time of the Temple, when we ran through the Inn, and you nourished me so quickly. I still get so caught up in you that it makes all this other stuff seem superfluous. I still only adore you. You are everything, my beloved Rachav. My erotic dream that forever comes true!"

"You made me so mad with lust; I couldn't help that time of the Temple. I had been outside the door watching the procession, getting pretty worked up at their stupidity, when I spotted you in the crowd. I thought on that day that you'd be rather supernatural if I let you do all you wanted to me, but I couldn't see back then how much I had fallen in love with you already." She grinned in the star-spangled darkness. Baba reached over and kissed her deeply.

"I still remember so clearly, you coming into the Inn and putting the pouch of coins on the bar. How you looked at me then, I knew exactly what would happen. But, the thing is, you could've had me for free, darling."

"What? How?" Baba questioned.

"You're Baba. You can get anyone to do anything you want. If you had tried romancing me, maybe you could've saved yourself some money, darling."

"I wouldn't change anything, my darling. Besides, you sure did make me work for you!"

"Rachav giggled. "Oh, and I loved the part of your proposition where you asked if we could have a 'transaction'. That was gorgeous!"

"Woman, you're making fun of me!" He slapped her bottom, to which she responded by licking his ear.

"Well, now you've gone and woken the beast," whispered Baba.

"I do hope so. He has a transaction to fulfil," murmured the aroused Rachav.

With that, Baba again tended his wife. Afterwards, they quietly snuck back to their tent, undressed and fell asleep warmly in each other's arms under the fleeces.

24

Love Matters

Abiah and Novac were elated. As part of their marriage contract, Novac was ordered not to work for a year. This would give the bride and groom time to 'know' one another. Whilst they understood the custom, they also had 'known' each other for quite some time.

Abiah awoke early, and as it was her custom, she made the early morning coffee and served her husband in bed.

Novac loved this new custom. He loved Abiah. He loved making love to Abiah, and he particularly loved making love to Abiah after morning coffee. She, in turn, loved serving her new husband, herself, on his bed of fleeces. She found ways of making his eyes grow wide, pop, and altogether jump for joy, and she loved pleasing him.

His new wife so entranced Novac. She was a sexual goddess. There was nothing she wouldn't try or do for him. But he wasn't a god. He didn't have the stamina or the know-how to titillate and tease his beloved for hours on end.

It was time to seek advice, and so, Novac approached Baba.

Baba smiled. He knew this day had been coming for a while now. "Alright, Novac, out with it. Tell me, what is the matter?"

"Baba, I am so in love with Abiah. I want to please her so desperately, but I cannot keep up with her insatiable appetite. How the heck do you keep up with Rachav?"

"Firstly, brother, I am a demi-god in the bedroom. Rachav has had to learn to keep up with me! And secondly, what the hell is wrong with you?" Baba boomed.

"Obviously, something is; that's why I'm talking to you, Baba." Novac was frustrated.

"Hmmm, okay then. Let's apply some reason and logic here. You're young. You're fit and healthy. You make love every day. Yes, to all of these?"

"Yes indeed."

"So, do you instigate things, or is it always Abiah?"

"Generally, it is her, and I don't want to offend her, so I oblige."

"Well, that's your problem, Novac. A woman knows when a man is just going along with things. She wants to feel wanted. She wants to feel beautiful and that you utterly adore her! She wants to feel sexually appealing to you. But if you take it for granted, you will soon get bored."

Novac shook his head in agreement whilst listening to the older man.

"Rachav and I have been together many years, and there's never been a time that either of us has turned the other away nor not been able to carry out our pleasure. But, and it's a big but, I used to travel abroad a lot with my work, so there were days and sometimes weeks when we weren't near each other. I'm not saying you need to get away, but if you're going to have this year be blissful, you've got to get brave and tell your woman to pace herself!"

"Would you speak to Rachav like that?"

"I do. She bellows back and calls me a brute, of which I am!" Baba laughed.

"Brother, don't stress. The two of you obviously are deeply in love and lust, but measure it out, and tell her to stop going off in the desert, please!"

"What are you talking about, Baba?"

"The two women went for a walk together and ended up sunbathing out there in all their glory! My god, man, our women must be brought into line sometimes." Baba humpfed.

"Well, I didn't know that. And I am none too pleased. If she's going to sunbathe anywhere, it will be right by me; thank you." Novac was flustered!

"Good Novac, good to see you getting a backbone. Now, go and deal with your wife, tell her who's the boss, and stop your whining!!"

"Good talk Baba, thanks brother."

Novac returned to his tent to find his lover wife, in the chair. How the heck was he going to pull her back into line when she was sitting there, wantingly, lusting after him?

"No, I've got to be strong and put my foot down, at once!" Novac chided himself.

"Darling, please. I have a matter that I need to discuss with you immediately." Novac pleaded with his wife.

"Of course, my love. What is the matter?" She donned her shift and looked at him questioningly.

"Sweetheart, I adore you. You are my world. You are my sunshine; my dream come true. But if we're to have a blissful year, don't you think we should pace ourselves, sexually speaking?"

Abiah looked somewhat amused. "Okay, sure. Where did this come from, though?"

"The problem is, I am so attracted to you, but I can't keep up. You are heaven to me, but I get a bit, um, sore." He looked at her, embarrassed.

"Novac, oh, darling, I would never want you to feel uncomfortable. Oh, darling, I'm so sorry." Abiah flung herself at her husband, kissing him and hugging him.

Novac moved away momentarily from his wife. "Now, there is another matter that I've just been made aware of. What's this about you and Rachav going off for a walk, sunbathing in the desert?"

Abiah giggled. "Oh. Yes, well, um. Before the wedding, we were mainly separated at night, and I was going up the wall crazy with lust because....well, we couldn't make love often. But Rachav and I were lamenting our former life and all we have left behind. Since it was quiet, we decided to sunbathe for a while. When we got back, we got in trouble with some of the older women of the tribe. I understand we were putting ourselves in harm's way. We won't do that again."

"What am I going to do with you, Abiah?"

"I can think of some things," flirted his wife.

"Please, Abiah, don't ever go out in the desert again without me. And darling, don't sunbathe in the desert without me." Novac's eyes started to smoulder.

"I thought you were sore, darling?"

"I was. I'm not now. I want you back on that chair and remove your shift, if you please." It wasn't a request, more a demand.

"Yes, my darling." Abiah obeyed whilst giggling. Then she stopped. "Are we okay, husband?"

"We are more than okay, my beloved. Now please concentrate on your duties to me as a wife!" He laughed, knowing that would never sway with his beloved Abiah.

They spent the afternoon pleasing and pleasuring one another - at Novac's lead.

Novac and Abiah came up for air. Since the conversation with Baba, the two couples had not seen each other. When the newlyweds ventured out for air, they were greeted with great cheer and music playing.

It was time for one of the Israelites' festivals. They were a tribe that liked to honour their God with feasting, dancing, music, wine and song, but they were very modest regarding sexuality. Or at least, that is what Rachav and her family had thought.

They were unsure of what particular festival it was today, so they enquired of one of the older tribesmen?

"Today is the celebration of the destruction of Yericho. We must meet with all the other tribesmen, elders and leaders. Today we make an oath before Adonai, which will produce either life or death."

As all the people gathered in an area like a natural amphitheatre, Y'hoshua spoke loudly and clearly.

"Adonai has spoken. With the destruction of Yericho and all its inhabitants, except for those chosen to be saved, we must bind ourselves with an oath to heaven. Will you willingly bind yourself to this oath?"

The crowd yelled, "Yes. We will bind ourselves with an oath, for we have seen Adonai do mighty miracles in our midst."

Y'hoshua continued. "A curse before Adonai on anyone who rises up and rebuilds this city of Yericho; he will lay its foundation with the loss of his firstborn son and set up its gates with the loss of his youngest son."

The crowd repeated the oath, much to the horror of the former residents of Yericho.

"So be it. Omaine."

The crowd roared, and then dancing ensued.

Baba and Rachav, along with Novac and Abiah, groaned in mourning. Did these tribesmen know their former gods had ordained the same thing in their former culture? Rachav was mad. She shook her head in utter dismay. "They make these oaths and pledges like frenzied worshippers! They are acting like illiterate ingrates!" She stormed off, knowing she may be hauled before the council and dealt with severally if she said anymore.

Baba watched as his beloved took off and stopped Abiah from following her.

"Leave her be. She needs time. This is still raw and foreign for her, indeed all of us."

"You're right, of course, Baba. I hate seeing her so upset." Abiah went and stood by her husband, who embraced her warmly.

After some time, Rachav returned and found Baba sitting in the shade, just inside their tent. He had raised the flap so that a cool breeze blew in.

"I'm sorry, husband. I'm still getting used to these new ways of ours, of theirs. How long until you think we will feel like we belong in their midst?"

"My beloved, it will take time. That is all I can say. I understand your anger. Just make sure you keep it in check. I don't want you hauled before the council – I'm quite partial to my wife." Baba winked at Rachav.

25

The Girl's Chat

Rachav and Alexandria had been walking and talking for the longest time, so they took a moment to sit down on a seat and ponder all that had been shared.

Alex wasn't blushing; instead, she was curious about how Rachav could share such intimate details without worry.

"Oh, dear child, I'm no longer human; that's why! I am a spirit being, and we can banter on for millennia about all sorts of things and completely forget we are now eternal, and that time is still a 'thing' here on earth. I do apologise – I've been reminiscing an awfully long time," Rachav burst into laughter.

"I guess one could be rather embarrassed offering up these intimate details of my life, but I believe they will be of great importance to many women AND men, Alexandria."

"How so, Rachav?"

"Well, dear child, we have watched from the balconies of heaven the twists and turns of people's lives and their love lives for millennia. We often wonder why they don't read their scriptures correctly or at least consider how things were done back in the biblical days. I am convinced that so much of the body of Yeshua is enslaved to an idea of sexuality, yet they are so afraid of being caught up in lust that they do the opposite – they run, then they do nothing!

"Darling child, Papa – our Abba Father – created sexuality and intimacy. He created all those feelings and pleasures for man and wife to enjoy within their covenant. Yet, the church has taught that this is bad, that is bad, this is evil, that is evil – when it's the furthest thing from the truth. I don't advocate that every couple spend every waking minute in sexual pleasure, but it should be the norm within a covenant relationship. That there is so much adultery, fornication, pornography, and addictions, can be traced to viewing sexuality apart from our heavenly Father – and that is where the distortion lies."

Alexandria sat there listening and pondering her own journey of sexuality. It had been quite a journey and one that she would not want to write about, yet here she was, writing about the very thing that had been a source of extreme frustration and pain, for many a year.

The two women went silent for a while. Then Alex was dying to ask a couple of things of Rachav.

"Rachav, how did you learn to have such unbridled passion and love for Baba? If no one taught you, and you didn't know Papa at this stage, I am curious to know."

"As we have covered ample times prior, my culture – the worship of multiple gods – was very orientated towards Astarte and Ba'al. So essentially, it was in my blood before I was even born. My parents were very affectionate with one another, but

I never saw them do anything untoward as such. For that, I'm glad," Rachav chortled.

"There was something supernatural about our love, and we both acknowledged that. He gave me full license to be whoever and whatever I was. There was no such thing as rebuking a spirit of lust or casting out a demon of lust, or anything like that. In our worldview, physical union was sacred and binding. Once you gave yourself to someone willingly, they were yours, and you were theirs. That was simply understood. I'm not referring to Sacred or Temple Prostitution, but to consensual intimacy between two people. In our culture, the formal marriage was just the legal contract that followed what the heart and body had already sealed."

Alex exclaimed, her voice carrying a hint of frustration, "It's absurd! Nowadays, if someone feels any kind of arousal, they're made to feel like they're possessed by a demon."

"That's what we're taught. We're taught to fear anything remotely sexual," Alex said, her frustration rising. "Apparently, Jezebel, Succubus, Incubus, spirits of fornication, lust, and uncleanness are all waiting to pounce. But most of those teachings are so vague and unclear—they barely make sense." She shook her head, incredulous. "The more I think about it, the more ridiculous it all sounds. Completely absurd!"

Rachav glanced at her friend, sharing a knowing smile. "You are right to be angry. What you've been accused of is unjust and untrue," Rachav said gently. "Those spirits do exist, but not always in the way people are taught today. More often, what binds people is not a demon, but deep wounds, old traumas, and unhealed abuse. The body remembers. And sometimes what people call a 'spiritual problem' is really a memory that needs to be acknowledged and healed." She paused, thoughtful. "We can pray over our bodies, bless them, and release what no longer belongs. It can be done — but it takes discernment, wisdom, and honesty to know what we're truly facing."

Rachav continued, "The Scriptures make it clear what Papa wants from us: 'Keep yourselves from sexual promiscuity. Learn to appreciate and give dignity to your body, not abusing it, as is so common among those who know nothing of God – like the pagans.'" Alexandria nodded in agreement.

The women got up from their seat and continued walking along the beach.

"What was Baba like as a person, Rachav?"

Rachav giggled. "He was really straightforward and honest. He worked very hard. He was honourable, dedicated, loyal and faithful. Once we were together, there was no one else he ever thought of; it was just him and me. Also, he was tender and kind-hearted. He loved me truly and deeply."

"Don't get me wrong; he was also petulant, selfish, arrogant and a giant show-off! But I needed those elements; otherwise, I would've been able to walk all over him, and that's not healthy." Rachav smiled at his memory.

"He's in heaven, you know. I've never really lived without Baba, not even when I was married to Salmah."

"As you know, when Baba died, I saw his spirit leave his body, and just before the Angel of the Lord took him heavenward, he turned and waved goodbye to me. I haven't told you that Baba would often visit me in my dreams, and sometimes I would feel him around me. I know that sounds contrary to what you get taught in church, but it's true, and that was my experience." With this revelation, Rachav seemed sincere, if not a wee bit sassy.

"I believe you wholeheartedly, Rachav. I know from my own experience that death doesn't truly separate us. It just means that we usually can't physically see our loved ones. But they are there, and I know that for a fact."

"What about Abiah and Novac? Are they with you in the afterlife, Rachav?"

"Oh goodness, yes! She's still 'spicy,' but now in a holy sense. And Novac, he is so beloved of our Father."

"What does that mean, if you don't mind me asking?"

"It means people think we have personality transplants when we enter Paradise, but that's simply not true. To some degree, the essence of who we are on earth remains and is intensified in the afterlife. It's a riot of joy and laughter up there! And, oh, how we worship Yeshua, so deeply and passionately – that quite simply we can't experience here on earth in any great measure." Rachav wept and laughed simultaneously. Alex did the same.

"Isn't it all about Yeshua, Rachav? Really, of all the books written, the conferences, the churches, the seminars, the courses, the endless meetings – isn't it all about the lover of our Souls, Yeshua – our soon coming Bridegroom?"

The women wept, worshipped and giggled as they continued on this journey.

"Tell me about Salmah, Rachav."

Rachav swooned. "Ah, my beloved Salmah. Such a handsome man. Such a lovely friend. And oh my, could he sing, Alexandria. He melted my soul with his voice.

"Salmah was a little taller than me, a few years younger, and very dark in looks. Brown eyes, wavy dark brown hair. Olive skin. He looked like a Jew before we even knew we were Jews," Rachav said, her humour bubbling up again.

"He was fit and healthy, but he didn't have the kind of physique Baba had—no one did!" she giggled.

"Salmah was born and raised in the wilderness. He'd never known any other life than that of a Nomad. Imagine his expression when he and Azriel came to spy out the land and ended up on my doorstep. He'd never slept in a building before, so even walking into one of our rooms was a treat for him. Several items he'd never seen, such as my women's commode or even a bed with a mattress and a frame.

"So it was Salmah who was a great source of help to Baba, myself and the others when we were integrated into the Israelite tribe. He would offer a lot of help and was my greatest source of help when, as a widow, I had to pack up my tent when we were yet again on the move, out there in that delightful desert," Rachav's eyes glinted with sarcasm.

"His family would open their tent to me and allow me to sup with them whilst regaling me with tales of wonder and supernatural acts that Adonai/Papa had done in their midst. They spoke of the ten plagues that hit Egypt, which was a takedown of the ten greatest gods at the time in the Egyptian region, and that was fascinating to hear.

"The irony with that story is that Baba had told me some of it when he came home from several of his trips. Most people assume the plagues happened over ten consecutive days, but in reality, they unfolded gradually over the course of about a year. It was a terrifying time. I assure you, I was grateful to be far from it."

Rachav continued. "As a widow, there were certain things that the tribe had instigated towards us, but I was a person of excellent means. I was wealthy, and so was Baba. He brought a lot of gold coins and other treasures with him before we fled Yericho, so I never needed that kind of help.

"I needed reminding that I couldn't eat certain birds, any sort of pork, or shellfish of any kind, and that particular meat and animals were off-limits too. I wasn't terribly fussed with this 'unclean' business around that time of the month because Baba had never seen me have a cycle. I had fixed things so that it would never seep out. But, when Baba died, I removed it all, and for the first time in the longest time, I actually had a cycle. That I had to be banished for seven days? Utter bliss for me!"

Rachav didn't stop. It was like she had so much to share because there had never been the opportunity to get the truth out there.

"Salmah and his family loved to celebrate. They played their flutes, tambourines, drums, lyres, harps and all manner of instruments and sang for hours. They worshipped the Lord openly and freely and would spend great times dancing and enjoying wine, whilst putting on big feasts and enjoying the moment. I loved that. It was organic, unpretentious and beautiful.

"I feel so fortunate to have entered a family that was so exuberant. They absolutely embraced my elderly parents, and I watched my Eema and Abba grow younger for a time. It was beautiful, Alex. Seeing these people I hadn't spent much time with because of my introverted life with Baba come alive and enjoy their remaining years in joy and harmony was such a sweet gift for me."

"In time, I will share the romance I had with Salmah, but there is still so much more to share before he became a permanent person in my life."

26

Salmah

He had noticed her when they knocked on the door of her Inn. Such beauty, he felt, was either divine or a cruel joke. Who but Adonai could create a being such as this? Why did he have to notice this woman, who was already married, and a heathen at that?

Putting her out of his mind and getting on with the task at hand, Salmah and his cohort Azriel were sent by Y'hoshua to spy out the land and report back to the council. Their quick-thinking hostess had saved their lives and given them time to formulate their escape. They knew if the King of Yericho found out their whereabouts, it would be death, for them both.

Salmah kept his thoughts to himself. What was the point of dwelling on something that would never happen? The young man felt a sense of dread as they ran through the countryside and returned to the Israelite camp.

They had spent some time speaking with the couple and instructed them on what must happen before the siege occurred.

Salmah's heart was so profoundly moved for Rachav, Baba and their loved ones. Only just finding out that Adonai was the one true God after healing Baba of a strange ailment, he was sadly empathetic to the knowledge that these people were about to lose their entire world. It couldn't be helped. Adonai had ordained this. It was Helel, the Evil One, who had dispatched his monstrous watchers who had taken for themselves wives in exchange for all the modern technological warfare and scientific spells and blood mixture, creating a blend of beings that were never supposed to roam the earth – the Nephilim, or Giants, as they were commonly known.

So many didn't even know that the Nephilim blood was running through their veins and that Helel, the Evil One was the instigator of this heinous crime. How many women had lost their lives birthing these giants? How many people had lost their lives due to being seduced into a world of magic, lust, technology and scientific impurities that were never meant for this earth?

Salmah was distraught. Yet he knew. Adonai was merciful, but he was also just. There was a job to be done, and he and Azriel, of all the men of the tribe, had been chosen for this. Unlike his forefathers, who died out in the desert due to their whining, complaining, and defiance of Adonai's laws, he didn't want to let the council down. A generation that could have inherited the promised land was now buried in the wilderness. *"Such a waste,"* thought Salmah.

He shook his head as if to rearrange these thoughts, then continued.

Now, these very people who he had helped save, were part of his tribe. "*What are the odds of that happening,*" he had pondered? Doing his best to stay respectful and wanting to be helpful, Salmah became a friend to Novac and Abiah, as well as Rachav and Baba, and Rachav's elderly parents. He found the parents to be an absolute delight, knowing that most of their lives had been lived and their remaining lives would be lived as wandering nomads. It almost seemed unfair, but Rachav's parents never did complain. They embraced this part of their story as if it were the greatest of adventures! Maybe it really was to them – Salmah didn't know. He did know that he was glad their paths had met.

Baba entertained Salmah and his family with tales of adventure and travel from his trips abroad. He spoke of the different regions he and Rachav had visited and some unusual places they had the good fortune to see. Salmah laughed whilst Baba regaled tales of Egyptian bandits out in the desert trying to rob them in the middle of the night; wearing an extraordinary suit from Bharat for his wife that had been custom-made for him yet was too fitting; fishing bare-handed up the coast of Lebanon near some incredible caves, then cooking the fish on the beachfront, and other great stories.

Salmah had been born in the wilderness, and travelling as a nomadic tribe had been the only life he had ever known. Living in a building was such a foreign concept to him; he had no idea when Baba or Novac would mention specific aspects of the building trade nor of Novac's Master Wine Making.

Being the son of Nahshon and Miryam, Salmah and his siblings were all privy to the intimate story of Moshe, Harun and

Miryam, from their exodus from Egypt to the eventual death of the siblings, before the tribe crossed the river Yarden.

Miryam, Moshe and Harun had all been born in Goshen, and whilst Moshe was raised in the Royal Palace of the Great Pharaoh, Miryam and Harun had been raised as enslaved people. The Hebrews had become a thorn in the side of the current Pharaoh. Since the original Hebrew, Yosef, was no longer honoured or remembered in Egypt, life became exceedingly difficult for the enslaved Hebrews. Adonai had heard their prayers and sent their deliverer, Moshe, at the appointed time.

Nahshon became a tribal leader of the Judahites during the wilderness wanderings of the Hebrews. He was renowned for being the person to initiate the Hebrew's passage through the Yam Suph by walking in head deep until the sea parted. The Israelites had stood at the sea banks and wailed with despair, but Nahshon entered the waters. The sea parted once he was up to his nose in the water. He had complete faith in Adonai and, thereafter, was crowned by Moshe as prince and military commander of the tribe of Judah.

Miryam sang with the voice of an angel. She passed her gift of music down to her son, Salmah. Miryam led the entire tribe into a triumphant jubilee once they had all crossed the Yam Suph and were safely on dry land. She loved to sing and dance with her tambourine, and whilst she was rather exuberant, later on in her life, she would be struck down with leprosy due to her accusations against her brother Moshe. For his part, Moshe would plead her case to Adonai, who healed her even though she had been disobedient.

To Salmah's dismay, both his parents had passed away in the wilderness. Their entire generation, save Y'hoshua and Kalev, had disappeared. This was partly due to their constant whining to return to Egypt, the land of 'garlic, leeks and onions'. They seemed to keep looking back to the past instead of claiming the promise of Adonai, to conquer the land of Kena'an – the land flowing with milk and honey. Meanwhile, this new generation had learned from the previous one that they would do whatever it took to conquer this new land and make it their own.

27

Novac

Novac, from a young age, had exemplary knowledge of the different types of grapes, the colours of their skins, the soil that would produce different varieties of wine, and the make-up of spices that would enhance the flavour. The Master Wine Making position he had secured as a youth had been his only job. Such was his expertise; the Kings' Court had snapped him up quickly. Novac loved his vocation, and it had afforded him many opportunities to which he would never have met his now-wife if he hadn't been willing to take a risk. His wealth of knowledge and expertise had afforded him the great pleasure of travelling to other wine-making facilities throughout the Levant. There was also the occasional trip through Europa – to strange countries that froze in the winter with snow. It was surely a sight to behold and too cold for the boy who'd been raised in the desert. And yet now he was married to a woman who came from that cold region. He smiled at his good fortune.

Novac was in charge of cooperating with all the viticulturists in the region. It was originally the Phoenicians who developed viticulture practices that were later used elsewhere in the Levant, a fact that Novac held with pride. The young man knew the most significant factors to producing Master grade wine successfully, were known as *terroir*: climate, slope and soil. Learning that each grape variety had a uniquely preferred environment for ideal growth was crucial in Novac's education. Understanding temperature variation and the role of climate within each region was paramount to good wine production. The knowledge of soil, which allowed for better root systems, was imperative too. If the soil quality was terrible, there was no point in having good growth and health of the vine.

Along with mastering the terroir, Novac also had to learn the hazards of wine growth. A plethora of mildew and viruses could take out a good crop and make for a low-producing harvest. There also needed to be the guarding of the vines against pests. After all, it is the little foxes that spoil the vine.

Alongside understanding and cooperating with the viticulturists, Novac needed to monitor the grapes to ensure their quality and predict the right time for harvest. In fact, it was Novac who determined the harvest time within his region.

Other factors that Novac's job entailed testing the wine, crushing and pressing the grapes, the fermentation of the grape material—filtering the wine to remove the solids, placing the filtered wine in their storage tanks/pots for maturation, and adding the right balance of additional flavours and spices, to achieve a high optimum wine.

The last part of Novac's wine production was having the finest pottery jars and amphorae to house the wine, and export to their customers in the region and beyond. The young man had determined his storage containers would be beautiful yet simple, much like him.

Coming from quite a large family and being the eldest son, there had been a lot of pressure applied to him to meet and marry the right kind of person. Novac's family had arranged a bride from his early youth, but he wasn't having a bar of it! Being of a determined mind, he knew that he would only be satisfied long-term if he married for love – such was his conviction.

After meeting Abiah and seeing how hard she worked, alongside being such a beauty in her own right, there was never a doubt that he would one day ask to marry her. But he wouldn't ever think of asking her parents; it would be directly to Abiah, to which he would confess his love and ask for her hand, and he knew that their union would be one of equals. She may not have owned the Inn, but she had spent many years there and had been trained by Rachav and then Baba, in all aspects of the business. Like her Madam, she was not afraid of hard work. Nor was she afraid of pleasure.

Novac had been courting Abiah for quite some time, when eventually, he almost begged to lay with her! He didn't realise that she hadn't been educated in the ways of love and sensual pleasures. She became defensive when he approached the subject until he suggested she approach Rachav. He knew that Rachav was a woman of the world and knew her own mind too. He wanted to experience his Abiah in all the ways the gods would allow, and he wanted her to be comfortable with him.

Looking back, there was nothing to worry about. She was so instinctual in the ways of love, that Novac had felt he was flying in the air when he was around or near Abiah. Their love transcended anything he could've ever asked for, so it was a natural progression from lovers to husband and wife eventually.

Answering the door that fateful night at the Inn, when Abiah was fresh from her love lessons with Rachav, Novac never expected to find her in her full glory, and ready! He was besotted with her.

After their time of love had been consummated, Novac lay as the sleeping beauty next time him slept, and he sighed. She was his goddess, and he worshipped her entirely—the feeling of being one with her. The teasing and taunting she put him through. Her desire to please him which led to sultry, seductive tones of lust, in and out of bed. The chair and all the pleasure that had brought. All of it was such a bank of sweet memories. He adored his bride and prayed always to make her his highest and most precious priority.

Now, here he was, living as a nomad, in his year with Abiah and with no job per se other than getting to know his beloved lover-bride. Part of him ached to be at work; it was something he had trained so long for and was so exemplary at. He knew in time that Adonai would make way for him and Abiah; for the time being, being with her was enough – she was more than enough!

PART TWO

The Reluctant Hero

28

War & Covenant

Baba returned from fighting another tribe in an area called Beit-El, to the west of Ai. Over twelve thousand men and women had fallen, and only the livestock and the booty had been retrieved. The King of Ai had been hung from a tree until that evening; at sundown, Y'hoshua gave an order, so they took his carcass down from the tree, threw it at the city gate entrance, and piled a big heap of stones on it.

Then Y'hoshua built an altar to Adonai, the God of Isra'el, on Mount 'Eival, as Moshe, the servant of Adonai, had ordered the people of Isra'el to, an altar of uncut stones that no one had touched with an iron tool. On it, they offered burnt offerings to Adonai and sacrificed peace offerings. He wrote there on the stones a copy of the Torah of Moshe, inscribing it in the presence of the people of Isra'el. Then all Isra'el, including their leaders, officials and judges, stood on either side of the ark in front of the Cohanim, who were L'vi'im and who carried the ark for the covenant of Adonai. The foreigners were there, along with the citizens. Half of the people were in front of Mount G'rizim and half of them in front of Mount 'Eival, as Moshe, the servant of Adon, had ordered them earlier in connection with blessing the people of Isra'el. After this, he read all the words of the Torah, the blessing and the curse, according to everything written in the book of the Torah. There was not a word of everything Moshe had ordered that Y'hoshua did not read before all Isra'el assembled, including the women, the little ones and the foreigners living with them.

Baba was exhausted. He wanted to live his life in peace and was resentful that because of his size and strength, he'd been chosen by the council to fulfil a commandment given before the former Yericho residents' integration.

This wasn't what he had signed up for, but again, out of respect, Baba pushed on.

Rachav worried furiously over her giant warrior. Being used to him going off on travels all across the Levant and elsewhere, she never gave a thought to his safety. She had always known he could care for himself, but this felt different. A foreboding that wouldn't lift. Rachav would share her concerns with her husband and occasionally with some of the tribe in confidence, and they would pray. They had seen the mighty hand of Adonai move in their midst and on their behalf, so Rachav felt she could trust Adonai with Baba and her life.

Finally, the time came that the land rested from war. Many kings had been killed, and the Israelites had overturned many cities.

Finally, Baba and Rachav were able to relish in this time of peace and make some plans for themselves. They still longed to head off to a place where they could be alone and enjoy themselves whilst appreciating a different land and culture.

They felt the right thing to do was approach the council and inform them of their plans. For now, they were encamped at Gilgal, with no immediate plans to move, so it made sense that Rachav and Baba could travel while the tribe remained where they were.

The council forbade it. They couldn't understand, nor wanted to understand. They were told under no uncertain terms that they wouldn't be welcome back if they left. It was such a blow for the couple, particularly after Baba had fought so hard on behalf of the Israelite tribe. In this instance, they made the only decision they could - they prayed.

Neither one of them had peace about travelling after seeking Adonai. To them, it was the strangest thing. Something that had been a true source of joy and adventure now seemed to be another piece of their past that needed to be laid down.

It was decided that since they weren't going to travel, they might start getting a little more integrated into the community. They both had done the minimum, aside from Baba fighting in all the endless wars, and maybe they should move from the periphery into a more community-based life.

During one of those times, when Baba and Rachav walked around the encampment's outer perimeter, Baba started to feel somewhat unusual. Memories of her beloved fainting on the boat whilst on their travels flashed back to Rachav's mind. She was frightened of Baba not being the strong, robust man he had always been.

Baba was trying to reassure his wife that he would be fine. He just needed rest. Heading back to the tent, Baba fell just before the door of their dwelling. Rachav yelled for help, and several men came running, helping get the large man into their tent.

An older man, who seemed to be wise in the ways of medicine, came and examined Baba. This was like déjà vu for Rachav, and she was worrying nonstop. With every breath Baba took, his body seemed to shake. His heartbeat seemed faint and erratic. There didn't seem to be a solid diagnosis other than his heart was giving up.

Baba – her demi-god, supernatural lover, closest friend and ally- was slipping away from her. They had matters to discuss, so everyone left the tent so they could have some privacy.

"Rachav, my love, come closer to me. I want to feel your breath on my face," whispered Baba faintly. Rachav moved as close to him as she could without lying on him. Leaning in, she listened as he spoke.

"My darling, you are the joy of my life, my soul and my heart. But I am dying. I know you will mourn me, but please don't return to having a hard heart. Adonai has placed us in a community that loves us, and you will continue on. Remember when you told me after I was having those horrible dreams, that you and I are two separate bodies, but one heart and one soul? That is true, my love. I may be gone soon, but I will never be gone from your heart." Rachav wept, but kept listening. While he breathed and wanted to talk, she was willing to be silent and listen. She wouldn't argue, for she knew Baba was speaking the truth.

"My darling lover wife, you have bought me untold joy and happiness. You are my goddess, remember?" She nodded. "Don't shut yourself away or withhold yourself from joy." Baba, too, wept. Wiping the tears from his eyes, Rachav gently touched his face. She was tracing every curve, every line. She knew this face. She had loved, worshipped and adored this face for as long as she could remember. She wanted to remember every detail. She had to, for she knew he was slipping away.

"Beloved, there is something I have never told you, and maybe it will help you understand where we are now." Rachav was intrigued.

"Did you ever wonder why I didn't have family around?" Rachav thought momentarily and then spoke, "Yes, I did. But I thought you would speak of them when you were ready. Why is it you are only ready now, darling Baba?"

"Because my siblings and my parents all died quite young. Though they were strong as oxen and had supernatural blood in their veins, their hearts gave out before they reached middle age. My brothers were older than me, but I never really knew them. I think they moved to other areas. I really don't know. But my parents died before I was out of my youth. It's really just been me. Then I saw you and fell in love with you, and it's been just us. Well, until all this happened." Baba grinned a little. "You see, darling, I couldn't risk us having children either, as I wouldn't be here to be their father as they grew." He wept. "I am sorry I didn't tell you earlier. I wouldn't blame you for feeling like you married a dud." Rachav shushed him. "Darling, you are perfect in my eyes. We have had over two decades together. The happiest and most wonderful years of my life. How could I ever regret a moment with you or accuse you of anything? Oh, Baba, some of this makes sense now – your assertion in your career and in the bedroom. Oh, darling!" Rachav laughed as she held Baba's hand.

"I'm tired, my love; I would like to sleep now."

"I'll be here, darling. You rest well." Rachav held his hand and bowed her head in prayer.

"Oh, Adonai. I still don't know you very well, but I know that you know us. These people tell me that you know every hair on our heads, every cell in our beings. If that's true, I ask that you be merciful to my Baba and not allow him to suffer. Adonai, you are so gracious and have been kind to us; I ask that you allow Baba and me one more night to say goodbye. Omaine."

Rachav awoke in the early morning hours and could hear the laboured breathing of her beloved. His colour had grown pale. Baba opened his eyes, and the iridescent blue still gleamed as he looked at his wife.

"Rachav," he whispered. "It's time."

Rachav stroked his hair as tears streamed down her face. "You have given me so much life and love, and I don't know how to do this without you, Baba." Her voice wavered.

"You must trust in Adonai now, my beauty. He will hold you and protect you. He will guide you. This I do know."

"But life without you won't be worth living." She was trying hard to be strong yet felt powerless and weak.

"Darling, you know what to do. You are so strong, so absolute in all you do. But please remember to keep your heart soft. I love you, Rachav. I adore only you...." With that, Baba breathed his last breath. "I love you, Baba. I adore only you." She cradled him as he slipped into eternity.

Looking up after burying her face in his flaxen hair, Rachav became aware she wasn't alone. She turned and saw a gleaming angel, who smiled at her. She then watched as Baba's spirit got up and left his body. The two of them looked at Rachav, who was gobsmacked, and they walked towards the tent door. Looking more beautiful and radiant than his earthen body, Baba looked at her, smiled, and waved as they walked through the tent fabric. She sat on their bed, unable to move, in utter shock at what had just transpired. Looking down, was the body of her beloved. Now she had to bury him.

As the day dawned, Rachav got off the bed and went to the tent door. Touching the fabric that the angel and Baba had walked through, she stood silent for a minute, gathered her courage and opened the door.

Outside were her parents Yaffah and Ever, alongside Novac and Abiah, all kneeling and weeping together.

Slowly word went through the enormous camp, of the death of their beloved warrior, Baba.

Azriel and Salmah were among the first to come and offer their help. Trailing behind them, were Salmah's family and friends.

This was unfamiliar territory for Rachav. She had never organised a funeral before and was completely out of her depth. She listened intently to the advice that was being given to her by the council and, of course, from her parents. Somewhere in the middle of those two suggestions, Rachav would have to find a send-off fitting for a one-of-a-kind man, such as Baba.

A hand reached out and placed itself on her shoulder. Rachav turned and saw it was her father, Ever. Never having been one to shy away from affection, Ever took her in his arms and allowed her to cry. Her body heaved with grief, realising the life she had once lived, was now over.

Baba was laid to rest in a newly carved tomb. Rachav had ensured he was wearing his best colourful tunic, his wedding band and favourite sandals and wrapped in fresh linen from the Levant. They sang and wept with her, then ate a feast worthy of the warrior he had been.

Quietly, Rachav slipped away into her tent. She had private matters to attend to. She lifted up a beautiful blanket they had brought abroad and put it aside, then opened up an elaborate trunk with some items of Baba's remaining items within it. Rachav decided that the dresses she would only wear in private for Baba, needed to go into the trunk. She also gathered all of Baba's clothing, knowing it was far too big for anyone else in the camp, extra jewellery and sandals, and placed them in there.

A cloak that Baba had worn regularly stayed draped over their favourite chair. It was warm and doubled as a blanket when there had been the need for one.

Rachav was exhausted. She removed the pins from her hair, blew out her oil lamp, and quietly got into the bed of fleeces. Laying on her side, she wept. The pain of his loss was far worse at night. The nights had always been theirs, but this aching wouldn't subside. Just as she was about to enter slumber, she felt someone holding her. She felt around the bed and realised no one was there – but it sure did feel like it. This would happen a lot in the early days. She wondered if, somehow, Baba was allowed back at times to bring a form of comfort to her grief. The beautiful widow didn't contemplate it too much; she was grateful nonetheless.

29

Life After Baba

Learning to live after the death of Baba was something that Rachav never anticipated. In her mind, she had thought this would be the most challenging transition. However, there seemed to be a sense of ease and peace that surrounded her during this time.

She had listened to the requests of her beloved husband and made a mental note that hiding away and withholding herself from a life lived from the heart wouldn't honour him. It was essential to Rachav that in all she did, she honoured her beloved. Rachav knew that Baba was with the Lord, and this gave her great comfort, if not making her a little jealous!

One of the first things Rachav made inquiries to her tribe about was finding out about this thing they called 'Shabbat'. Rachav, Abiah and Yaffah went and spoke to Salmah's relatives to see if they would be willing to teach them what it was and why it was necessary? There seemed to be a lot of preparations around this weekly ritual, so Rachav became a student in all things Hebrew.

Salmah's sister explained. "The Shabbat is twenty-five hours, from sundown on Friday to one hour after sundown on Saturday. According to the scroll of Vayikra, Moshe instructed us to stop all work and gather together for a 'solemn assembly'. Shabbat is gathering of ourselves physically, emotionally and spiritually to rest and turn our attention entirely to Adonai, family and friends."

The women were intrigued and motioned for the sister to continue.

"Interestingly, the ancients tell a story of Avraham and Sarah and Sarah's Shabbat Lamp. Centuries ago, Avraham and Sarah embarked on a journey to bring the idea and morals of monotheism to a predominantly pagan world. Their journey took them from their native Ur Kasdim to Charan and from there to the land of Kena'an, where they settled first in Hevron and later in Be'er-sheva. They pitched their tents at the desert crossroads and offered food, drink and lodging to all wayfarers of every tribe and creed. Wherever they went, they taught the truth of the One God, creator of heaven and earth.

In Sarah's tent, an extraordinary miracle proclaimed that the Divine Presence dwelled therein: the lamp she lit every Friday evening, in honour of the divine day of rest, miraculously kept burning all week, until the following Friday eve. When Sarah died, the miracle of her Shabbat lamp ceased. But on the day of Sarah's passing, Rivka was born. And when Rivka was brought to Sarah's tent as the destined wife of Sarah's son, Yitz'chak, the miracle of the lamp returned. Once again, the light of Shabbat filled the tent of the matriarch of Israel and radiated its holiness to the entire week.

"Remember the day, Shabbat, to set it apart for God. You have six days to labour and do all your work, but the seventh day is a Shabbat for Adonai, your God. On it, you are not to do any kind of work — not you, your son or your daughter, not your male or female slave, not your livestock, and not the foreigner staying with you inside the gates to your property. For in six days, Adonai made heaven and earth, the sea and everything in them; but on the seventh day, he rested. This is why Adonai blessed the day, Shabbat, and separated it for himself." Sh'mot 20:8–11.

A prayer we pray during the Shabbat is, "Blessed are You, Lord, our God, King of the universe, who sanctifies us with His commandments and has been pleased with us. You have lovingly and willingly given us Your holy Shabbat as an inheritance in memory of creation. The Shabbat is the first among our holy days and a remembrance of our exodus from Egypt. Indeed, You have chosen and made us holy among all peoples and willingly and lovingly given us Your holy Shabbat for an inheritance. Blessed are you who sanctifies the Shabbat. Omaine."

"We also prepare food, such as Challah bread, which is sweet, and ensure these things are ready before sundown. It is wrong of us to make preparations afterwards, as it violates the rules of Shabbat – no working at all. So it is imperative that I teach you to go about the day before and the morning of Shabbat to ensure everything is right. Adonai has given us six days to work, but the Shabbat is holy to him. We must honour that in every way."

Rachav and Abiah went about making their preparations, albeit rather nervously, for fear of getting things wrong.

The women were adept at cooking, so making the Challah bread was relatively easy for them. Noting they also needed wine for the table, Novac retrieved one from the stores he had brought from Yericho. Realising it wouldn't be kosher, he spoke to the family, and they didn't think Adonai would mind – "His blessing upon the table would be enough to negate any pagan residue," they had stated. Once the table was set, the loaves covered, and the wine glasses readied, the candles were put into the candelabra. Lighting the candles just before sundown, the women remained silent. Prayers and blessings were offered up, and then the wine was poured. The leaders of each table washed their hands ceremoniously praying as they did. Then came the blessing over the bread, and finally, the delicious Shabbat meal itself was consumed. Much singing and celebration ensued, healing the grief and becoming salve for Rachav's soul. Afterwards came the blessing after the meal, followed by cheers, hugs and more celebration.

As she stumbled through the various stages of this ritual, Rachav would often giggle, knowing that Baba would have swatted her bottom, and they would have laughed heartily together.

At times, Rachav would sense his presence, and rather than run to her tent and cry, she would embrace that feeling, breathe it in and thank Adonai that she wasn't alone.

Like her parents, Abiah and Novac would often be by Rachav's side. Whilst keeping a respectful distance and honouring the grieving process, Salmah visited more than when Baba was alive. Rachav found that to be quite humorous and nothing to take seriously. There was no way that Rachav would be with another man. There would be no one like Baba, not for her. Ever. So she thought.

Rachav was never one to be outgoing or attract a crowd around her. Being the only child and being that she had been an Inn Keeper for so long, she was used to her own company. However, the time had come, she and Baba had spoken of this, and she knew that at her age, she had to step up and make some effort to get to know some people and allow others into her inner world. This, to her, was so foreign, but she embraced the changes and started to revel in some of the women who ingratiated themselves to her.

Being a widow brought its challenges. Rachav knew she had the support of a select few, but allowing others to step in where once Baba was in control, took some getting used to.

She would often smile when watching others struggle with menial tasks that Baba seemed to do so naturally. Rachav had to remind herself that he actually was from a supernatural lineage.

Knowing that she needed time to grieve privately, others would watch out from a distance as she walked around the encampment. There had been times when foreigners had tried to infiltrate their camp, but the tribe knew how to circumvent these invaders.

Rachav was held in high regard, as was Baba, knowing that they had risked their lives to save the spies when they had done their reconnaissance back in Yericho. No one would forget the sacrifice of their gentle giant Baba, who fought so valiantly in the army and gave them great victories. But the time had come for mourning to come to an end, and life had to move on. Would Rachav be ready to meet that challenge?

According to the Israelites, Moshe had written in his scroll, that it wasn't good for man to be alone. Therefore he needed a wife. But Rachav bucked at this. She had been a wife and lover for many years and felt no need to share herself ever again. However, this was definitely against their custom. She apparently was still of child-bearing age, so she needed to be at least open to the possibility of marriage again.

"No! I have just lost my husband. How could you even think there would be room in my heart for anyone other than Baba? How could you even suggest such a thing? Eema, Abba, I love you; truly, I do. But that is enough. My mind is made up – there will never be another man for me! Please, stop this nonsense at once!" Rachav stormed off. There was no way that she would even consider another man, let alone these funny Hebrew men and their appendages that had been circumcised. *"Good grief, they weren't even real men anymore!"* Rachav thought to herself whilst giggling a little. She remembered a conversation that Novac and Baba had when they first joined the tribe, and both the men were utterly insulted at such a thought. They would be Hebrew in every way the tribe wanted, but there was no need to take matters that far and give permission for themselves to be deformed now.

Rachav had removed her sponges and, for the first in a very long time, had allowed herself to cycle. It was a very odd thing to do, and now she was privy to the benefits of leaving the camp for seven days, as she was now considered 'unclean'. She relished the idea! *"Oh my, I have been unclean my whole life then,"* she murmured to herself. Baba would've baulked at the changes she had to make now. He would've understood, but he wouldn't like to have been separated when she would be on one side of the camp and he on the other. He would've broken all the relevant laws and rules concerning that. The giant man was a brute when he wanted to be and a stubborn child at times. Still, that was in the past, and Rachav welcomed this new change.

Alongside allowing herself to follow the natural rhythms of her body, Rachav no longer wore her hair up in fancy adornments or wore make-up now. She didn't feel the need to do herself up for anyone, so she went about with her long brunette hair either down or tied in a knot on her head. Her shifts replaced the beautiful coloured brocades and shimmering fabrics she had been afforded back in her Yericho days, and for the first time, Rachav delighted in feeling more 'earthy'. She loved being unpretentious and not worrying about Baba and his demands. The whole side of her sexuality that had been the mainstay of their lives had grown solidly dormant, and this was a beautiful time for the widow. Locking those things away was easy. She longed to understand the culture she was immersed in now but had to take some things within her own time.

30

Y'Hoshua Speaks

After the appointed time of mourning had passed, Rachav was summoned to have a meeting with Y'hoshua, Kalev and the council. Feeling somewhat troubled at the summoning, she took along her parents, Ever and Yaffah.

Rachav rarely had seen or spoken with Y'hoshua; therefore, the woman was nervous. Thinking the worst, he immediately put her at ease and invited Rachav and her parents to sit amongst the cushions as they were served coffee and sweet pastries.

"Rachav, sister and friend. We owe you a great debt," boomed the loud voice of the head tribesmen.

"I am honoured you feel that way, Y'hoshua, but there is no need to thank me. Baba and I had started to pray to Adonai, and we had asked for a sign that we were heading in the right direction, and then the spies turned up. So, you see, we are deeply indebted to you." To Rachav's surprise, her eyes welled up with tears, and she felt a swelling within her chest. It was like she was in the presence of someone great, and she wanted to honour that feeling for the first time in her life.

"I'm glad you bought up Baba. How are you doing now that he is with Adonai?"

"Some days are easier than others, but I have great support and know where Baba is. Did you know I saw his spirit leave?"

"No, I did not. The Lord deeply honours you for allowing you to see this." Y'hoshua seemed to be perplexed.

"Does this bother you, Y'hoshua?"

"No, dear sister, this makes my heart very glad. Adonai is so merciful to us, eh?" The older man smiled.

"Indeed, he is." Rachav returned the smile.

"Rachav, I need to address matters concerning Baba and his heritage. You are certainly aware that he descended from an ancient tribe of giants – the Gibborim?"

"I've never heard them called that, but Baba had spoken to me a couple of times about this ancient blood. It was often something we laughed about."

"Hmmm. I do not believe it is a matter to be laughed at, Rachav. It is deeply serious and was of great concern to us when we invited you and your family to join us from Yericho. Are you aware that these descendants come from the two hundred watchers that descended from Heaven to Mt Hermon?"

"Yes, Y'hoshua. Baba explained that his line comes from an angel called Azazel. Is that correct?"

"That is partially correct. His name was Azazyel, and he was responsible for teaching many things, including warfare, of which Baba was a true warrior. However, they were fallen angels."

Rachav gasped. "You mean, these were the fallen ones who left their estate with Adonai?"

"Yes, Rachav."

"And this means they were now enemies to Adonai and no longer his servants? Do I have this correct?"

"You do."

Rachav sat in a state of shock. Words and conversations circled her brain's inner workings as her mouth fell open and groans leapt forth.

"What does this mean then, Y'hoshua? Am I doomed? Is my husband with Adonai? What.... how.... What?" Rachav raised her voice in anguish.

"What of my beloved Baba?" She couldn't help but give in to the tears and anguish spilling forth from her soul.

"Now, dear sister, be at shalom. Your beloved Baba is with Adonai. You saw him leave with the angel of the Lord, did you not?" Rachav nodded.

"He was beloved by all of us, dear one. His heart honoured Adonai. Whilst he had part of the story's origins mixed up, that wasn't his doing. He had given himself to the work of Adonai, this no one doubts. And while the Gibborim were not allowed into paradise, there are rare occasions where Adonai allows things to change a little. He is, after all, sovereign and entirely merciful."

Rachav managed to calm down as her mother and father sat on either side of her and held her. "So why are you telling me this, Y'hoshua?" Rachav wiped her eyes whilst speaking.

"We, the council, felt you needed to hear the truth from us. There is more to the story, but not more concerning Baba.

Understanding why we have had to wage so much war and overtake some cities whilst leaving others uninhabited is imperative. If you and the tribe don't understand the commandments given to us by the Lord, then I fear we will forever remain as Nomads roaming in the desert as our tribe did for forty years under Moshe's command."

"What is there to understand?" enquired Rachav's father, Ever.

"Ah, Ever, such a great Hebrew name! Do you understand the meaning of your name?" Y'Hoshua asked directly to Rachav's father.

"No, sir, I don't," responded Ever.

"Your name means 'to go over'. That's very poignant considering the recent events of Yericho and our tribe, wouldn't you say, Ever?"

"I see. That is indeed very peculiar, Y'hoshua. I thank you for explaining that to me." Ever smiled at the older tribesman.

"Well, Ever, Yaffah and Rachav, here is where the story gets fascinating. Are you aware that Yericho was a stronghold for the Gibborim in times past? You may know them as the Anakim?"

The trio shook their heads, somewhat perplexed.

"The very foundations of Yericho are built on an ancient Nephilim citadel. An energy source that was in use when the giants roamed freely all across the known world. This was ground zero, if you like, the world's centre and the Nephilim's capital. The whole area was demonically charged, and until we conquered your former city, it carried that charge until it was burned to the ground. You, of course, are aware that your former gods and goddesses demanded human foetal blood to keep the citadel charged and the favour of the divine upon your walls?"

The trio looked horrified. None of them had been too interested in the gods and goddesses, other than minor concessions over the years. Yaffah looked pale, almost as if she was going to be sick.

"Yaffah, do you need some air?"

"No, Y'hoshua, I will be fine. However, this is a bit to take in, and it will take a while to understand what we didn't know, or should I say, refused to acknowledge, about our own city and culture."

Y'hoshua continued.

"The citadel was part of a complex of cities spread throughout the Levant after the watchers had come down and formulated their demonic plans. In essence, they acquired women to mate with in exchange for sharing secret heavenly knowledge with man. The women were taught the art of seduction through making up their faces with various paint and jewellery, which formerly hadn't been known by mankind. The introduction of weapons of warfare became an obsession with man, who gave themselves entirely over to warring with one another and leaving behind the worship and honour of Yahweh. He became just another god amongst these watchers.

"How it grieved the heart of Heaven to see their former citizens creating gross havoc on the earth. They came to a point in their iniquity where they began mating with all the different forms of animals, both on the land and in the oceans. Nothing was sacred to these beings. They created scientific experiments within laboratories they built and thought in their devious minds how wonderful it would be to create crossbreeds of humans and animals alike. They are called chimeras. You have known them as gods. Just look around the cultures in the Levant and over in Egypt to all their known gods, and you will see what I mean."

Rachav spoke up. "Would you mind going back to the destruction of our city, and explain why you marched around the city, and blew the shofars? We were utterly perplexed when this occurred but didn't think to question you at the time?"

"Certainly, Rachav. As I have mentioned, the citadel under Yericho was a demonic power source. We had to use divine energy and vibration to break that source completely and return the land to Adonai. This whole earth has energy and vibrations mixed with colours and sound, but that is a mystery for another time." Y'hoshua smiled and then poured himself another coffee.

Yaffah, Ever and Rachav poured themselves another coffee and enjoyed a sweet pastry as they pondered all the information Y'hoshua had given them.

"One of the key factors in this whole sordid tale was blood. The watchers knew the plans of Adonai and knew there would be a time when pure blood would be needed on the earth. Their evil father, Helel, devised his plan, including the absolute destruction of pure blood. His desire was for Adonai to have no pure humans left; therefore, a future Messiach could not come. All the laws and commandments we follow are a type and shadow for a day when Messiach will come and fully redeem all things. However, for that to happen, Adonai had to step in and raise a righteous man who would do his bidding here on the earth. That man was Noach. You have heard of him, dear ones?"

The trio smiled. Yes, they knew the myth of Noach. He had been called other names, but they too, were captured by the story of the boat, the flood and the animals.

"Noach would spend over a hundred years building a boat, such as the earth had never seen before, and he preached a righteous message pleading with man to repent of their depravity and iniquity. Not one man, other than Noach's family, would bend. How Adonai wept. He even repented of creating mankind – his crown and glory! His mercy has always been extended to all who would bow their knee and soften their hearts, but man had gone too far. They enjoyed their sin so desperately that they saw no reason to bow to Adonai. In their hearts, he was no greater or lesser than that which they were worshipping already. Ah, the grief we humans cause him, eh?" Y'hoshua beat his chest and wiped his eyes.

"I have lived a long time, my friends, and I have seen the hand of the Almighty do things that these gods only wish they could do! Nothing is too hard for Adonai, nothing!" he bellowed.

"However, as man wouldn't repent, the flood came. Such destruction was rent upon the whole earth. Continents were now formed where the whole earth was once a land mass. New oceans, rivers, and seas appeared as the cisterns of the deep earth exploded. Mountains arose higher than before. Fault lines appeared, and tectonic plates shifted greatly, causing deep divides in the earth's structure. Many man-made structures that were on high places, temples and altars, fell into the waters.

The oceans are full of remnants of a world gone mad. Although half-divine and half-human, the Nephilim lost their place on the earth. The watchers – all of them, were taken below the earth and are currently in chains until the end of times. But even though Noach and his family were considered righteous and were given the charge to govern the earth once more and populate it, the sin that had been prevalent within the world, still dwelt within some of their hearts. That is why we need rules, laws and commandments – we are born with sin, thanks to the original sinner, tempted by Helel – the beautiful shining one."

Yaffah, Rachav and Ever sat with their mouths wide open, not knowing what to say. No one had ever attempted to enlighten this family with the truth before.

Y'hoshua continued. "My friends, I have shared a lot with you, but now, I think it is time that you go and have time to think and pray on these matters. I still have things to share with you, but that will wait for another time." With that, Y'Hoshua bowed his head slightly, and walked out of the tent, leaving the trio in a semi-state of shock.

Rachav was the first to arise, helping her parents off the cushions; the three of them strode out of the tent and walked back to their dwellings. The silence between them betrayed the loud ramblings within each of their minds. Thankfully, they all knew they could pray. That is what they did.

Rachav stood outside her tent and looked at the vista before her. Dusk was settling over the encampment, with its pale pinks and golden hues appearing in the sky. She never got tired of seeing this scene. It harkened her back to times with Baba on their various trips when they would've been seated outside on a boat waiting for dinner. Rachav shook her head and went into her tent, gathering her food so that she and her family, including Abiah and Novac, could have their communal dinner. Tonight, however, she wished that she could eat alone.

After celebrating their meal, Rachav took herself off to her tent. Still on her mind, was the formation of Yericho. Then suddenly, there it was – the foreboding sense she had up in the mountains of Anatolia. The complex they had stayed at had been part of this Nephilim civilisation. Of course!

Rachav sat on her chair, connecting all the pieces within her mind, knowing that Baba would have been both intrigued and enlightened by this newfound knowledge.

She moved off the chair, hopped into her bed, whispered a prayer of thanksgiving to Adonai, then blew out her lamp.

<h1 style="text-align:center">31</h1>

Present Day

Alex and Rachav were sitting on a cluster of rocks, watching as the tide went out. Their times together had become so precious to Alex, with Rachav sharing, teaching and imparting great knowledge, wisdom and understanding to the younger woman.

The wind rose and blew Rachav's beautiful brunette locks off her face. Alex looked at the older woman's profile. She was stunning, *"Even more so than when she walked the earth,"* thought Alex. The Jewish sages had said that Rachav was one of four women who walked the earth that possessed such incredible beauty. Yet Alexandria knew that Rachav wouldn't have been happy with this summarisation, then or now. Whatever the case, Alex was profoundly humbled and cherished every moment spent with this gracious woman.

The two looked at each and laughed. Such great friends they had become, it was difficult to distinguish what reality they were in at times.

"Rachav, when did you grasp the enormity of the task before you?"

"Which one, Alex?" Rachav questioned.

"Understanding the festivals, holy days, feasts and all the traditions that you not only had to learn but embrace and eventually live by? I couldn't fathom being thrown into the deep end and having to do that in a short space of time."

"That's where your world and mine were exceptionally different, Alex. We had a lot of time. We weren't governed by schedules, clocks, watches, timetables, planners and calendars as you know them, or anything else of that nature. We were governed by celestial times, which had been written by Adonai in the skies, alongside his commandments he gave Moshe, on stone and in our hearts. It was a joy to live in such a way that there was purpose and meaning. We were united in our servitude and honour of Adonai, which was beautiful. It seems that modern-day faith, indeed just living, is so difficult and harsh. Our world was open to the foreigners, the strangers and aliens, as it were, and we were particularly admonished to look after the widows – the ones who had been abandoned, divorced and left behind, as well as the orphans. Modern society would do well to look back in ancient history and see how we handled situations. There was great wisdom in what Papa/Adonai ordained from the start."

"So, for you, having to unlearn and relearn – letting go of one culture, and embracing another, was that difficult or painful in any way, Rachav?"

"In a sense, it was, particularly at the start. I often walked off to avoid upsetting others with my opinions and outbursts!

Baba was very good at understanding where I was coming from. Still, Salmah and his siblings taught me and showed me the inner workings of some of the more peculiar commandments, in reference and context to the cultures we were living amongst."

"How so, Rachav?"

"People seem to interpret the Scriptures these days within the context they live and dwell in. But that isn't helpful in the slightest. One only needs to do a little research to understand that all the commandments and rules were diametrically opposed to how cultures operated back when we walked the earth. It seems odd that I watch from the balconies of Heaven and see people applying their lens over scripture. It needs to be viewed through the lens through which it was written – a Middle Eastern document for a Middle Eastern people. A time when giants really did walk the earth, and pleasing the gods and goddesses was at the centre of what the collective culture did. Our lives were circular. Everything was connected, and there were no particular carving areas into little boxes and tucking them away. As you have learnt through the years, Alexandria, the river of life – Yeshua – flows into every area of life."

"It's fascinating that you word things that way, Rachav, as I've struggled to understand the Western Christianity for which I seem to be stuck inside of. I understand that Yeshua was a Jew, and therein lies all sorts of problems for someone who lives on the other side of the world. One of my key frustrations being in the southern hemisphere is that we are diametrically opposite seasonally to when all the feasts and festivals are taking part – in the northern hemisphere. I find it difficult to keep myself in the right frame of mind, the right rhythm, when I am coming from the opposite side of the world."

"I sense and understand your frustration, Alex; however, don't you think Papa knows this? Of course, he does, and whether you feel it or not, you are in the right place for this very season. Don't try and shape your world to fit your beliefs; just let Papa's river flow through and make the changes as necessary."

"Thank you, Rachav. I sometimes get deeply frustrated with my culture and the mindset of supposed Christians around me. I realise I cannot afford to get carried away and make this beautiful time with you all into a sense of legalism and folly. Because I am still learning all the basics of first-century Jewish thought and understanding, I need patience and gentleness – things that aren't necessarily naturally easy for me."

Rachav got up from the cluster and started to walk towards the distant tide. "You don't get to control the tides, Alexandria; the moon does that. How Papa has framed all creation and made things work in their miraculous intricacy is beyond me. But I trust him now as I trusted him then. It's simple, Alex. Don't push so hard. The learning is happening, but at the same time, the unlearning is happening too. You must remember that time is on your side, and you're not walking any path other than what Papa has ordained for you."

"Yes, I know you are right, and I appreciate your wisdom; thank you, my dear friend."

32

Love Song

Salmah sang with all his heart and mind. Not realising that anyone was around as he tended the flock, as David would in generations to come, Salmah loved to sing praises to Adonai.

His heart would soar in worship as the songs poured forth from him. When he would hit a specific note, he would sense the presence of Adonai drawing him closer, pulling him into his love and adoration even more. For Salmah, it felt like he had crossed over into another realm; such was the passion and intensity. He adored Adonai and longed with all his heart to honour him in all he did. Loving the creator this way was the most natural thing in the world to him. It was what he had seen his mother, Miryam do as he was growing up. She alone led the tribe in a victorious celebration of jubilant worship when the Pharoah and his army that had chased them, drowned in the Yam Suph. From that time to her death out in the wilderness, she would use her voice to worship Adonai, and this gift was passed down to her children, specifically Salmah.

Whilst Rachav was used to a culture with music and song as part of life, she was not used to seeing a man, or a tribe of people, break out in spontaneous praise towards this invisible deity. Alongside the worship, she saw and heard instruments she'd never known existed: shofar, harp, lyre, string instruments, flute, and cymbals. To watch them as they took their sound and tuned it into their constant praise, was a sight to behold. She found herself getting caught up in the moment and was caught off guard when words came tumbling up and out of her mouth! Alongside, she had a certain feeling, much like euphoria that happened. Was she, for the first time, consciously worshipping Adonai?

33

Pesach

"Not so many years ago, the Hebrew people were plagued by the Egyptians and trapped in slavery for several generations. Adonai heard the cries of their hearts and told Moshe via a burning bush he was the man to set them free. Along with Harun as his mouthpiece, Pharaoh proves unwilling to let his slaves go and cause an economic downturn for his country. In reaction to Pharaoh's decision, Adonai plagues the Egyptians in ten different ways, the tenth plague being the death of the firstborn son in all the Egyptian households.

"In reality, the ten plagues were a direct assault on the ten main gods over Egypt.

"Water turning to blood was Hapi, the Egyptian god of the Nile. Frogs coming from the Nile River was Heket, the Egyptian goddess of fertility, water, and renewal.
Lice from the dust of the earth was Geb, the Egyptian god of the earth. Swarms of flies was Khepri, the Egyptian god of creation, movement of the sun and rebirth. Death of Cattle and

Livestock was Hathor, the Egyptian goddess of love and protection.

Ashes turning to boils and sores was Isis, the Egyptian goddess of medicine and peace.

Hail rained down in the form of fire was Nut, the Egyptian goddess of the sky.

Locusts sent from the sky was Seth, the Egyptian god of storms and disorder.

Three Days of Complete Darkness was Ra, the sun god. Death of the Firstborn was Pharaoh, the ultimate power of Egypt."

Rachav was mesmerised by the storytelling of Salmah over this, her first Pesach celebration. She urged him to continue.

"Adonai commanded Moshe to take a lamb for each family, slaughter it at dusk on the set day, take some blood and smear it on the doorframe and lintel, and afterwards eat the meat, roasted in the fire, hurriedly. For that night, Adonai will pass through the land of Egypt and kill all the firstborn in the land, except for the houses that have the sign of the blood on them."

"Adonai spoke to Moshe and Harun in the land of Egypt; he said, "You are to begin your calendar with this month; it will be the first month of the year for you. Speak to all the assembly of Isra'el and say, 'On the tenth day of this month, each man is to take a lamb or kid for his family, one per household — except that if the household is too small for a whole lamb or kid, then he and his next-door neighbour should share one, dividing it in proportion to the number of people eating it. Your animal must be without defects, a male in its first year, and you may choose it from either the sheep or the goats.

"'You are to keep it until the fourteenth day of the month, and then the entire assembly of the community of Isra'el will slaughter it

at dusk. They are to take some of the blood and smear it on the two sides and top of the door frame at the entrance of the house in which they eat it. That night, they are to eat the meat roasted in the fire; they are to eat it with matzah and maror. Don't eat it raw or boiled, but roasted in the fire, with its head, the lower parts of its legs and its inner organs. Let nothing of it remain till morning; if any of it does remain, burn it up completely.

"'Here is how you are to eat it: with your belt fastened, your shoes on your feet and your staff in your hand; and you are to eat it hurriedly. It is Adonai's Pesach. For that night, I will pass through the land of Egypt and kill all the firstborn in the land of Egypt, both men and animals; and I will execute judgment against all the gods of Egypt; I am Adonai. The blood will serve you as a sign marking the houses where you are; when I see the blood, I will pass over you — when I strike the land of Egypt, the death blow will not strike you.

"'This will be a day for you to remember and celebrate as a festival to Adonai; from generation to generation you are to celebrate it by a perpetual regulation." Sh'mot 12:1-14.

Next, Salmah explained about leavened bread. "Adonai gave us strict instructions that, as well as Pesach, we are to eat matzah – unleavened bread for seven days. As there was no time to let the bread rise on the night of the Passover, we replicated that with the matzah. Also, leavened bread symbolises sin and the evil inclination. That is why we are commanded to have it out of our house before the observance can begin. If we don't, we are banished for the week."

"'For seven days you are to eat matzah — on the first day remove the leaven from your houses. For whoever eats hametz [leavened bread] from the first to the seventh day is to be cut off from Isra'el. On

the first and seventh days, you are to have an assembly set aside for God. On these days no work is to be done, except what each must do to prepare his food; you may do only that. You are to observe the festival of matzah, for on this very day, I brought your divisions out of the land of Egypt. Therefore, you are to observe this day from generation to generation by a perpetual regulation. From the evening of the fourteenth day of the first month until the evening of the twenty-first day, you are to eat matzah. During those seven days, no leaven is to be found in your houses. Whoever eats food with hametz in it is to be cut off from the community of Isra'el — it doesn't matter whether he is a foreigner or a citizen of the land. Eat nothing with hametz in it. Wherever you live, eat matzah.'"

"Then Moshe called for all the leaders of Isra'el and said, "Select and take lambs for your families, and slaughter the Pesach lamb. Take a bunch of hyssop leaves and dip it in the blood which is in the basin, and smear it on the two sides and top of the door-frame. Then, none of you is to go out the door of his house until morning. For Adonai will pass through to kill the Egyptians; but when he sees the blood on the top and on the two sides, Adonai will pass over the door and will not allow the Slaughterer to enter your houses and kill you. You are to observe this as a law, you and your descendants forever.

"When you come to the land which Adonai will give you, as he has promised, you are to observe this ceremony. When your children ask you, 'What do you mean by this ceremony?' Say, 'It is the sacrifice of Adonai's Pesach [Passover], because [Adonai] passed over the houses of the people of Isra'el in Egypt, when he killed the Egyptians but spared our houses.'" The people of Isra'el bowed their heads and

worshipped. Then the people of Isra'el went and did as Adonai had or-dered Moshe and Harun — that is what they did.

"At midnight Adonai killed all the firstborn in the land of Egypt, from the firstborn of Pharaoh sitting on his throne to the firstborn of the prisoner in the dungeon, and all the firstborn of live-stock. Pharaoh got up in the night, he, all his servants and all the Egyptians; and there was horrendous wailing in Egypt; for there wasn't a single house without someone dead in it. He summoned Moshe and Harun by night and said, "Up and leave my people, both you and the people of Isra'el, and go, serve Adonai as you said. Take both your flocks and your herds, as you said, and get out of here! But bless me, too." The Egyptians pressed to send the people out of the land quickly, because they said, "Otherwise we'll all be dead!"

"The people took their dough before it had become leavened and wrapped their kneading bowls in their clothes on their shoulders. The people of Isra'el had done what Moshe had said — they had asked the Egyptians to give them silver and gold jewellery and cloth-ing; and Adonai had made the Egyptians so favourably disposed to-ward the people that they had let them have whatever they requested. Thus they plundered the Egyptians.

"The people of Isra'el travelled from Ra'amses to Sukkot, some six hundred thousand men on foot, not counting children. A mixed crowd also went up with them, as well as livestock in large numbers, both flocks and herds. They baked matzah loaves from the dough they had brought out of Egypt, since it was unleavened; because they had been driven out of Egypt without time to prepare supplies for themselves.

"The time the people of Isra'el lived in Egypt was 430 years. At the end of 430 years to the day, all the divisions of Adonai left the land of Egypt. This was a night when Adonai kept vigil to bring them *out of the land of Egypt, and this same night continues to be a night when Adonai keeps vigil for all the people of Isra'el through all their generations.*

"Adonai said to Moshe and Harun, "This is the regulation for the Pesach lamb: no foreigner is to eat it. But if anyone has a slave he bought for money, when you have circumcised him, he may eat it. Neither a traveller nor a hired servant may eat it. It is to be eaten in one house. You are not to take any of the meat outside the house, and you are not to break any of its bones. The whole community of Isra'el is to keep it. If a foreigner staying with you wants to observe Adonai's Pesach, all his males must be circumcised. Then he may take part and observe it; he will be like a citizen of the land. But no uncircumcised person is to eat it. The same teaching is to apply equally to the citizen and to the foreigner living among you."

"All the people of Isra'el did just as Adonai had ordered Moshe and Harun. On that very day, Adonai brought the people of Isra'el out of the land of Egypt by their divisions." Sh'mot 12:15-50.

Rachav gulped. No wonder they hadn't shared this story when Baba was alive – he would have had a fit! She wondered how her father and Novac would react to this commandment now?

Unlike Shabbat, this festival had a lot of steps to take and lessons that needed to be learned. Rachav ensured she stayed by Salmah's family and asked many questions as each step was introduced. She could see there was a deep reverence and seriousness about each aspect of Pesach and determined she would learn and understand what currently was a mystery to her.

Rachav thought to herself how hard it had been remembering, learning and absorbing all these new rituals, traditions, feasts, festivals and holy days. She would fall into her bed at night, absolutely spent. Having run an Inn and being responsible for every aspect of that business was second nature to her, but this was different, somehow. The exhaustion was mental, physical and spiritual. However, Rachav loved the celebratory nature of the culture she was now in. They loved their celebrations, and they weren't in the hedonistic orgiastic ways of her previous life – they were genuine celebrations of life, as the Israelites attested to when raising their cups and goblets at a feast – L'Chaim!

34

Remembrance

A tear coursed down Rachav's cheek. The pang of remembrance. She wondered what might have been, remembering her beloved in all his glory. Time had moved on, the tribe had become established at Gilgal, the inheritances had been given and established by Y'hoshua, and now, Rachav had some decisions to make.

By the light of her oil lamp, she went over to the large chest and opened the lid. There, untouched for many months, were all of Baba's tools, implements, smocks, tool belts and plans, which had been rolled up and carefully put away. Removing one of the ledgers at the bottom of the chest, Rachav opened its pages and was mesmerised by Baba's writing. His penmanship had been impeccable -something one wouldn't naturally attribute to her beloved brutish thug! She went down his columns and realised that Baba had been an astute businessman, tallies showing his profit and loss and the most popular items he had crafted. Another ledger recorded all of Baba's contacts within the Levant and beyond. Alongside sourcing expensive woods and trimmings, Baba had spent many evenings in front of Rachav, carving bowls and utensils for the Inn. He made the most exquisite goblets that held the King's Wine, alongside many cups that housed the beer they had imported from other regions. Only the best had been served to Rachav's patrons – whether they knew that fact or not.

She uttered a prayer, knowing that Adonai was with her and, indeed, was listening. She needed to know what to do with these things. There must be some men within the tribe who were experienced woodturners, carvers and carpenters? She made a mental note that she should enquire of the elders.

Unrolling some of the plans, Rachav found numerous maps dotted with places Baba had visited – with and without her. Waves of feelings washed over her until she had to sit on her bed and let the emotion out. Memories came flooding back. Times of profound, intimate moments, times of much laughter, times of arguing, and times of beautiful adventures.

Rachav knew that the emotions would pass and allowed herself a few moments to get herself together. As she wiped her tears away, she heard someone outside her tent.

"Rachav, are you awake?" It was Abiah.

"Yes, beloved Abiah, come in."

Abiah looked at her friend and immediately hugged her. Tears flowed freely from their eyes until they were spent. The women parted and sat on the bed.

"My dearest friend, thank you for coming here when you did. I am at a loss as to what to do with Baba's work gear. All his records, implements, tools, work belts, ledgers and maps are here. Maybe I should speak with the elders and see if anyone within the tribe would benefit from these things. What do you think, Abiah?"

The younger woman sat for a moment, then responded.

"Let's ask Adonai what the best thing to do would be. Is that all right with you?" Rachav was amazed that Abiah had suggested this and nodded her head in agreement.

Together, they beseeched Adonai for his wisdom, and soon enough, Rachav knew what to do.

Rachav then looked at Abiah and queried, "Beloved; it's late evening. Why did you come?"

Abiah broke into a large smile, lighting up her already beautiful face.

"Ah, my friend, I am with child," exclaimed the young woman enthusiastically.

Rachav jumped up and rejoiced with her best friend.

"Abiah, how do you feel? Are you okay? What made you think you were with child?"

"Oh Rachav, I feel wonderful. I thought I might be pregnant because my breasts feel twice as large as normal!" The women giggled at this.

"And Novac? How is he with this news?"

"He is ecstatic, of course! He thinks he will help grow the twelve tribes of Isra'el and keep me in this state for the next few years!" Again, the women laughed.

"But in all reality, Rachav, I am scared. This is so new and exciting, but how I wish my Eema and Abba were here." Abiah looked off at the opening of the tent, misty-eyed.

Rachav held her friend, and together they prayed for shalom to enter her heart and mind. Abiah hugged her friend and then exited the tent.

Rachav went and sat in her chair and marvelled at the goodness of Adonai. Although young and inexperienced, she knew her two dearest friends would have all the help and knowledge they needed. Yaffah and Ever, alongside many within the tribe, would see to that. Besides the pregnancy news, Rachav was extremely grateful for Abiah's prayers. Although still somewhat of a new concept, they had all integrated a prayer life into their everyday lives.

The only other thing that had Rachav thinking was the contact ledger. Would this be useful in the future, or was it best for her to let that go too? She was somewhat unsure about this particular aspect of her findings within the expansive chest.

35

Inheritance

After much discussion amongst the elders, Y'hoshua went before Adonai in the Tabernacle and sought him to divide the land.

Each tribe would inherit according to the commands of Adonai, but He had something special in mind for his servant Kalev alone. After many years of serving Adonai faithfully, whilst at times going against the common thought, Kalev and Y'hoshua were the eldest and only two remaining members of the original tribe. They had left Egypt as adolescents and grown up in the ways of Adonai – even going against their families' rebellion and serving Adonai with true hearts.

The men were still active warriors within the tribe, even though their age was advanced in years. Within these men beat the hearts of the true warrior kings, as long as they remained devoted to their God and followed His commands.

Rachav and her small clan remained in deep awe and reverence towards the two elder statesmen. They had been kind, truthful and honouring to Rachav and her family, and their loyalty in return was non-negotiable.

Today, the tribes would know how much and where their newly acquired land would be.

They understood that because of their connection with the two spies, Salmah and Azriel, Rachav and her family would be part of the inheritance of Y'hudah. When they heard where the boundaries would lay, they all smiled. It would not be far from their former land; therefore, they could take some of what had been planted beforehand and transplant it into their new territory.

Before the great assembly, Y'hoshua honoured Kalev with his allotment first. Remembering their original surveillance of the land and the promising report they brought back to their elders, Kalev had received a promise from Adonai through Moshe, "Surely the land where your foot has been will be the inheritance for you and your descendants forever because you have followed Adonai, my God, completely."

Kalev himself spoke, "Now, look: Adonai has kept me alive these forty-five years, as he said he would, from when Adonai said this to Moshe, when Isra'el was going through the desert. Today I am eighty-five years old, but I am as strong today as on the day Moshe sent me — I'm as strong now as I was then, whether for war or simply for going here and there. Therefore, give me this hill, the one Adonai spoke about on that day; for on that day you heard how the 'Anakim were there with great, fortified cities; perhaps Adonai will be with me, and I will drive them away, as Adonai said."

Y'hoshua embraced his friend and brother before the crowd, nodded and announced to all, "Now Kalev, alongside his family and tribe, will inherit Hevron as his own land. We bless you, brother and the work of your hands, the fruit of your loins, the animals in your care and all generations from you. May you know Adonai's shalom at all times. Omaine."

The crowd resoundingly cried, "Omaine!" Great rejoicing ensued.

Once the crowd had settled again, Y'hoshua called up Salmah and Azriel.

"Because of your courage, faithfulness and reconnaissance within Yericho, yourselves and your tribe will now be blessed within the land of Y'hudah." Salmah and Azriel were profoundly humbled and returned, standing near their families.

Y'hoshua went on to read out all the clans that made up the tribe of Y'hudah and realised their territory would be vast. It was to Salmah and Azriel, their families and their adoptive clan of Rachav, Yaffah, Ever, Novac and Abiah that would move to Beit-Lechem.

Much rejoicing went on as tribes and clans discovered their new lands. The fires had been lit and roasted freshly slaughtered sheep. Alongside this, many loaves of bread had been baked, alongside pots of stew, fresh herbs, and dates picked off the nearby palms. Jugs of wine, taken from Yericho's stash of amphorae that Novac had located outside the city walls, were being drunk in great measure.

The celebrations lasted through the night and into the next day.

<h1 style="text-align:center">36</h1>

Realisation

Rising early one morning from a particularly fitful night, Rachav went about her morning duties. Taking a cup of warm brew, she opened the tent flap and sat inside, watching the sunrise. To her surprise, Salmah was outside tending to some animals nearby, so she invited him to partake of some warm brew. He came and sat beside her, which wasn't unusual.

"How are you this fine morning, Rachav?"

"Ah, my friend, I am fine. I had a restless sleep, but I guess that would be nerves for the upcoming move. How do you feel about this next part of the journey, Salmah?"

Salmah looked wistful. Rachav had never noticed this before, but somehow he seemed more handsome than she realised.

"I wonder how life will be in Beit-Lechem, but I trust Adonai to guide us and grant us favour. This is the only life I've ever known, being part of a nomadic tribe, and the thought of living in a solid dwelling, well....you understand what that's like." Salmah smiled at the woman.

"Yes Salmah, I do. I had to adapt to living in a tent, but it hasn't been all bad. I am grateful wherever Adonai leads me now."

"We're unfamiliar with this land of our inheritance, and I wonder if some of us will be sent out to do reconnaissance. I must speak with the elders and see what they have planned. You must understand that much of this life is new to us all. From having fields to feed and nourish our flock to having crops to grow and harvest, it sure beats all the years of quail and manna. Please don't think I'm being ungrateful, but the same thing day in and day out was a tad monotonous, so we're all grateful for a bit more variety in our life and food palate now!" Salmah laughed, with Rachav smiling at his newfound joy. *"He really is lovely,"* she thought, then shook her head as if to empty those thoughts out.

"Time to get back to the animals now. Thank you, Rachav, for the warm brew. It's been lovely chatting with you."

"Yes, it has Salmah. Shalom to you."

"Shalom Rachav."

He walked over to the animals and gathered his stick, cloak and water skin. Rachav knew Salmah would be off with the flock for a few days, watching them as a true shepherd and protector. She felt a twinge of pain in her stomach, then got up, replenishing her cup, taking a small hunk of bread, and eating her fill for breakfast.

"Adonai, what am I feeling and sensing with Salmah? Surely you're not saying anything about a romance between us, are you? Oh Lord, that is not in my plan!" Rachav felt a depth of emotion as she prayed, then continued on. "Still, Lord, let your will be done in my life. I choose to stay open to your ways, no matter where they lead me. Omaine."

Rachav wiped her face with a cloth, then fully opened her tent. She looked out and saw Abiah and Novac embracing, and then he left to help Salmah.

Walking over to Abiah, the two women embraced.

"How are you feeling this morning, Abiah?" Rachav patted Abiah's tiny stomach.

"I'm very well. No morning sickness, just feeling rather round in all areas." Abiah laughed, pointing to her chest and belly.

"Novac loves my new shape and says he can't wait to see my stomach grow bigger." Abiah lowered her voice and leaned into Rachav. "He partakes of my breasts often!" The two women giggled. Rachav was so happy they kept their passion and zest alive. They wouldn't be Abiah and Novac without that.

"My friend, I'd like to talk to you about something. Would that be alright?"

"Of course, Rachav, of course."

The two sat down, and Rachav shared her heart, her concerns and her prayer to Adonai.

"Oh Rachav, surely you know how much Salmah loves you?" Enquired Abiah.

"No, I truly didn't. I've been so blind in my grief and processing all that this tribe is to me now, I hadn't given that a thought. But I fear it is a silly folly of my mind. I'm too old for someone like Salmah, and I fear my child-bearing days are almost over. I couldn't offer him anything other than my now wrinkling skin!" The women laughed again.

"Oh, my friend, you are still as beautiful as the day I came to start working for you. In fact, Rachav, I think you're more beautiful. You have this sereneness about you, and you shine all the time. Even in your grief, you've always radiated such goodness and beauty. Let's keep this matter between Adonai and us and see what transpires. In the meantime, Rachav, I need food – I'm always famished!"

After Abiah had finished her meal, the two women arose and walked around the encampment.

"How are you feeling about moving to Beit-Lechem, Abiah? You'll be having your baby there."

"Yes. Novac and I have been doing a lot of talking and praying to Adonai about this. I know we will be fine, but as I've not travelled much, I wonder how that will be. Starting yet again in another new place, especially while pregnant, isn't the easiest thing to deal with, but I know I have you, my family, to help me through it all."

"Of course, darling friend. Whatever you need, I will be here, as will my parents and, of course, Novac. I understand your hesitancy, but after what we witnessed and have endured these past months, surely nothing is too hard for Adonai, eh?" Rachav took Abiah's arm in hers, and together they walked and talked.

"Novac had wondered about uplifting some of the vineyards outside Yericho. We thought we could start a vineyard in Beit-Lechem from the vines he already knows. It's what he has trained for and studied for his whole life. You know the astute businessman and his reputation throughout the Levant. Maybe those contacts will still be there, but we at least would like the freedom to try again. What do you think, Rachav?"

"What a fantastic idea! Yes, I love it. Maybe we will be taking these animals with us too, and we won't be starting again, more like continuing on, but in more permanent abodes and such? That sounds fine to me."

"I agree, Rachav. We're looking forward to something with more permanence that we can call our own. The tribe has been so wonderful to us, and I am grateful for all their help and input, but a solid dwelling will be nice again. Especially with a baby coming."

The women ended their walk and chat and parted company.

As Rachav went about her afternoon duties, she couldn't help but think of Salmah. She felt both silly and giddy and resigned herself to knowing that Adonai would take care of it all.

37

Shavuot & The Ketubah

The small group of adopted foreigners, sat around the fire with some of the elders and listened whilst they explained Shavuot and why the likening to a Ketubah.

Kalev took the reigns this time and started speaking in his rather animated way.

"You have to remember, brothers and sisters, myself and Y'hoshua witnessed many miracles during those early years when we were still in Egypt and then beyond. It was as if Adonai put on a spectacular production just for us. The miracles; watching staffs turn into snakes and Moshe's snake eating the others – that made us laugh indeed. Seeing all the plagues and yet not one came near us in our town of Goshen. We were blessed indeed. That very first Pesach, witnessing the Angel of the Lord bypass all of us who had placed blood upon the doorposts and lintels of our dwellings. It was as though Adonai himself had come down to protect us. We were in deep awe of our God and momentarily forgot the deep anguish and suffering that had become our lives' mainstay. Can you imagine us, the slaves of Egypt, going to all the houses upon our departure and asking for all their silver and gold? Ah, the look of terror in their eyes when they ran to grab all they had and threw it into our outstretched hands. They were so deeply fearful after the miraculous displays of power Adonai had wrought through Moshe and Harun – they wept with tears of joy when we left. They believed they would never again have to worry about us, the slaves of Egypt, but how wrong they were. In their wildest dreams, they never thought they would lose their large army, watching these brave warriors drown along with their royal horses and chariots of gold. But alas, Adonai still had more showing off to do!

"Water from a split rock, the size of which would strain your neck if you were standing near the base and looking up at it. I still remember the fear of Adonai upon Moshe's face when he struck that rock, yet it nurtured our animals and us for the longest time. The quail and manna dropped down so that we would be fed every day of our lives. Our clothes and shoes never wore out and lasted until we came here to Gilgal. Near on impossible, and yet it really did happen. Imagine, if you will, the knowledge that there was not one feeble or sick amongst us. The only time disease came near us was when there had been disobedience in the camp. Ah, dear one, Adonai was so good to us. But in reality, he had to be. We endured hundreds of years of suffering, not knowing when a redeemer would rise and come to our rescue. But who knew our redeemer would be the Prince Regent of Egypt, a Hebrew baby boy who had been rescued from the reeds and raised in the King's palace? Praise Adonai.

"Our hearts were sick. We had endured such severe poverty and abuse. After Yosef died, the Pharaohs did all kinds of wickedness to our people. Instead of the blessing we had once been, we became the scourge of society. We became a curse, an anathema, a people treated worse than their enemies. We were living on so little and yet were expected to work nearly every moment from sunrise to sundown, in the blaring heat, with little to nourish our depleted tongues. Yes, indeed, Adonai needed to show himself off to us.

"We were a people who had become the very thing Adonai wanted to free us from – idolaters. We were surrounded and imbued with pagan worship everywhere we turned. We spilt our blood and sweat in building monuments to man and idols. Think of all those huge cities that Egypt is famous for – we built many of those, and in return, we turned our backs on the one True God that matters – Adonai. Ah, Lord, forgive us. We weren't much better with our freedom. People who are full of idols, who have been raised with violence and abuse, don't know how to manage freedom. We learnt the hard way, this I tell you for certain." Kalev openly wept.

"At first, we were grateful, but then we were an insolent bunch of brutes. We were running off and complaining about our newfound freedom. Taking the precious gold we had gained and making a ridiculous idol in the form of a cow, just like we had seen and known back in Egypt. I am still surprised that Adonai didn't strike us all down then and there. We know that Moshe had to mediate on our behalf and that we may have been killed if it were not for him. It would have been our own fault.

"It took the longest time to get Egypt out of us, even Y'hoshua and myself. Whilst we didn't outwardly sin, we sure grew tired and fed up with our lot in the desert. No wonder a journey that should have only taken a few weeks took forty years! Stubborn, obstinate people we were, eh Y'hoshua?"

The elder statesman nodded. Kalev continued. "It wasn't until all the tribe was circumcised recently that the whole process finally concluded. And now, here we are in our 'Promised Land', and we are all truly grateful for that.

Rachav and the group asked Kalev to continue on. "Ha, let me have some wine and bread; a man could die of thirst with all this talking!" he bellowed.

Afterwards, he got up and started again with his animated storytelling.

"Upon Sinai, Adonai proposed to us, the Ketubah, in the form of the Ten Commandments, much like a bridegroom would to his potential bride. Of course, we considered the terms and conditions and were all in accord with our resounding, 'Yes', but oh, how faithless and nagging we have been as Adonai's 'wife'. We have tested and tried Him to the nth degree, and I still don't know why He established a covenant with us. Oy vey, we have had some very trying times. But He is our God; we are His people, and we love each other. Despite our sins, though they are many, He is merciful and just and doesn't punish us according to our many rotten deeds. I, in particular, having seen with my own eyes the miracles and wonders Adonai wrought on our behalf, am so thankful that His mercies are new every morning. Oh, how great is His faithfulness! Such wonders and miracles pour from His heart of grace; it is a wonder that we are still here. Then I think of His fame around the Levant and how many have heard of His mighty deeds, that others shudder and lament at the sound of His name."

Rachav interjected. "Kalev, I was one of those people. I heard many things when I was an Inn Keeper, and I found it both amazing and frightful to hear the stories that would trickle through to our establishment. You may have also heard that when Baba grew sick coming back from Bharat, I got on my knees and beseeched the One True God, Adonai. I too, am so thankful for His glorious mercies. Then, as you know, we prayed together upon our return to Yericho and asked for people who knew Adonai to be brought onto our path, and then the two spies, Salmah and Azriel, appeared at our Inn. It was a true miracle."

Kalev smiled and then slapped Salmah on the back. "Son, who knew the miracle that would occur when you arrived at the Inn? Imagine one's fate if Rachav had refused to help you two men. Oy vey, it could have been a very different story." Salmah looked at Rachav and grinned. She felt the familiar feeling in her stomach, and looked away.

Salmah, knowing the answer but asking the question on behalf of the group, spoke, "What was it like when you all gathered on Sinai, and all of you witnessed the thunderings and flashes of lightning, along with the shofar trumpeting and the mountain smoking?"

"Ah, Salmah, you have asked well, dear boy. It was wild! Awful in that we shook from the fear of the Lord. And when Moshe appeared with the tablets – oh, we were deathly afraid. This was yet another miracle. This was the Ketubah – Adonai betrothing himself to us in the form of the Ten Commandments. We had all been through the ritual mikvah and cleansed ourselves, but I don't think any of us knew what to expect. Just like that, Adonai blows our minds again!" More laughter exploded throughout the group.

"Seeing nature perform as it did above Mount Sinai was incredibly wild. We were desert dwellers, a nomadic tribe, and seeing this weather wasn't normal for us. We were witnessing Heaven come to earth and mingling with us. I tell you, Adonai tabernacled with us in the most meaningful way. Providing a flame of fire all through the night and a cloud throughout the day. He protected us from the harsh heat and covered us with light during the night, when it was the safest to travel at times. We came across many groups of bandits who were intent on raping and pillaging our camp, but seeing that supernatural sign put the fear of Adonai in them, and they would flee seven ways." Kalev roared with laughter at the folly of the bandits.

The elder statesman continued his narrative after Kalev and the group calmed down.

"Shavuot. This is a holy day, celebrating the giving of the Torah to us, the Hebrews, on that blessed day on Mount Sinai. Every year we renew our acceptance of Adonai's gift of the Torah. On THIS day, seven weeks after leaving Egypt, Adonai came to be with us, on the earth, as a bride and a bridegroom. Also, Shavuot is the celebration of the wheat harvest and the ripening of the first fruits. Unfortunately, we haven't been able to celebrate this holy day properly until now, so we are incredibly grateful that we can finally do that.

B'midbar 28:26-31, *"On the day of the firstfruits, when you bring a new grain offering to Adonai in your feast of Shavu'ot, you are to have a holy convocation; do not do any kind of ordinary work; but present a burnt offering as a fragrant aroma for Adonai, consisting of two young bulls, one ram, seven male lambs in their first year, and their grain offering — fine flour mixed with olive oil, six quarts for each bull, four quarts for the one ram, and two quarts for each of the seven lambs — plus a male goat to make atonement for you. You are to offer these in addition to the regular burnt offering and its grain offering (they are to be without defect for you), with their drink offerings."*

"We celebrate Shavuot in several steps, much like the other festivals and holy days.

We Tikkun Leil Shavuot: Hold an all-night vigil during which we devote ourselves to the learning of Scripture. This prepares you to receive the Torah and the entirety of God's word anew. Like a bride who can't sleep on the eve of her wedding day, an all-night study on the eve of Shavuot helps us to demonstrate a deeper sense of appreciation, love and longing for Adonai and his word. This comes from when we Hebrews slept so soundly at Mount Sinai just before receiving the Torah, that Adonai himself had to wake us with the thunder and lightning!" Kalev was grinning at Y'Hoshua at the memory of that evening.

"On Shavuot, we eat two meals – dairy and meat. We eat dairy because Torah is compared to milk lying under the tongue. Just as milk is the perfect food for sustaining wee children, it is the key to nourishing our human souls. The meat signifies a feast, a celebration, a way to delight ourselves in Adonai.

"We then decorate our dwellings with any type of flowers or greenery that can be found. This represents our lives becoming lush and green at the giving of the Torah.

"We always gathered at the foot of Mount Sinai during Shavuot to hear the Ten Commandments read and reaffirm our commitment to Adonai and the Torah."

"The last thing I think you should know is that Adonai gave us a new title at the giving of the Torah. Sh'mot 19:5-6, "'*Now if you will pay careful attention to what I say and keep my covenant, then you will be my own treasure from among all the peoples, for all the earth is mine; and you will be a kingdom of cohanim for me, a nation set apart.' These are the words you are to speak to the people of Isra'el.*'" We are a Royal Priesthood and a holy nation now. Impressive, but true!"

Kalev took a bow, then sat down amongst the group. They all clapped their hands and rejoiced in this animated and informative lesson.

Relaxing on the pillows, some attendants brought wine, bread and sweet pastries. Salmah reached for a pastry at the same time as Rachav, brushing her hand. The woman blushed and turned her head; however, Salmah insisted he look at her.

Finishing their pastries in silence, Salmah then spoke. "Rachav, would you please walk with me? There are matters I wish to discuss with you."

Rachav blushed again, then looked him in the eye and simply said, "Yes."

The two walked out into the cool of the evening, walking at a slow pace as they admired the stars that had just peaked out against the darkening night sky.

"Rachav, if I may be so bold, I must share something with you."

"Of course, Salmah. You are free to share what you wish."

"Rachav, please look at me." She slowly turned toward him.

"I went and spoke with your parents about the possibility of courting you," Salmah blurted out. "I am terrible at this kind of thing, but I wanted to do everything right. Please forgive me if I have overstepped things, but I just wanted to ensure that Ever and Yaffah would give us their blessing, should you agree to a courtship." Salmah breathed and let out a large sigh. Rachav stood utterly speechless.

"Wow, that was a lot, Salmah," grinned the surprised woman. "Out of curiosity, what did they say?"

"Oh, they were wonderfully kind to me. They reiterated that you have your own mind but respected that this was the right thing to do according to Adonai's laws. They have given us their blessing if you want to pursue this."

Rachav couldn't wipe the smile off of her face. She looked at Salmah with sheer delight and nodded her head. "Yes Salmah, I would love to be courted by you. Very much so!"

Salmah looked at her grin and stood with his arms crossed, feigning annoyance. "Just what are you grinning at, Rachav?"

"You, Salmah – I'm grinning at you!" She kept looking straight at him and then spoke again. "A few days ago, I realised I had feelings for you and have been praying to Adonai about it all."

"Ah, I see," spoke Salmah. "Are you sure you would like to do this? I have tried respecting your time of grief and heartache, and only ever wanted to offer friendship to you during this time, but I fear my heart longs for more than friendship now."

Rachav raised her hand to silence the man, then replied with a slight smile.

Rachav stepped closer to Salmah and looked deep into his eyes.

"I never thought I would want to be with someone else after being with my giant brute, Baba. And yet here we are...."

Rachav continued. "What happens now, Salmah? I'm unfamiliar with courting rituals from any culture, actually."

"Hmm, me too. I guess we approach the council and ask. We must do things correctly, eh Rachav? I don't want Adonai smiting me because I long to kiss you!" They both laughed again.

"So, let's approach them in the morning and see what we do afterwards. Is that a plan?"

"Sounds good to me."

Salmah walked Rachav to her tent, lifted her hand and gently kissed it. "I shall see you in the morning, dear Rachav."

In the morning, Salmah and Rachav walked the distance to the Elder's Tent. They had sent word they wanted to discuss a personal matter with Yaffah and Ever in attendance. Representing Salmah's family were his brother Doran and his two sisters, Ariela and Bat-Shiva.

Y'hoshua, Kalev and the rest of the council listened as Salmah spoke.

"Esteemed elders, council members, and beloved family, I come before you today with a heart overflowing with faith and gratitude.

Today, I stand here not only as a man of faith but also as a man overwhelmed with love and adoration for Rachav. Her courage in saving our spies and her unwavering faith in Adonai have deeply touched my soul. I could never replace beloved Baba, neither am I trying to. In fact, I have tried to not feel as I do, but that has failed dismally. However, in Rachav, I have found a partner whose love mirrors the love that Adonai has for His people. Rachav, with her grace and strength, has captured my heart. I am overcome with a love so pure and profound that words fail to express its depth. I vow to honour and cherish her, to protect and provide for her, and to love her with every fibre of my being.

Together, Rachav and I will walk hand in hand, not only as husband and wife but also as faithful servants of Adonai. Our union will be a testament to the power of love and faith, a beacon of light in a world often darkened by doubt and fear.

I ask for your blessings and your prayers as we embark on this journey together. May Adonai's grace and mercy guide our steps, and may our love for each other be a reflection of His infinite love for us. Thank you."

Both his brother and sisters were deeply moved by his speech. Ever and Yaffah had tears in their eyes while Rachav sat grinning from ear to ear. When Salmah had finished his speech and set out the terms and conditions that he had spoken privately with Rachav's parents, the two elder statesmen rose.

"Well, dear friends, it seems love is in the air," motioned Kalev theatrically, pointing his nose up and sniffing the air. Met with a smack on his arm, Y'hoshua brought the sense into the meeting.

"Argh, Kalev, enough with the jesting. These are serious matters!"

"Hmph. This is how Adonai made me, so calm down. Besides, love is fun too – ask my wife!" The group all giggled to themselves.

"I shall do no such thing, you old fool! Keep silent and let me finish, or so help me, Adonai might take me right here and now, and it will be all your fault!" Y'hoshua, in his gruffness, had a glint in his eye and winked at the women.

"As I was saying, this is serious business and something that should not be rushed. Rachav, are you willing to walk in courtship with Salmah, with the view of betrothal and marriage? Do you agree to the terms and conditions that Ever, Yaffah and Salmah have agreed upon?"

"Yes, Y'hoshua, I do."

"Salmah, are you willing to walk in courtship with Rachav, with the view of betrothal and marriage? Do you agree to uphold the terms and conditions you have agreed to with Yaffah and Ever?"

"I do."

Alright then. Further down the track, at an appointed time, I would ask the parties concerned to come and sign contracts, and fulfil their legal obligations, and then there will be a marriage set forth at a time agreed upon by all parties. Are we all in agreement together?"

"Yes, we are." The party all agreed.

Y'hoshua and Kalev motioned for all the parties in the tent to arise, and they walked over to Rachav and Salmah. Joining their hands and blessing them upon their heads, they both spoke the words commanded as the Priestly blessing in the book of B'midbar 6:24-26, "Y'varekh'kha Adonai v'yishmerekha. [May Adonai bless you and keep you.]
Ya'er Adonai panav eleikha vichunekka.
[May Adonai make his face shine on you and show you his favour.]
Yissa Adonai panav eleikha v'yasem l'kha shalom. [May Adonai lift up his face toward you and give you peace.]."

38

Rosh HaShanah, Yom Teruah

Vayikra 23:23-25, *"Adonai said to Moshe, "Tell the people of Isra'el, 'In the seventh month, the first of the month is to be for you a day of complete rest for remembering, a holy convocation announced with blasts on the shofar. Do not do any kind of ordinary work, and bring an offering made by fire to Adonai.'"*

"This is our new year, Rachav. A time for starting again, a clean slate, a do-over from anything in our lives that is wasted or unworthy. This is remembered as a holy day, sanctified by many prayers, honey-dipped apples, and challah bread with celebration and cheer. The shofar blowing is why this holiday is known as the Feast of Trumpets. We, as Israel, sound the shofar to recognise Adonai as our Creator and King. We read from the first scroll of B'resheet, *"In the beginning God created the heavens and the earth. The earth was unformed and void, darkness was on the face of the deep, and the Spirit of God hovered over the surface of the* water. Then God said, "Let there be light"; and there was light. God saw that the light was good, and God divided the light from the darkness. God called the light Day, and the darkness he called Night. So there was evening, and there was morning, one day. God said, "Let there be a dome in the middle of the water; let it divide the water from the water." God made the dome and divided the water under the dome from the water above the dome; that is how it was, and God called the dome Sky. So there was evening, and there was morning, a second day.

God said, "Let the water under the sky be gathered together into one place, and let dry land appear," and that is how it was. God called the dry land Earth, the gathering together of the water he called Seas, and God saw that it was good. God said, "Let the earth put forth grass, seed-producing plants, and fruit trees, each yielding its own kind of seed-bearing fruit, on the earth"; and that is how it was. The earth brought forth grass, plants each yielding its own kind of seed, and trees each producing its own kind of seed-bearing fruit; and God saw that it was good. So there was evening, and there was morning, a third day. God said, "Let there be lights in the dome of the sky to divide the day from the night; let them be for signs, seasons, days and years; and let them be for lights in the dome of the sky to give light to the earth"; and that is how it was. God made the two great lights — the larger light to rule the day and the smaller light to rule the night — and the stars. God put them in the dome of the sky to give light to the earth, to rule over the day and over the night, and to divide the light from the darkness; and God saw that it was good. So there was evening, and there was morning, a fourth day. God said, "Let the water swarm with swarms of living creatures, and let birds fly above the earth in the open dome of the sky." God created the great sea crea-

tures and every living thing that creeps, so that the water swarmed with all kinds of them, and there was every kind of winged bird; and God saw that it was good. Then God blessed them, saying, "Be fruitful, multiply and fill the water of the seas, and let birds multiply on the earth." So there was evening, and there was morning, a fifth day. God said, "Let the earth bring forth each kind of living creature — each kind of livestock, crawling animal and wild beast"; and that is how it was. God made each kind of wild beast, each kind of livestock and every kind of animal that crawls along the ground; and God saw that it was good. Then God said, "Let us make humankind in our image, in the likeness of ourselves; and let them rule over the fish in the sea, the birds in the air, the animals, and over all the earth, and over every crawling creature that crawls on the earth." So God created humankind in his own image; in the image of God he created him: male and female he created them. God blessed them: God said to them, "Be fruitful, multiply, fill the earth and subdue it. Rule over the fish in the sea, the birds in the air and every living creature that crawls on the earth." Then God said, "Here! Throughout the whole earth I am giving you as food every seed-bearing plant and every tree with seed-bearing fruit. And to every wild animal, bird in the air and creature crawling on the earth, in which there is a living soul, I am giving as food every kind of green plant." And that is how it was. God saw everything that he had made, and indeed it was very good. So there was evening, and there was morning, a sixth day."

Salmah's eldest sister Bat-Shiv continued on. "We remember Avraham and his obedience to Adonai, by reading the account of him taking Yitz'chak and binding him to the altar. This speaks of Adonai's supernatural provision for us if we are obedient and faithful to Him.

"To celebrate, we have a large family meal, greeting everyone with, 'L'Shanah Tovah!', which means 'A good year!' We light candles and recite ritual blessings over ourselves. We repeat the blessing over some wine and challah bread. We pass the challah around for everyone to break off a piece and dip it into honey, along with apple slices, symbolising the hope that the new year will be sweet. We then gather together as a congregation and have songs, readings, and a sermon about the binding of Yitz'chak from the Torah. We then go to a body of flowing water for a ritual known as Tashlich. We toss bits of bread into the water, symbolising letting go of and completely releasing our sins.

"After that is complete, we go and help those less fortunate around us, to be a blessing to them, and therefore to the heart of Adonai."

Rachav thanked Bat-Shiv, for the lesson and bid them all good night.

Laying her head upon her pillow, she fell into a deep sleep, dreaming of ram's horns, apples and challah bread.

39

Yom Kippur

"Adonai said to Moshe, "The tenth day of this seventh month is Yom-Kippur; you are to have a holy convocation, you are to deny yourselves, and you are to bring an offering made by fire to Adonai. You are not to do any kind of work on that day, because it is Yom-Kippur, to make atonement for you before Adonai your God. Anyone who does not deny himself on that day is to be cut off from his people; and anyone who does any kind of work on that day, I will destroy from among his people. You are not to do any kind of work; it is a permanent regulation through all your generations, no matter where you live. It will be for you a Shabbat of complete rest, and you are to deny yourselves; you are to rest on your Shabbat from evening the ninth day of the month until the following evening." Vayikra 23:26-32.

Salmah's brother, Doran, began his narrative to explain Yom Kippur for the evening. His booming voice was animated in style. "Rosh Hashanah is followed by ten days of repentance and awe, culminating in Yom Kippur; the Day of Atonement is the year's most holy and solemn day. Rosh Hashanah focuses on individual repentance, while Yom Kippur focuses on national repentance. During Yom Kippur, we cease our work and observe a twenty-five hour fast from food and water. The extra hour of fasting is added to "put a fence around the law," to be sure we obey God's command completely. The day is set aside to 'afflict the soul' to ask for atonement for the sins of the past year. Some even wear a kittel, a white robe. They do it to remind themselves and others that life is finite and that everyone must be prepared to stand before the Lord at the time of death.

"Yom Kippur is the only day the high priest would dare to enter the Most Holy Place. In that most sacred place, he would offer atonement for the sins of the people of Israel.

"Of the various Day of Atonement sacrifices, the most important was that of the two he-goats. They were to be of equal height, weight and cost. Lots were cast determining the he-goat that would be sacrificed as a sin offering upon the altar to the Lord, and which one would be designated the scapegoat for Azazyel. The high priest lays his hands upon the head of the sacrificial goat to symbolise the transference of sins from him, the nation's representative, to the animal, who would bear the burden. The priest fastens a scarlet woollen cord to the horns of the goat and ties a second scarlet cord to the entrance of the Kodesh section of the temple. The high priest lays both hands upon the scapegoat again, reciting the following confession of sin and prayer for forgiveness:

"O Lord, I have acted iniquitously, trespassed, sinned before Thee: I, my household, and the sons of Harun, Thy holy ones. O Lord, forgive the iniquities, transgressions, and sins that I, my household, and Harun's children, Thy holy people, committed before Thee, as is written in the law of Moshe, Thy Servant, "For on this day He will forgive you, to cleanse you from all your sins before the Lord; ye shall be clean."

"When the high priest lays both his hands on the scapegoat, he is transferring the iniquities of Israel upon this solemn creature.

"After the nation prays this prayer, a cohen takes the goat to the precipice in the wilderness, where he throws it over the steep jagged cliff, so that its body would be completely torn apart before it reaches the bottom.

"Once the sacrifice was complete, the red cords that were tied to the horns of the scapegoat and placed at the entrance of the Holy Place, supernaturally turn from red to white, symbolising that although Israel's sins were crimson, Adonai has washed them as white as snow. When this occurs, it publicly bears testimony that Israel has been forgiven." Doran was rather pleased with the explanations and dramatics that accompanied his narration. He then continued.

"To prepare for Yom Kippur, you must understand there are five prohibitions from which we abstain to fulfil the commandment 'to afflict our souls'. You cannot eat or drink for the fast nor use oils to anoint yourself. There is no bathing for pleasure or wearing leather shoes – making sure that there is no barrier between the feet and the ground to feel the pain of the pebbles walked upon. Also, marital relations are to be abstained from. This is to focus your mind on spiritual things, like the angels in heaven. Also, men and women are to wear a white kittel, as this represents purity and the angelic.

"To approach Adonai, you must first approach those you have trespassed against throughout the year. When you have asked for their forgiveness first, you can ask Adonai to forgive your sins.

"We are to celebrate together within our community. While it is a solemn occasion, you are to sing songs of thanksgiving to Adonai together. At the appointed time, you are to break the fast together with a hearty spread of food."

Rachav sat back on her cushions, utterly aghast at the requirements. Rules and regulations so bound these Israelites more than the pagans were, and yet, there seemed to be a sense of freedom and wonder within it all. She wasn't so sure about the poor old goats, but compared to what she had seen when she was once a pagan, it made sense.

Doran made his way over to Rachav and asked if she had any questions.

"I believe, Doran, I understand much of what you have shared. I appreciate your animation and delightful demonstrations, though." With that, Doran took a bow. Rising with a smile on his face, Salmah approached his brother and mockingly slapped him on the back. The family then burst into laughter.

40

Sukkot – The Feast of Tabernacles

"Adonai said to Moshe, "Tell the people of Isra'el, 'On the fifteenth day of this seventh month is the feast of Sukkot for seven days to Adonai. On the first day there is to be a holy convocation; do not do any kind of ordinary work. For seven days you are to bring an offering made by fire to Adonai; on the eighth day you are to have a holy convocation and bring an offering made by fire to Adonai; it is a day of public assembly; do not do any kind of ordinary work."
Vayikra 23:33-36

This time, Salmah's sister, Ariela, took the narrative for the evening. "Sukkot means 'the time of our rejoicing.' Sukkot is also the plural of sukkah, which means 'booth' or 'hut'. Adonai has charged us with building open booths and dwelling in them for seven days as a memorial to Him being our provider and caring for us in the desert. The materials are supposed to be impermanent and fashioned so that stars are visible at night through the branches that make up the roof. This is all to remind us that our security is Adonai, not what we can do and provide for ourselves. This is a time to realise our abundant blessings. Oh Rachav, this is a time of great joy as we remember the intimacy of those forty years when Adonai 'tabernacled' with us, sustaining us daily with manna from Heaven.

"*But on the fifteenth day of the seventh month, when you have gathered the produce of the land, you are to observe the festival of Adonai seven days; the first day is to be a complete rest and the eighth day is to be a complete rest. On the first day you are to take choice fruit, palm fronds, thick branches and river-willows, and celebrate in the presence of Adonai your God for seven days. You are to observe it as a feast to Adonai seven days in the year; it is a permanent regulation, generation after generation; keep it in the seventh month. You are to live in sukkot for seven days; every citizen of Isra'el is to live in a sukkah, so that generation after generation of you will know that I made the people of Isra'el live in sukkot when I brought them out of the land of Egypt; I am Adonai your God.*" Vayikra 23:39-43.

Rachav enquired, "Why give up your normal homes for a booth or hut? I'm afraid I don't quite understand the reasoning."

"No, that's a good question, Rachav. We Israelites can't separate Adonai's presence from His protection. His manifest presence was the glory that led us during the days of the wilderness, forming a canopy of clouds over us. He enclosed us on all sides – from the north, south, east and west, above and below us. He protected us from the sun, wind, sandstorms, scorpions and snakes; in the evening, He protected us against predators and the cold and lit our way as a firey column in our midst," shared Ariela.

"We decorate the sukkah with harvest vegetables hung from the ceiling beams or placed throughout the corners. We also find vines, flowers, palm fronds, herbs, and anything that will make the sukkah look festive, and we encourage our young ones to be creative and include their decorations as well. Then we take a lulav – a palm leaf, two willow branches and three myrtle branches held together by woven leaves. We harvest etrog – a lemony fruit, then with that in our left hand and the lulav in our right, we bless them and shake them in the six directions mentioned before, symbolising Adonai's presence everywhere.

The blessing: "Barukh atah Adonai, Eloheinu, melekh ha-olam kidishanu b'mitz'votav v'tzivanu, al n'tilat lulav. Omaine. Blessed are you, Lord, our God, sovereign of the universe, who has sanctified us with His commandments and commanded us to take up the lulav. Amen."

"We do this according to the scroll of Vayikra 23:40, "*On the first day you are to take choice fruit, palm fronds, thick branches and river-willows, and celebrate in the presence of Adonai your God for seven days.*" We eat, sleep and play in the sukkah, inviting others to join us if we have the room. It is a wonderful time of feasting and merriment, and we leave it up for eight days."

Ariela could see that Rachav was quite overwhelmed with more instruction. Walking up and placing her arm around her, Ariela led Rachav outside the tent of meeting.

"My dear sister, please don't be concerned. We are all still learning the various aspects of these feasts and festivals together. You must realise that as nomads, many of these couldn't be celebrated the way Adonai commanded, so we are learning too. With us by your side, it will become normal and natural, but be at shalom, dear sister."

Rachav breathed a deep sigh of relief. She had grown accustomed to these long evenings in the tent of meeting, learning all the reasons and requirements for these holy days and seasons. Despite her misgivings, she was determined to understand and fully celebrate these times with her new tribe and family.

Looking over at Ariela, Rachav spoke. "I'm so grateful for your friendship and encouragement, Ariela. This means so much to me. I'm used to doing most things alone, with Abiah and occasionally my parents. So, I thank you for looking out for me, dear friend." The women hugged, and then Rachav returned to her tent to collapse in exhaustion.

<h1 style="text-align:center">41</h1>

Love Calls

The days became filled with glory and wonder for Rachav. Having never known courtship or romance per se, she lapped up all this attention from Salmah and revelled in her new status. What a year it had been. From Baba suddenly dying to becoming a widow; learning a whole new culture, putting away old ways and embracing a new mindset; Rachav was amazed at her world's transformation. Now, here she was, courting an Israelite with the view to betrothal and marriage. Oh, how Baba would be laughing from the balconies of Heaven if indeed, he could see all this.

Salmah and Rachav learnt to appreciate their different viewpoints and ways and relished in their budding courtship. Aware that all eyes were on them at all times, they remained an approved distance at most times, but on the odd occasion, there had been hand-holding and a kiss or two.

For his part, Salmah was in utter ecstasy. He had never bothered too much with the thought of marriage and children, but all that had changed during this new season upon their entry into their promised land. He could only fall to his knees and offer up his song of praise to Adonai, as a gift of his devotion and love to his Maker. All that he had been taught, all that he had ever known, was now becoming infused with light, joy and the greatest love on earth he'd ever known. His heart swelled with unspeakable joy, and his time with Rachav was unlike anything he'd ever experienced.

Soon, there was talk of the betrothal, which brought on another set of contracts, legalities and meetings.

Rachav swooned. She felt like a foolish girl, but oh, how she loved this feeling!

Salmah picked her up and swung her around in his arms, then planted a kiss on her lips. More electricity shot through them, to which they both giggled.

"Salmah put me down!" Rachav pleaded half-heartedly. The two carried on walking and sharing their hearts with one another.

"My concern, Salmah, is that I am older than you, I am near the end of my child-producing days, and my skin is starting to sag. You would almost have a dud on your hands."

"Rachav, nothing could be further from the truth. You are stunning, absolutely exquisite, and children are from Adonai. If he wills it, then he shall provide. I haven't gone into this with the eyes of a naïve child; I understand the complexities before us – but I do believe that Adonai has chosen us to be as one."

Salmah looked at Rachav, who was glowing in the moonlit night, and drew her to himself. Pushing her hair off her face, he held her head and leaned in to kiss her fully. As they parted, they both sighed, giddy from the emotion and the knowledge that their destiny together had just started.

"Oh Adonai, you have made my heart so glad, that all I can do is offer you these tears of joy as a sacrifice of praise!" Rachav wept deeply as she buried her head into her bed. Kneeling before her maker, she was utterly undone and wildly overcome with emotion. Not expecting this to happen and nearly middle age, she suddenly thought about how life might be now that she had agreed to marry Salmah. "Adonai, I don't know how to be a godly wife to Salmah. He has always known you and has been brought up in the faith. I haven't, Lord. I fear I don't know all the traditions and protocols you teach, and I will bring great shame to such a dear man. Please Adonai, help me. As you have used several dear folks in the tribe to teach us the feast and festivals, please send someone to teach me how to be a good wife. I long to get this right, oh Adonai, and honour both Salmah and you in all I do. Thank you for hearing my prayers. Omaine."

Rachav was exhausted. Leaning over to blow out the lamp, she smiled and immediately fell asleep. Waking the next morning, she heard a muffled noise and looked up to find Salmah standing in the corner of the tent. She motioned for him to sit on the bed, but the look of shock on his face told her that perhaps she should get up and refresh herself, then converse with her beloved.

Salmah breathed a sigh of relief. "I am so sorry, Rachav. I don't know what I was thinking, coming into your tent so early this morning. I just couldn't sleep well, and honestly, I just wanted to see you." He looked at her, so beautiful and glowing, still. "I don't have immoral intentions; I can assure you, my beloved. I just wanted to see you." He seemed coy and awkward, and then Rachav guessed why.

"Salmah, having been raised within this community, apart from your mother and sisters, you haven't really experienced women, have you?"

"No, not really. I mean, of course, I can converse and interact with women, but no, I've never been in love or anything like that. I'm sorry I seem so awkward." For the first time, Salmah was the one blushing.

"Oh Salmah, it will take some time for us to be entirely comfortable around each other, but it will happen. However, I guess there are some conversations we need to have, and as uncomfortable as they may seem, it's necessary for a good marriage. Well, at least, I think so."

"I agree, and of course, you were with Baba a very long time, so you know what you're doing. I feel like a young boy fumbling in the darkness, that's all." Salmah smirked and then grinned fully.

"I spent much time praying for Adonai's help last night. I feel so unprepared, mostly because I've come from a pagan culture where everything was diametrically opposed to what this nation stands for. I love all the commandments, traditions, feasts, festivals and holy days, but I fear I may shame you greatly if I don't do everything perfectly the first time. Oh Salmah, I would never want to embarrass you." Rachav started weeping, not understanding her angst when she was usually so calm and at peace.

"You could never shame or embarrass me, my beloved. It is because you come from a different background that I was immediately drawn to you, and I see that as a blessing, not otherwise. I should think with the two of us joining together, we shall be able to teach each other a great deal. Don't you?" They both started laughing again, nodding in agreement.

"So, my beloved, do we need a contract and official ceremony? I have my own chattels and money, and have want for nothing. However, I'm guessing we will be required to approach the elders alongside our families and flesh out some agreements between us all?" Rachav didn't like the thought, but respected it was the Israelite way.

"I guess we should ask; then we know for sure," added Salmah. "But in the meantime, can we eat some breakfast? I'm starving!" Rachav threw her arms around Salmah and hugged him. He lifted her chin, kissing her lightly, then grabbed her hand, and they both ran towards the delicious aromas making their stomachs grumble loudly!

42

Til Death Do Us Part

Weeks had passed since the initial betrothal ceremony, whereby all contracts had been agreed upon and signed. The women went about getting wedding preparations underway, and the men went about choosing their choicest and fattest animals to feed up and use during the most enormous wedding feast known to mankind!

This wouldn't be a small affair; this wedding feast would include the whole tribe – all represented by the twelve tribes of Isra'el. It was decided upon for two reasons: the wedding itself, and this would be the last celebration as a nation and tribe before departing to the lands of their inheritance.

Rachav wasn't worried or fussed at all. She had a beautiful dress all picked out that had been made for her back in Yericho, which to date, she had never worn. It was white brocade with gold thread weaved throughout in a lily pattern. Along the edges of the garment and the boat neckline were thick strips of gold, making the dress stand out. The bodice was very fitted, with the skirt being full length and flaring out from the waist. The sleeves were full-length and bell-shaped.

Rachav's hair was placed up in a bun, high on her head, accentuating her cheekbones and finely chiselled nose. To her eyes, Abiah and Yaffah applied a small amount of kohl, and also to her lashes, giving the effect of looking longer. To her cheeks, they applied some bronze powder and also to her eyelids. On her lips was a hint of deep burnt red stain.

Over her head, Yaffah had made a beautiful white veil, translucent and delicate, that her handsome Abba pulled down over her face before escorting her down the aisle.

Salmah stood looking at her, tears forming in his eyes, captivated by his betrothed's exquisite beauty and appearance. He wore long white linen trousers and a long tunic jacket identical to Rachav's dress. By some miraculous deed, the material had appeared from someone's stowed-away chest and had been made especially to fit the handsome man. His hair was shoulder length, dark and wavy, with beautiful red and auburn tones shining in the sun's light. On his feet were dark tan sandals, new and pristine.

Ever and Rachav approached Salmah whilst the crowd looked on. This was their boy, and shouts of joy went up as Ever placed Rachav's hand in Salmah's. Once the vows had been spoken, another contract signed, and the glass been smashed underfoot, the two newlyweds were ushered into a tent for a private meal. They bowed their heads in recognition that Adonai had bought them together, then ate their delicious meal. Toasting each other with Novac's special wine, they leant over and kissed each other, relishing their newfound status in a quiet moment. All too soon, they celebrated with the whole nation – a sight to behold and remember for many years.

After much dancing and celebration, the newly married couple stowed away to a private dwelling erected for their honeymoon. Whilst still within the walls of Gilgal, it was secluded enough that they could relax and enjoy their first days as husband and wife without the constant noise and pressure from well-meaning people.

Rachav looked at her husband in the glow of the oil lamp, and reached for his hand. He took her hand and pulled her into himself. Leaning down and kissing her deeply and passionately, he swooped her up in his arms. Walking over to the bed that had been decorated with lamps, flowers and a garland of leaves, Salmah lay his wife on the bed, closed the thick heavy curtains surrounding them and then proceeded to remove his tunic and trousers. He longed for her and found the fastenings to undo her dress. Removing the pins from her hair and watching it fall down upon her breasts, Salmah gulped in both excitement and dread. Here he was, an inexperienced virgin, unsure of what to do, so he lay next to her and traced the curve of her body with his hands while looking at her adoringly.

Rachav felt the tingle grow into a flame of passion, unfelt for such a long time, and she reached up and pulled Salmah's face towards hers.

Movement and motion - Rachav encouraged Salmah to touch her, to explore and taste all he desired. She explored her new husband and groaned in delight at his touch.

When they could wait no longer, the two gently melded together as one. The longing was replaced by a burning flame of desire ignited in both of them. The crescendo was reached, and the two lay on the bed, weeping in delight and wonder.

"My love, you are wonderful. I am blessed beyond measure to have you as my wife. I love you, Rachav." Salmah held his wife in his arms and kissed her softly. She, in turn, whispered in his ear and straddled him. She wanted more of her lover, and he responded in kind.

Afterwards, he grinned cheekily, looking at his beloved. "You are amazing, wife!" She giggled at his words and kissed him on his neck, brushing her lips towards his ear. The two became entangled and entered a world of whispers, groanings and desires. Afterwards, they fell asleep, ecstatic and exhausted.

The next morning, the newlyweds smelt fresh bread and realised their breakfast awaited them on a sideboard. Someone must have snuck in and left them this wonderful feast when they were asleep.

They refreshed themselves and then drank some lovely spring water to nourish their loved but parched bodies.

Sitting on the bed, Rachav smiled at her husband.

"You are stunning, Salmah. You have filled my heart and soul to overflowing. I thank Adonai for you and the chance to love again." She smiled, feeling the flush of new love once more. Salmah sat back and admired his wife. She had worried that she was getting older, but in his eyes, she was perfect. Rachav radiated a more profound joy than mere beauty; his soul rejoiced in her.

"My darling Rachav. You have ignited my soul as never before and given me more than you could ever know. Adonai has indeed blessed our union, and I am forever grateful to him for this journey that we have embarked upon."

The two found robes hanging in the tent and then devoured the food that had been left for them. After a time, they both lay on the bed and slept for a while.

When they awoke, Salmah found Rachav had drawn a bath in the outer tent near the sideboard. She had filled the water with herbs and flowers, and motioned for her husband to join her in the warm water. After washing and enjoying the deep soak, they returned to the bed and again made love. Salmah was fascinated with every part of his new wife. Touching, tasting, breathing, laughing and melding into one, they wept in delight and thanksgiving for the gift of marriage. Rachav responded in such wonder to Salmah's touch. She felt renewed and resplendent in his presence, almost like she was experiencing the pleasures of love for the first time.

In the quietness, laying next to her dark-haired beloved, she felt the tears of thanksgiving fall down her face onto her pillow. Rachav was so grateful to live this new life and participate in the most incredible adventure ever.

43

The New Wine

Novac looked over at his wife and smiled. He found her even more attractive while she was pregnant and delighted in telling her so. He couldn't keep his hands off her – and at times, this annoyed the young expectant mother-to-be! To keep himself out of trouble, he had started thinking about their future in Beit-Lechem and wanted to go and stake out the land to test the soil for his future vineyard.

Because of his expertise in the wine-making field, the elders had permitted him, if he agreed to take another couple of men along with him, for company and protection. Novac was not a natural-born warrior; however, he was happy to have these men along with him.

Abiah was happy for him to leave on the journey, promising to bring back a treat, if at all possible. She didn't usually ask for anything, so Novac planned a surprise for his beloved wife.

Having arrived with his travelling companions in the land of Beit-Lechem, Novac looked around and felt underwhelmed.

There didn't seem to be much of a village there, and what was there seemed to be a rocky outcrop that didn't possess much flat land for planting.

After commiserating with his companions, they explained that though the land seemed irredeemable to him, they knew of a way that planting could be done: terraced planting. As with other cultures they had travelled near in their time in the wilderness, they witnessed different types of agriculture and permaculture and kept note of these things for their future. As they explained the process, Novac grew excited about the possibility. Of course, they hadn't scouted out the whole of the land, and there was a genuine chance that flat land and paddocks might be around, but they hadn't seen this as of yet. Novac took notes, made plans and sketched the locations that would suffice for a future vineyard. He was grateful they would be transplanting some of the vines from outside of Yericho but also knew starting again would be hard work, and he had to have this as his long-range goal. With Adonai on their side, they would be drinking new wine in a few short years and celebrating the birth of, hopefully, many sons and daughters.

Novac thought of his wife and how fortunate he had been to meet and marry her. Now, he would have to learn from the men in the tribe how to be a good father. This wasn't something he felt particularly encouraged over, yet he knew again that with Adonai on their side, they would make it. All he did and ever wanted was wrapped up in his abiding love and desire for his wife, Abiah. She was his dream come true. He quietly gave thanks to Adonai for her.

Chatting with his companions, he explained he promised Abiah a present for allowing him to go on this reconnaissance trip. The men were able to direct him to a small village that sold all sorts of handmade goods, crafts, food, wine and clothing. Amongst all the beautiful offerings that could be purchased, Novac spotted a tiny tunic and a little pair of shoes. He bought them immediately for the baby. He also looked and found an exquisite long-flowing tunic that would keep Abiah cool and comfortable in the hotter months, especially whilst pregnant. The fabric was bright and colourful and reflected Abiah's vibrant nature. To top things off, he found some scent that smelt of a combination of musk and vanilla and hoped his wife would appreciate that too.

It was a productive trip, but he would be glad to be home and in the loving arms of his gorgeous wife.

44

Life in Beit-Lechem

Abiah struggled the most. She was, by now, heavily pregnant and not at all excited about their move to their promised land. Although Novac had provided a donkey for her to ride on, she was none too thrilled about being on this beast of burden for the day. Novac sensed her discomfort and planned for stops along the way, so she could dismount and move around a little. After what seemed forever, the tribe stood atop a hill and surveyed the land. This was theirs, to do with as the Lord commanded, and now their hard work was about to begin.

Marking out territory and near some of the rocky outcrops he had previously visited, Novac made plans for building a permanent dwelling as soon as possible. He wanted his wife settled and ready with everything she needed before the arrival of the little one.

Rachav and Salmah helped attend Abiah while watching Novac run around like a madman! They were greatly amused and also a little concerned. Whilst Novac was a brilliant master winemaker, his skills in building houses were left to be desired, and therefore Ever, Salmah and his family stepped up and offered to help build their abode. Novac was very grateful and none too proud to accept the offer. Abiah was grateful too. She loved her husband dearly but knew that if it were up to them, their abode would include the donkey in the middle of the home too!!

Within days, the abode was built, with Rachav, her new sisters-inlaw and Abiah, helping to furnish the home with fabrics, furnishings and all that was needed. Rachav's mother, Yaffah, cooked up a lot of food, including some recipes she had been famous for back in Yericho. Abiah, in particular, was very thankful. Though she was a great cook, it was getting more challenging to stay on her feet now. The baby would be here soon; she knew this intuitively.

Within days, Abiah had gone into labour. Novac panicked, so Salmah took him off while the women gathered in the birthing tent with Abiah.

Bearing down, with a leather strap gritted between her teeth, she pushed out the baby, with Yaffah catching him and wrapping him gently in a soft cloth. Shocked at how quickly the baby arrived, Abiah took hold of her newborn son and wept tears of joy. She asked for Novac to join her, of which he was summoned only after mother and baby had been checked and attended to.

Abiah was a natural mother. She let the baby suckle on her breast and felt the magical tinge as her newborn baby drank from her. It was unlike anything she'd ever known. As he took his fill, his father, Novac, entered the birthing tent. Weeping for joy, he kissed his wife on the lips and held both of them gently in his arms. He felt the tender presence of Adonai hovering over him as he looked into the beautiful face of his son. Taking the baby and walking around with him, he hummed and sang over the child. Lulling him to sleep, he looked at his wife with absolute love and pride. She had done so well and produced this baby in record time but still needed time to rest. Abiah lay sound asleep, and Novac sat in a seat, still holding his newborn son.

Rachav entered the tent and took the baby, placing him in a crib by Abiah's bed. She whispered for Novac to rest; before he knew it, all three of them were asleep.

Later that evening, all three of them awoke, and Abiah tended to their son.

"Darling, what shall we call this beautiful boy of ours?" asked Novac to his tired but satisfied wife.

"What about Gilad? It means 'endless joy'."

"Yes, I like that." Looking at his son, Novac spoke again. "Welcome, little Gilad. You, indeed, are already our endless joy. We love you, son. And we praise you, Adonai, for the safe arrival of our boy and for looking after my beautiful Abiah during the delivery." Novac wept openly. Abiah did too. Together they kissed and snuggled with their little treasure.

Life proceeded for the little family, with all the usual ups and downs that come with a newborn baby. Fortunately for Abiah and Novac, they had many families surrounding them, able to give advice, help and support when needed.

Rachav and Salmah marvelled at how their friends had taken to parenthood, despite Novac's fears and concerns. Abiah loved being an Eema and cherished her new role.

After a while, Novac started thinking about his winemaking business and decided it was time to go full steam ahead. Having transplanted the vines from his former home, he was pleased to see they had all taken to their new home and were flourishing. The winemaker put out the word he was looking for workers to help him build up the vineyard. He reconnected with his former contacts within the industry and was met with amiable responses. Knowing there was a lot of groundwork to cover, he approached his friend Salmah to see if he was willing to give some time to the business. Salmah was delighted to help and also learn from the ground up.

After a conversation on a particular evening, Rachav made a proposition to Salmah and Novac: with her knowledge and expertise within the hospitality industry and their expertise in their fields of operations, why not try opening another Inn, catering food and wine to the locals and as well as the travellers who would come through town? As they had now put down roots in Beit-Lechem, it would make sense that they return, in a modest form, to the industries they had all been trained in. Novac would provide the best wine in the region, Salmah would provide the choicest of meats, and Rachav and Abiah could run the Inn for both man and beast. It was certainly something for them all to think about. Of course, nothing would go ahead without seeking Adonai about this and asking the elders' wise counsel. They were, after all, no longer slaves to their old ways but wanted to honour Adonai in all they put their hand to.

After meeting with their village elders and seeking Adonai's ways, they all met together to share the outcome. The elders were thrilled with the idea and wondered if the community could be a part of the business, in some small way. Would any of them be willing to train some younger folk and introduce them to the various industries they represented in exchange for free help? Would they be willing to retrain some of the folk who had been nomads and had no formal training beforehand? In this instance, Rachav could now see a lot of the men could utilise the tools once belonging to Baba, and be able to glean from his written journals and also garner from his contacts. The friends all thought these were terrific ideas and loved that they could inspire another generation of folk and give a helping hand to those who would like it. Abiah loved the concept of the village helping with the raising of Gilad as well.

Rachav and Salmah set about finding the perfect spot to build an Inn. As the excitement rose, they stopped and looked at one another. "My love, in all our planning, prayers and preparations, I haven't asked you how you feel about all of this. Does this bring up bad memories or feelings for you, Rachav?"

"My Salmah. You are sweet to be concerned, but I would have told you if there had been. You know I don't keep anything from you." The two hugged and kissed each other warmly.

Rachav then spoke. "I'd really like Eema's input into this business. Back in Yericho, she was renowned for her hospitality and culinary skills, and on the odd occasion, she would help Abiah run the Inn when we were out of town. I never had to be concerned because her reputation was so esteemed; no one would dare try anything on her! Believe me, under that kind exterior, is the heart of a lioness!" They both laughed at this notion.

"I do believe, darling, that's a fine idea. Maybe your Abba would like to do some of his famous mosaics somewhere on or in the building too? Although, we probably shouldn't go about putting up scenes of the pagan gods, now should we?" Novac gave Rachav one of his cheeky smiles.

"A brilliant idea, my love." The two walked hand in hand to speak to Ever and Yaffah.

"Oh darling girl, what a great idea. We would be honoured to help you in any way you would like. Thank you, Rachav and Salmah, for considering us in your new venture. It seems you've got the whole village buzzing. How very exciting for everyone!" Ever and Yaffah gave praise to Adonai for this fantastic opportunity.

It was decided that the Inn would be built upon the plateau rather than on the steep hillside where the new vineyard and new abodes were being built. The reasoning behind this was that travellers, who are already tired and weary, would not want to walk up a steep hill near the end of the day, whereas this had a gentle incline. Rachav and Salmah also decided having a separate abode near the Inn would be best, giving them a little privacy away from the business.

The men gathered their resources together and devised a list of what would be needed to build the Inn. Salmah had a pouch of gold coins from some business he had conducted before shifting here. Alongside some of Rachav's profits, there was more than enough to build a quality Inn with all the necessary fixtures, lighting, furnishings, kitchen and, of course, a stable for the animals.

Some of the men went off to nearby villages to source materials for the build.

Before long, the bones of the Inn were taking shape, and Rachav was getting excited. She had given up her precious Inn back in Yericho and never dreamt that she would be part of owning another one. All praise to Adonai. This Inn, however, because it was freestanding and not built into the walls, was much larger than what she previously owned. Therefore, she could use some of the goods she had insisted she and Baba rescue before Yericho fell. She was grateful for the foresight to salvage these items, some of which had been brought on their many different travels.

45

With Child

Rachav was in shock. She'd known that there were changes in her body, but being of more middle age, she thought she was going through 'the change' as it was called. Never once did Rachav believe that she would be pregnant.

Salmah was elated! He picked her up and twirled her around, which didn't help the nausea she was already feeling. She looked pale, so he put her down suddenly and profusely apologised with his beaming smile.

What were her parents going to think? What would Abiah say? *"Oh my, what will I do? I've not been around many babies and children before – I don't know what I am in for."* Rachav was fraught with anxiety, and after the wave of nausea left her, she promptly went to her parents for advice. Dragging Salmah along, who was still beaming and was like a petulant little puppy wanting to get into mischief, Rachav sat both Yaffah and Ever done and started a little speech.

"Eema, Abba. You know I haven't been feeling my best of late. So, it would seem that I am with child – me, who is middle-aged and starting to go grey! Argh, what on earth will I do?"

Immediately Yaffah and Ever jumped up and embraced their only child. "We're going to be Savta and Saba? Are we going to have a wee grandbaby? Oh, Rachav and Salmah, our prayers have been answered by Adonai! We are indeed truly blessed!" Yaffah and Ever started to dance around their abode and then stopped, looked at each other, and started laughing. Rachav and Salmah looked on and giggled at her parent's youthfulness and enthusiasm. Then Rachav knew. She knew that with the love of her husband, her parents, her friends and the tribe, this child would be fine – she would be fine.

However, the most pressing matter of the moment was to stop feeling so nauseous. As Rachav was spending so much time in the kitchen at the Inn, preparing food and cooking culinary delights, it wouldn't be good to keep running off every time something smelt 'off' to her.

After speaking to her Eema about these matters, Yaffah took Rachav to one of the Herbalists living in the village, who gave her some special tonic to use. Fortunately, it started working immediately.

"You're pregnant?" squawked Abiah. "I can't believe it, Rachav! This is wonderful news. How are you? Are you okay? Do you need help?"

"Abiah! Shoosh! One question at a time, dear friend." The women started giggling.

"Oh Rachav, if you have a child such as Gilad, you will be blessed indeed. He's so sweet and kind. I hope that for you, too." The two women hugged.

"He's been wonderful for me to be around because, as you knew when we met, I wasn't interested in children. Salmah changed that in me. He's so level-headed, so loving and cheerful. Not like that petulant brute, I was married to beforehand." Rachav smiled at Abiah. "The memories remain, but the present is so much more fulfilling. I just cannot believe I am having my first baby at this age."

"Well, we will raise our newborns together, Rachav." Abiah gave a sly smile to her friend.

"You're pregnant too?"

"Ah, yes. That has always been Novac's plan. Barefoot and pregnant for ten years!"

"Well, if Adonai hadn't wanted us to be fruitful and multiply, he wouldn't have made the practising so much fun," retorted Novac.

"Oh darling, very true," grinned Abiah.

"Any sickness for you, Abiah?"

"No, just a little tired these days. I fall asleep around the same time that Gilad goes down in the evening, so poor Novac has to entertain himself, for the most part now."

"I have plenty to keep myself busy – for the most part," winked Novac at his wife.

Rachav was thrilled to see the two of her friends so deeply in love with each other. They were still cheeky and occasionally naughty, but were a delight to be around.

"I guess this means things will change at the Inn, not immediately, but in a few months. You, Abiah, will have your hands full with two babies, and I will have one to keep me preoccupied. I guess we will have to train up more young ones, who have the time and energy to run the place, while we care for our little ones?"

Abiah agreed. "Still, let's not worry about that now. We have to prepare the dinner for tonight and see about making sure the stables and rooms are ready to receive some guests."

After serving supper to the guests and directing them to their rooms, the women went about their duties, and then left for the evening. They were confident with their two young trainees on board and the ever-watchful Yaffah.

<h1 style="text-align:center">46</h1>

<h1 style="text-align:center">Yaffah & Ever</h1>

The elderly couple wandered around their surroundings, having just received the news of Rachav's pregnancy. They were elated! Never in their wildest dreams did they think they would live to see this dream come true. Surely Adonai had smiled down on them.

Ever entwined their hands as they continued their stroll; how he loved his wife tremendously. She had never complained, never caused a day's worry for him. He simply adored her for all the beauty she still possessed, her kind and gentle heart, her courage and strength in the face of adversity, and the simple fact that she was the love of his youth, which had been sustained into their old age.

They started out as any other couple in their culture. They longed for a big family, prosperity, love, and all the usual things. But their gods hadn't looked down on Yaffah's womb too kindly. Rachav was their only success, and what a beauty she had been right from birth. With a strong and fierce independent streak but with the same kind and gentleness about her as her mother, she would be their only child who lived. Even Rachav didn't know the miscarriages and stillborn births that had transpired before her life came forth. After Rachav was born, The couple had decided not to try for more children – their prayers had finally been answered, and their lives were complete – albeit a slightly differing vision of what they once shared, they were happy with what they had been given.

Yaffah took to motherhood like a duck to water and enjoyed every moment with her infant child. Ever adored coming home after work and seeing his two girls shining their glorious smiles at him. He loved them deeply, and vowed to do all he could to care for them and make them happy.

The family grew to be incredibly tight-knit until the horrible incident with the aforementioned man, who took it upon himself to spoil their beautiful daughter. They had done all they could to protect and shield this young beauty from the dastardly deeds of a few evil men that lurked within the city walls, but unfortunately, it didn't work this time.

With time, Rachav grew to trust again. She lost the sweet innocence she once carried, for it to be replaced with a hardness and a tenacious spirit that wanted everything, and under the watchful eye of her parents, she got everything she wanted.

Ever had installed a strong work ethic in his daughter, who was unafraid of doing all he asked her to do and getting dirty too! Rachav often could be found in the fields, tilling and ploughing the soil, sewing crops, reaping the harvest and having a good laugh with all the other workers. Ever was intensely proud of his daughter and would tell her so. However, the day came when they realised that her strength and tenacity had been coupled with a hint of pride and arrogance. Using her God-given beauty and persuasion, she was able to forge ahead in her chosen career with the help of a few wealthy men and her body. The couple were not impressed, but rather than make an enemy of their daughter, they sat tight and trusted it would be a phase she would grow out of. Thankfully, Baba came along, and the rest is history.

Ever had once been a humble artisan, crafting some of the most beautiful mosaics in all of Yericho. His skill and artistry had gained him a reputation for excellence, and he had gradually risen to become the owner of his own mosaic business. Now, he employed several men and was known as a successful businessman and provider for his family. He was grateful for the journey that had brought him to this point, from his modest beginnings to the fulfilment of his dreams.

Mosaic – the art of creating images with an assemblage of small pieces of coloured glass, stone or other materials- originated in Mesopotamia. The most popular mosaic subject was mythological scenes, such as the gods and goddesses, which are frequently found. The god of Enki, the god of freshwater oceans, and also closely associated with wisdom, magic, incantations, arts and crafts, was found in temples, gardens and private dwellings alike. Since this was a highly skilled and laborious art form, Ever had been able to charge a premium for his gifts and expertise.

Of course, after the initial help with her business, Rachav wouldn't accept another coin towards her costs and expenses. She wanted to do it all on her own.

And so, life became about Yaffah and Ever from that time on. Always on standby for their daughter, if needed, Yaffah busied herself keeping a beautiful home for entertaining her husband's associates and their wives, and of course, was a legend for her culinary skills. Most of Yericho was aware of the exquisite dishes she would cook, along with her expert hospitality. Many young women would come and inquire about Yaffah's knowledge and advice. She was, after all, the person who taught Rachav all her wonderful recipes that she made for the Inn – much to the delight of her patrons.

Over the years, Yaffah and Ever helped out with Rachav's Inn, to their joy and delight. They loved meeting the new patrons and the travellers and assisting with the livestock that would utilise the stables. Ever, in particular, would take great delight in the children who frequented the Inn and teach them some of his magic tricks or how to create art, with the curious parents looking on. Ever would take the children into the kitchen so Yaffah could spoil them with treats and goodies.

The two of them beseeched the gods and goddesses for grandchildren, but none came, even when Rachav married Baba.

When the talk began to spread like wildfire within the city about the amazing god who did miracles for the Israelite tribe wandering in the desert, both Ever and Yaffah paid attention. Imagine their good fortune when Rachav confided in her parents that two spies had come into the Inn, and she had hidden them, in exchange for her and her family's safety.

Rachav's parents were intrigued by this foreign god, but also were frightened. They knew they needed to make a decision, and they weren't ready to lose their lives for the sake of their King and city.

The decision was made, and Yaffah and Ever embarked on a new journey with their family and friends.

47

The Gifts

The time grew nearer for both Rachav and Abiah to have their babies. Rachav waddled around like a pregnant duck, exceptionally uncomfortable and past her due date. Feeling like this baby would never come, she waddled up the hill, albeit a gentle hill, to the Inn and then sat down in the cool shade. Her mother scolded her for having been out walking in the heat of the day and up the hill; Rachav ignored her complaints and fanned herself. Salmah came running into the Inn and scolded his wife – he had gone home to have the midday meal with her, and she had disappeared. Fortunately, she listened to him and saw why her family was worried.

Abiah was also full term, yet busy running around after her sweet toddler, Gilad. She adored being his Eema, but she was tired all the time. Novac helped where possible, but the vineyard took up much of his time. Abiah's neighbours were accommodating and did what they could to assist with Gilad, and other chores, such as carrying the water from the well, and babysitting the toddler so she could nap some afternoons, when he wouldn't. The community stepped in and helped both the expectant mothers, with several women offering to assist with the births, when their time came.

Abiah and Rachav would often get together and laugh about their lives now. How different things were now, especially with their burgeoning bellies, swollen ankles, and the busy Inn. Still, they were so grateful to Adonai for giving them a second chance at life, in a new town, and with each other close by.

Rachav awoke from an unusual sleep and tried to get out of bed so she could sip some water. She managed to stand and then gushed all over the floor. Immediately, there was a pang in her pelvis, and she knew the baby was coming. She found the oil lamp, lit it, and then woke Salmah.

"Darling, it's started."

A sleepy Salmah responded, "What's started?"

"My waters have broken, all over the floor, and I have pangs in my pelvis, spreading all over, and the baby is on its way!" She spoke rather loudly as each pang seemed to grow in intensity.

"Oh my....umm, what do you want me to do, beloved?" Cried out Salmah, who was panicking, which made Rachav smile a little.

"I need you to help me clean up this mess, get changed, and then go and get my Eema. Then I need you to awaken the midwife and tell her it's time. Can you do those things for me, please, Salmah?"

"Yes darling, I can. Let's get you sorted, and don't worry, I will clean this mess up shortly."

Rachav sat down in a chair, all cleaned up and breathing through the pangs that kept coming. Suddenly her Eema and the midwife burst through the door.

"Okay, Rachav, it's time to take you to the birthing tent, where we will examine you and proceed. Don't be afraid, this is all perfectly normal and natural, and besides, Adonai is with us, Omaine." It was more a statement of fact than a prayer, but the women spoke, Omaine in agreement.

"Rachav, darling girl, what can I do for you?" Yaffah was fussing over her only child and was utterly nervous, which Rachav could pick up on.

"Eema, please, I need you to relax and hold my hand while we walk to the birthing tent." Out in the dark of the night, Rachav asked Yaffah a question. "Eema, we've never spoken about my birth. What was it like for you?"

"My goodness, that was a long time ago, my love. Many hazy memories, but I remember your birth being quick and wonderful. Your Abba was present and actually caught you as you were born. I attest that to why you two are so close. You always have been, right from your first breath." Yaffah wiped a tear from her face and looked at her daughter. "You are such a joy to us, Rachav, my beautiful girl. And your child will be the same to you. There's nothing to fear, darling – Adonai created us to bear children, and we do it well!" The two women held hands, with Rachav squeezing her Eema's hand as her labour progressed.

Once inside the tent with her Eema and the midwife, Rachav asked, "Can I speak with Salmah, please?"

Salmah walked into the tent, feeling somewhat out of place, being the only male.

"My love, what is it? Is anything wrong?"

"No, Salmah, everything is fine. But I want you to be here. I know it's out of the ordinary, but if it's good enough for my Abba to attend my birth, then it's good enough for our baby's Abba to attend its birth. Would you mind, darling?"

"I'd love to be here. Mind you, this will be different to birthing lambs, I'd think!" The couple smiled at one another, then took a deep breath.

"I don't think it's going to be too long now, husband....ohhhh!" Rachav's labour was in full swing now, and she was feeling the urge to push.

Feeling pangs in her lower back and thighs, she flipped over to be on all fours. Salmah rubbed her back as the midwife, and Yaffah rubbed her thighs. Rachav swayed back and forth, and with each pang, she breathed and concentrated on a spot on the floor. Between each pang, she beseeched Adonai to help her through and labour in safety and shalom. Before too long, the head crowned, and within a few minutes, a beautiful dark-haired boy was born to Rachav and Salmah. Like his father-in-law before him, Salmah readied himself with a large blanket and caught the baby as he was birthed. Tears of joy sprung forth like pools of water in an oasis. Rachav managed to bear down and birth the placenta, and then the midwife and Yaffah attended to her. Sitting on the bed, Rachav held her newborn son and wept, giving thanks to Adonai and all who were present.

The new mother was given some herbs and a pleasant drink, then encouraged to allow her son to suckle at her breast. She sat in wonderment, looking at Salmah. "This is what I was created for, my love. I marvel at what Adonai has done." Salmah teared up, then went over and held his wife and baby, gently singing a psalm of praise, "My soul does rejoice in you, my King. My soul does magnify you, my Lord and Saviour. Surely you have done mighty things and beheld us in your majesty. To you alone, Oh Adonai, I rejoice and give thanks."

"Darling, what shall we call this beautiful wee boy?" Enquired Rachav of Salmah.

"I think we shall name him Bo'az. It means 'quickness', and he sure did get here quickly!" He kissed Rachav on the forehead.

"Bo'az, I like that. Welcome, sweet little Bo'az. You sure did come quickly, but oh, how wonderful to have you here and hold you in our arms, wee one." She gently kissed his forehead.

Soon, the little family slept for a time. Upon waking, Rachav felt strong enough to walk to their home, albeit slowly and awkwardly.

Abiah had been in their home and prepared a beautiful little basket for the baby to sleep in. Clothes had been made and gifted to the couple, along with all the mother's and baby's needs. Overwhelmed at the generosity of their community, Rachav broke down in tears. Of course, hormones and emotions were at play, but deep in her heart, Rachav was humbled and grateful for all Adonai had showered upon them.

Not many days afterwards, a very pregnant Abiah entered labour, bringing forth a beautiful wee baby girl whom they named Ziva. Unlike Gilad, who had a shock of dark wavy hair like his Abba, Ziva had beautiful golden locks like her Eema and a feisty little personality to go with it! Novac laughed at this, "Ah, my wee daughter, you are just like your Eema." Abiah smiled and was grateful the numbers had evened up!

The town of Beit-Lechem rejoiced with their two newest little lambs. Adonai had blessed their community indeed.

48

Y'Hoshua & Kalev

Rachav always had a soft spot in her heart for Y'hoshua and Kalev. Both men were giants of the faith, original witnesses, and servants of Moshe. She adored them and remembered all the times they would spend in the meeting tent, with Rachav learning all their ways, albeit at times, heartbreaking and with a pounding headache near the end of each session.

Today, they would gather at Sh'khem to hear Y'hosuha's last address. He was now getting on in age and was 110 years old. Still a mighty warrior, and an outstanding oracle, the crowd went silent when they saw him appear before them.

"I am old; age is taking its toll. You have seen everything Adonai, your God, has done to all these nations because of you, for Adonai has fought on your behalf. Here, I have allotted you land for inheritance according to your tribes between the Yarden and the Great Sea to the west; it includes the land of the nations I have destroyed and those that remain. Adonai will thrust them out ahead of you and drive them out of your sight so that you will possess their land, as Adonai, your God, told you.

"Therefore, be very firm about keeping and doing everything written in the book of the Torah of Moshe and not turning aside from it either to the right or the left. Then you won't become like those nations remaining among you. Don't even mention the name of their gods, let alone have people swear by them, serve them or worship them, but cling to Adonai, your God, as you have done to this day. This is why Adonai has driven out great, strong nations ahead of you, and it explains why no one has prevailed against you to this day, why one man of you has chased a thousand — it is because Adonai has fought on your behalf, as he said to you.

"Take great care to love Adonai, your God. Otherwise, if you retreat and cling to the remnant of these other nations remaining among you, if you marry them and have children with them and they with you, know that Adonai, your God, will stop driving out these nations from your sight. Instead, they will become a snare and a trap for you, whipping your sides and pricking your eyes until you perish from this good land which Adonai has given you.

"Today, I am going the way of all the earth. Therefore consider in all your heart and being that not one of all the good things Adonai your God said concerning you has failed to happen; it has all come to pass; nothing of it has failed. Nevertheless, just as all the good things Adonai your God promised you have come upon you, likewise Adonai will bring upon you all the bad things too, until he has destroyed you from this good land which Adonai your God has given you. When you violate the covenant of Adonai your God, which he ordered you to obey, and go and serve other gods and worship them, then the anger of Adonai will blaze up against you; and you will perish quickly from the good land which he has given you!"

Rachav and Salmah moved to the front of the crowd and met one last time with their friend, Y'Hoshua. There were no parting words of wisdom or advice, just a strong hug and a look of knowing. He patted them on their heads, blessed them with the priestly blessing, and then walked away.

Likewise, the couple sensed this would be the last time they would see Kalev. They made their way to him, and he glanced at them with his broad smile, pushing others out of the way, so he could embrace them. Knowing that Salmah, the unofficial Prince of Y'Hudah, was now an Abba, Kalev slapped him on the back and kissed Rachav.

"Well done, my children, well done! About time, eh?" Laughed Kalev cheekily. "Alas, I too am about to make my journey to the bosom of Avraham, but not before giving you some words of wisdom." The two looked intently at their elder and friend. "Fight the good fight of faith, dear one. In Adonai is all you will ever need. Teach your son the right way; he will not depart from it when he is older. Mark my words: greatness comes from your bloodline, Rachav the Beautiful!" She blushed but thanked Kalev and hugged him tightly.

"Go well, my daughter, and be at shalom. You are well loved." To Salmah, he looked, eyes glistening with pride. "My son. I have known you since your birth, and I have loved you for every second. Your parents, unfortunately, didn't make it to the promised land, but you, O Prince of Y'hudah, have greatness

49

Sailing The Seven Seas

The family had bid goodbye to their beloved Yaffah and Ever, who died naturally, of old age. Amongst the grief of losing her parents, Rachav taught her young son the ways of mourning, so that he would be prepared for the eventuality of their death, one day in the future. Both Salmah and Rachav had watched on as Yaffah and Ever took on their roles as Savta and Saba with generosity, amazement and love. From their input, such deep, abounding joy flowed, and Bo'az grew in character and kindness.

Having left an inheritance for the family as well as the greater community, Rachav spent some time in prayer, then approaching her husband, asked him an unusual question.

"Salmah, how would you feel if we went on a journey together? Just the three of us?"

Salmah seemed a little surprised, but not entirely. He'd wondered over the years if Rachav had missed her travelling days.

"Darling, I think it's a wonderful idea. Moments like these are a great life education for us all, particularly Bo'az. Where were you thinking of going?"

"I thought we could charter a boat, go around the Levant, and at least expose Bo'az and yourself to life outside Beit-Lechem. What do you think?"

"I say yes. I know you and Baba had wanted to leave and travel again in the past, but life has moved on from then. There isn't the immediate danger there once was, and now we have more freedom to do these things. Let's do it as soon as we can, my love." Salmah was exuberant, and couldn't wait to go aboard a boat and experience different cultures, albeit not partaking of the paganism that still surrounded them.

Plans were made, the Inn and house would be looked after, and before they knew it, they were travelling to the port town of Tyre to board their boat. Let the journey begin!

Travelling from Tyre, they headed south through the Syrian Sea and Gulf of Pelusium onto Alexandria. Stopping in at the great port, they marvelled at the architecture, the great library and university, and the massive lighthouse that greeted them as they entered the harbour. Moving through the large bustling city, the trio and a guide found the markets and discovered all kinds of exotic foods and drinks to sample, alongside Rachav picking up some fabrics and beauty items.

Their journey took them to the international port of Carthage, on the pinnacle of the Punic Sea, then heading north to the island of Sardinia. Whilst travelling around the island, they were mesmerised by the giant architecture they discovered, and Bo'az was entertained by the guide telling him tall tales of myths and legends that couldn't possibly be true – and yet, according to their own recent history, their own elder, Kalev had slaughtered the sons of Anak from Hevron. Maybe this was true after all?

Leaving Sardinia, they sailed towards Roma through the Tyrrhenian Sea, and anchored there for a few days. Rachav, Salmah and Bo'az marvelled at the large buildings that seemed to rise from the earth in this city, and Rachav sensed a familiar feeling – she knew all too well the various gods and goddesses, under the guise of different names, that were worshipped openly and freely in this place. Not wanting to dampen the joy and adventures of her husband and son, she kept quiet but kept in prayer and vigilant in what was appropriate for them as sightseers.

Then came the long journey to Athens, which meant crossing several seas, rolling waves, and inclement weather. These things didn't bother the males much, but Rachav preferred calmer waters. Bo'az loved the adventure of the oceans. The captain would take the time to show the young boy all the implements and tools needed to navigate the fine boat, and of course, Salmah was listening in, too, learning all about an industry he knew nothing about. Rachav was so pleased they had come on this adventure. It would be something they would remember for the rest of their lives, but it also gave them a greater sense of purpose and perspective when the days were long and arduous back in Beit-Lechem.

Finally, they arrived in Athens, and the monuments took their breath away. Although dedicated to various gods and goddesses, their beauty and craftsmanship were second to none.

Bo'az was a little confused at all the statues and wondered where their clothes were, but Salmah and Rachav took that all in their stride.

After discovering the interior of the island and then heading to some of the smaller islands, the trio headed out on the final leg of their journey. As much as they wanted to stop on the islands of Crete and then Cyprus, time was against them, and they needed to head back home. Across the Aegean and Minoan Seas, the boat came into some rough weather again but gained strength as they crossed the Egyptian Sea and headed into the familiar waters of the Syrian Sea.

Leaving the boat, Bo'az ran back to the captain and gave him a hug. He'd had a wonderful time with the old rugged man, who seemed at home with a pipe in his mouth and a rough straw hat on his head and offered no other name; he was just Captain. The old man mussed up the young boy's hair, then sent him off with a small coin in his hand for a treat.

Smiling and waving to the captain and his crew, Salmah, Rachav and Bo'az made their way into Tyre for the evening to rest, before travelling back to Beit-Lechem.

Waking in the bustling city the next morning, they found a camel caravan and joined them on the trek back home.

Within a couple of days, the trio were back in their homeland and entertained the townsfolk at the Inn with tales of wonder and adventure, high seas, myths, giants and legends.

Abiah and Novac were doing exceptionally well with the brood of children, which had reached five now. Three boys and two girls later, Novac exclaimed his dream had come true of keeping Abiah barefoot and pregnant for ten years. Of course, she protested, then quickly swatted her husband on his behind – typical behaviour for those two!

Ziva had missed her friend, Bo'az, and couldn't wait for him to share all of his stories with her. The two had been brought up together, having been born a few days apart, and had always been close. He was considered one of Abiah's children, which made Rachav and Abiah laugh.

As they continued growing, the children filled their respective households with cheer and delight. Rachav couldn't bear any more children due to her age, but this never concerned her or Salmah.

Their family, faith and community were the pillars of their life and world, until the fateful day Rachav fell ill.

50

Paradise Awaits

Her long silvery hair lay fanned upon the pillow. Salmah reached for a cloth and dipped it into a bowl of cold water. Wringing out the excess water, he lay the cool cloth upon Rachav's forehead, praying for the fever to go down. It wouldn't budge.

"My love," she gently whispered, "It's time. Don't fret, for I'm not in any pain. But you must release me, so I can go to paradise and live within Avraham's bosom." She implored him with her still beautiful brown eyes.

"Beloved, how can I let you go? You are my world, my light, my love." Tears fell down Salmah's face onto Rachav's gown. "All I am, all I have is wrapped up in you, my darling Rachav."

"Trust in Adonai, dear Salmah. He has never let us down. Though we may be parted for a while, we will be together again soon. Trust him, and don't let go of your faith, my darling." She motioned for Bo'az to draw nearer.

"The son of our love, you are our greatest joy. Never forget the stories I have shared with you, or forget your God, darling Bo'az."

"I won't, Eema. I will never forget." Bo'az lay his head on his mother's breast and wept. After a time, he lifted his head to see her looking at him with a beaming smile.

"Ah, how like my Abba you are, darling young man. Remain faithful to Adonai, and remain kind. Remember to always provide for the widow and the stranger who come to you. Remember to always do the right thing, Bo'az." She took a deep breath, then called out to Salmah.

"Beloved husband and son, please remain best friends and father and son. You will need each other when I am gone. Keep lifting your voices in praise to Adonai. Oh, how my heart has rejoiced when I hear you both sing. My two darlings, what a joy you both have been to me."

"Please tell Abiah and Novac; they have been like a brother and sister to me. I adore them and their brood of children."

"We will, Eema," assured Bo'az.

"I have lived a full life, an extravagant life, really. I have been blessed with so much. Salmah, please give Bo'az his portion of the inheritance when I'm gone. And Bo'az, use the money wisely. Don't be foolish in your youth. Instead, invest wisely, and find a good wife. One who will not only be your love but your best friend. After all, you must like the person you lay next to, and you need to communicate clearly with them. And darling, make sure you have fun! Laugh much, like you have seen Abba and I do throughout the years."

Bo'az and Salmah smiled. Ever the mother, even on her deathbed. Rachav murmured something softly, causing the men to lower their ears to her mouth.

"I love you both. I'll see you soon, my darlings." She let out a long breath, then gently, it stopped.

As a gentle breeze stirred the air in the room, a shimmering light coalesced into the form of an angel standing beside Rachav's bed. The angel was breathtakingly beautiful, with long, flowing dark hair that seemed to dance around her shoulders like liquid silk. She was dressed in a radiant white tunic that glowed softly in the dim light, giving her an otherworldly appearance.

Rachav, now looking youthful and radiant, gazed at the angel with a serene smile on her face. The room seemed to hold its breath as the angel reached out a hand towards Rachav, who took it without hesitation. With one final, loving glance back at Salmah and Bo'az, Rachav's form began to glow with a radiant light, and she disappeared from sight, leaving behind a sense of peace and wonder in her wake.

Salmah and Bo'az stood frozen, their eyes wide with awe and disbelief at the sight before them. The room was filled with a lingering sense of peace, as if the very air was infused with a divine presence. Salmah felt a mix of emotions swirling within him—grief for the loss of his beloved wife, but also a profound sense of wonder and gratitude for the glimpse of the heavenly realm they had just witnessed.

Salmah reached out and took Bo'az into his arms, and together they grieved.

Stepping out into the midday sun, Abiah ran down the hill and stopped. Seeing the look on the faces of Salmah and Bo'az, she instantly knew. She fell into Salmah's arms, crying hysterically. Novac finally caught up, and took his wife into his arms as she continued to sob for her dear sister and friend.

After the funeral, the villagers gathered at the Inn. Every part of the building had the hallmarks of Rachav upon it. From the luscious furnishings and fabrics to the coloured interiors and mosaics done by her Abba, the Inn was quintessentially Rachav. However, rather than make everyone sad, they were joyful and celebratory. This woman, their dear friend, sister, daughter, mother, wife and lover, had been the hero of a story generations ago that culminated in these people being here today. Were it not for her great courage and tenacity, they wouldn't have been there now.

Rachav was indeed a quiet, gentle hero with the rarest of faith, strength and courage.

One that is still being spoken of today.

51

Alexandria & Rachav

The two women looked at each other.

Rachav spoke first. "It is here our journey ends, my dear Alexandria."

Tears welled in the younger woman's eyes.

"After all this time, I can't believe this is the end, Rachav." The tears poured down her face, causing Rachav to enfold Alex in her arms.

"You have been so gracious to me, Alexandria. I can never repay you for your kindness. What an honour and privilege to share my whole story with you."

Alex wiped away her tears and smiled at the beauty before her.

"You have come to mean so much to me. But believe me, Rachav, the honour has been mine. Thank you for entrusting intimate details and your deepest heart's journey with me. I've never been so captivated by someone's story– all the different shades and everything in between!" The women laughed together.

Hearing the deep baritone voice of her beloved Papa, Alexandria whirled around and ran into his loving embrace.

"Papa. Thank you!" Alexandria gushed.

"I didn't realise with this assignment how much healing and transformation I would go through personally. Thank you for choosing me to write this and giving me the great honour of meeting such an outstanding woman, such as Rachav. People will not believe some of the events and tales that will eventually make their way onto paper." Papa and daughter laughed together.

Papa looked over at Rachav and smiled. "Daughter, how are you? Have you been able to share all your heart longed to?"

"Oh yes, Papa. I most certainly have. I believe that many who read this story will start to see the truth, which has been hiding in plain sight. I pray that many will be free from their personal prisons of pain and wounding, and they will allow your goodness and grace to come and heal them as only you can. Thank you, Papa, for this wonderful journey." Looking over at Alex, Rachav, too, became misty-eyed. "I shall miss this dear friend of mine. But I know, one day soon, we shall all be together in paradise, with you forever."

"Yes, you will. What a reunion, eh, my dear ones!" Papa gathered both his girls under his arms and squeezed them.

"Well, dear Alex, it's time you headed back to your world. I think you've got much to share with Drew, right?" Alex smiled. Giving them another hug, Alex walked over to the bench and sat down. She turned to wave goodbye; however, they both had disappeared.

"Ah, Papa. What will I do now?" Her heart felt sore and somewhat empty.

"Write, dear one. Write it down, and don't leave anything out. It doesn't matter if it's uncomfortable or makes others squirm. Sometimes, truth does that." She heard Papa's deep voice.

"Ah, Rachav. My dear, dear friend." She blew a kiss on the wind.

Waking in the morning, Alex looked over at Drew. "Darling, you will not believe what I dreamt about."

"Well then, tell me, honey."

"There's a whole book's worth of explanation, but I met with Rachav."

"Who's Rachav?"

"Rahab, who helped the spies in Jericho."

"Wow. Why her?"

"Papa wants me to write her story, some of it from the view of a 'harlot's heart'."

"Meaning?"

"You'll understand soon enough!" Alex rolled over and kissed her husband, then took off to the computer to begin...

Epilogue

Destiny of Bo'az

Bo'az couldn't help thinking of his beloved Eema. Of all the stories his parents would tell him, the one that fascinated him the most was when Eema and her family saved the spies from the King. That one good act saved their entire family and showed the strength and courage of this woman, who had no allegiance or responsibility to do anything for the spies. Her loyal character and fortitude served her well for the coming dilemma she would find herself in.

He couldn't help thinking about his wife Rut and his mother's similarities. They had not been born into the Israelite clan, yet they left behind all they knew and became true Israelites, in time. Leaving behind their pagan gods, culture, friends and family, Rachav and Rut shed all they knew and embraced the One True God. This fact alone astonished Bo'az. Rachav would be proud of this beautiful woman whom Bo'az had married. He felt his eyes grow teary. How he missed his mother, especially at a time like this. But she had lived a long, beautiful, wonderful life, and she was now in Avraham's arms. The bosom of Avraham, to be precise. He knew that one day, they would be reunited.

Bo'az reflected on the kindness of his Abba. Salmah had taught Bo'az all about worshipping his creator and being faithful, loyal, honest and true to all things in Adonai's heart. A man's portion was in the hands of his creator, that much he knew and taught his son.

As Salmah had been a shepherd all his working life, he taught his son how to handle, read, and work with animals. Bo'az and his Abba would spend countless nights under the stars, where Salmah shared his heart with his son, singing songs and psalms to Adonai, whilst being on guard with the animals.

Bo'az had been a good learner and a faithful son and was well rewarded for being so. Someday, Bo'az's name would be inscribed on one of the two pillars that made up the portico of Shlomo's temple.

Being a wealthy landowner, Bo'az was favoured by his workers for being a kind and just man. He was approachable and sometimes spent time harvesting crops with the men and women. He was also considered a judge in Beit-Lechem and proved to have favour throughout the land.

The man himself loved Adonai fiercely. He was a student of the Torah and would often meet with the Rabbis to midrash over the scriptures.

But in all his achievements, Bo'az deeply loved and adored his wife, Rut. Knowing her journey, he felt great pride in the woman who walked beside him. His greatest treasure was when Rut announced to him they would become parents – oh, how Bo'az rejoiced! He called for a celebration, a feast of the fattened calf, alongside beautiful, sumptuous delicacies and the choicest of wines from Novac's vineyard.

After a trouble-free pregnancy, Rut laboured and brought forth a beautiful son, Obed. Their prayers had been answered, and their lives were complete.

"One day, my son, in this small clan of Beit-Lechem, a future ruler of Isra'el, will come forth, whose origins are far in the past, back in ancient times. He will stand and feed his flock in the strength of Adonai, in the majesty of the name of Adonai, his God. What a time that will be, my son!"

"Abba, what does that mean?" Obed looked at his father, somewhat confused.

"Ah, my son. The Messiach will come forth from our line, our heritage. And he will come forth from this place we live. Imagine that, Obed! Our little town will be the birthplace of the Messiach of Isra'el! Glory to his name."

"Abba, that sounds very exciting. Will he be in Eema's tummy like I was?"

Bo'az chuckled to himself. "No, Obed. He will be in his own Eema's tummy, though I'm not sure who that will be. I don't think we'll be around to see this happen, but I know it will happen, just as the prophets have foretold."

"Oh, okay then, Abba. Can I go and play now, please?" Obed looked up into his Abba's face, full of delight and wonder." "Yes, you may, my son." Bo'az mussed his hair and kissed his forehead, then watched him run off to play with his friends.

A tear ran down the man's rugged face. Waiting, holding the silence as the holy and unexpected moment it was.

"Surely Adonai is in this place." He spoke in a whisper.

Appendix

Ancient Sources and Extra-Biblical Texts

The Book of Jasher

Chapter Two

"And it was in the days of Enosh that the sons of men continued to rebel and transgress against God, to increase the anger of the Lord against the sons of men."

"And the sons of men went and served other gods, and they forgot the Lord who had created them on the earth: in those days, the sons of men made images of brass and iron, wood and stone, and they bowed down and served them."

Chapter Four

"And every man made unto himself a god, and they robbed and plundered every man, his neighbour, and his relative, and they corrupted the earth, and the earth was filled with violence. And their judges and rulers went to the daughters of men and took their wives by force from their husbands according to their choice. The sons of men in those days took from the cattle of the earth, the beasts of the field and the fowls of the air and taught the mixture of animals one species with the other, to provoke the Lord. And God saw the whole earth, and it was corrupt, for all flesh had corrupted its ways upon earth, all men and all animals."

The Book of Enoch

Chapter 7

"And when the angels, the sons of heaven, beheld them, they became enamoured, saying to each other, Come, let us select for ourselves wives from the progeny of men, and let us beget children.

"Then their leader Samyaza said to them, I fear that you may perhaps be indisposed to the performance of this enterprise; and that I alone shall suffer for so grievous a crime.

"But they answered him and said, "We all swear and bind ourselves by mutual execrations, that we will not change our intention, but execute our projected undertaking."

"Then they swore all together, and all bound themselves by mutual execrations. Their whole number was two hundred, who descended upon Ardis, which is the top of Mount Armon (Hermon).

"That mountain, therefore, was called Armon because they had sworn upon it and bound themselves by mutual execrations.

"These are the names of their chiefs: Samyaza, who was their leader; Urakabarameel, Akibeel, Tamiel, Ramuel, Danel, Azkeel, Saraknyal, Asael, Armers, Batraal, Anane, Zavebe, Samsaveel, Ertael, Turel, Yomyael, Azazyal. These were the prefects of the two hundred angels, and the remainder were all with them.

"Then they took wives, each choosing for himself, whom they began to approach, and with whom they cohabited, teaching them sorcery, incantations, and the dividing of roots and trees.

"And the women conceiving brought forth giants, whose stature was each three hundred cubits. These devoured all the labour of men produced; until it became impossible to feed them. When they turned themselves against men in order to devour them and began to injure birds, beasts, reptiles, and fishes, to eat their flesh and drink their blood.

"Then the earth reproved the unrighteous.

"Moreover, Azazyel taught men to make swords, knives, shields, breastplates, the fabrication of mirrors, the workmanship of bracelets and ornaments, the use of paint, the beautifying of the eyebrows, the use of stones of every valuable and select kind, and of all sorts of dyes so that the world became altered.

"Impiety increased; fornication multiplied, and they transgressed and corrupted all their ways.

"Amazarak taught all the sorcerers and dividers of roots.

"Armers introduced the solution of sorcery.

"Barkayal taught the observers of the stars.

"Akibeel taught signs.

"Tamiel taught astronomy.

"Asaradel taught the motion of the moon.

"Men, being destroyed, cried out; and their voices reached to heaven.

"Then Michael and Gabriel, Raphael, Suryal, and Uriel, looked down from heaven and saw the quantity of blood which was shed on earth, and all the iniquity which was done upon it, and said one to another, "It is the voice of their cries; the earth deprived of her children has cried even to the gate of heaven. And now to you, O you holy ones of heaven, the souls of men complain, saying, 'Obtain Justice for us with the Most High.' Then they said to their Lord, the King, Thou art Lord of lords, God of gods, King of kings. The throne of thy glory is forever and ever, and forever and ever is thy name sanctified and glorified. Thou art blessed and glorified. Thou hast made all things; thou possesses power over all things, and all things are open and manifest before thee. Thou beholdest all things, and nothing can be concealed from thee.

"Thou hast seen what Azazyel has done, how he taught every species of iniquity upon the earth and disclosed all the secret things done in the heavens to the world.

"Samyaza also has taught sorcery, to whom thou hast given authority over those who are associated with him. They have gone together to the daughters of men; have lain with them; have become polluted, and have discovered crimes to them.

"The women likewise have brought forth giants. Thus has the whole earth been filled with blood and with iniquity. Now, behold the souls of those who are dead, cry out. They complain even to the gate of heaven. Their groaning ascends; they cannot escape from the unrighteousness committed on earth. Thou knowest all things before they exist. Thou knowest these things, and what has been done by them; yet thou dost not speak to us. What on account of these things ought we to do to them?"

"Then the Most High, the Great and Holy One, spoke and sent Arsayalalyur to the son of Lamech, saying, "Say to him in my name, Conceal thyself. Then explain to him the consummation which is about to take place; for all the earth shall perish; the waters of a deluge shall come over the whole earth, and all things which are in it shall be destroyed. Now teach him how he may escape and how his seed may remain in all the earth."

"Again, the Lord said to Raphael, "Bind Azazyel hand and foot; cast him into darkness, and opening the desert which is in Dudael, cast him in there. Throw upon him hurled and pointed stones, covering him with darkness. There shall he remain forever; cover his face, *that he may not see the light. And in the great day of judgment, let him be cast into the fire.*

"Restore the earth, which the angels have corrupted; and announce life to it, that I may revive it. All the sons of men shall not perish in consequence of every secret, by which the Watchers have destroyed, and which they have taught their offspring. All the earth has been corrupted by the effects of the teaching of Azazyel. To him, therefore, ascribe the whole crime."

"To Gabriel also the Lord said, "Go to the biters, to the reprobates, to the children of fornication; and destroy the children of fornication, the offspring of the Watchers, from among men; bring them forth and excite them one against another. Let them perish by mutual slaughter, for the length of days shall not be theirs.

"They shall all entreat thee, but their fathers shall not obtain their wishes respecting them; for they shall hope for eternal life, and that they may live, each of them, five hundred years."

"The Lord said to Michael, "Go and announce his crime to Samyaza, and to the others who are with him, who have been associated with women, that they might be polluted with all their impurity. When all their sons shall be slain, when they shall see the perdition of their beloved, bind them for seventy generations underneath the earth, even to the day of judgment, and of consummation, until the judgment, the effect of which will last forever, be completed.

"Then shall they be taken away into the lowest depths of the fire in torments, and shall they be shut up forever in confinement. Immediately after this shall he, together with them, burn and perish; they shall be bound until the consummation of many generations.

"Destroy all the souls addicted to dalliance, and the offspring of the Watchers, for they have tyrannized over mankind.

"Let every oppressor perish from the face of the earth; let every evil work be destroyed.

"The plant of righteousness and rectitude appears, and its produce becomes a blessing. Righteousness and rectitude shall be forever planted with delight. Then shall all the saints give thanks, and live until they have begotten a thousand children, while the whole period of their youth and their sabbaths shall be completed in peace. In those days, all the earth shall be cultivated in righteousness; it shall be wholly planted with trees and filled with benediction; every tree of delight shall be planted in it.

"In it shall vines be planted; and the vine which shall be planted in it shall yield fruit to satiety; every seed, which shall be sown in it, shall produce for one measure a thousand; and one measure of olives shall produce ten presses of oil. Purify the earth from all oppression, from all injustice, from all crime, from all impiety, and from all the pollution which is committed upon it. Exterminate them from the earth.

"Then shall all the children of men be righteous, and all nations shall pay me divine honours, and bless me, and all shall adore me. The earth shall be cleansed from all corruption, crime, punishment, and suffering; neither will I again send a deluge upon it from generation to generation forever. In those days, I will open the treasures of blessing which are in heaven, that I may cause them to descend upon earth and upon all the works and labour of man.

"Peace and equity shall associate with the sons of men all the days of the world, in every generation of it."

Ancient Sources

Many notable voices from early history document the bizarre events that took place between the fallen angels and women of earth. A careful look into past records reveals that for many centuries these happenings were understood to have actually taken place. In this next section, we present over a dozen quotes from renowned theologians, apologists, and historians that all verify the story of Genesis 6:1-4:

JOSEPHUS [37 – 100 AD] For many angels of God accompanied with women, and begat sons that proved unjust, and despisers of all that was good, on account of the confidence they had in their own strength; for the tradition is, that these men did what resembled the acts of those whom the Grecians call giants... the giants had bodies so large and countenance so entirely different from other men, that they were amazing to the sight and terrible to the hearing. The bones of these men are still shown to this very day, unlike any credible elations of other men.

CLEMENT OF ALEXANDRIA [150 – 215 AD] ...[Angels] partook of human lust, and being brought under its subjection they fell into cohabitation with women...but from their unhallowed intercourse spurious men sprang, much greater in stature than ordinary men, whom they afterwards called giants... wild in manners, and greater than men in size, inasmuch as they were sprung of angels; yet less than angels, as they were born of women...not being pleased with purity of food, they longed only after the taste of blood, wherefore they first tasted flesh... all things, therefore, going from bad to worse, on account of these brutal demons, God wished to cast them away like an evil leaven, lest each generation from a wicked seed, being like to that before it, and equally impious, should empty the world to come of saved men. And for this purpose, having warned a certain righteous man, with his children, to save themselves in an ark, He sent a deluge of water, that all being destroyed, the purified world might be handed over to him who was saved in the ark, in order [that there might be] a second beginning of life. And thus it came to pass.

IRENAEUS [120/140 – 200/203 AD] For a very long while wickedness extended and spread, and reached and laid hold of the whole race of mankind, until a very small seed of righteousness remained among them and unlawful unions came about on earth, as angels linked themselves with offspring of the daughters of men, who bore to them sons, who on account of their exceeding great size were called Giants. The angels, then, brought to their wives as gifts teachings of evil, for they taught them the virtues of roots and herbs, and dyeing and cosmetics and discoveries of precious materials, love-philtres [magic potions], hatreds, amours, passions, constraints of love, the bonds of witchcraft, every sorcery and idolatry, hateful to God; and when this was come into the world, the affairs of wickedness were propagated to overflowing, and those of justice dwindled to very little.

ATHENAGORAS OF ATHENS [133 – 190 AD] ...These [angels] fell into impure love of virgins, and were subjected by the flesh, and became negligent and wicked in the management of the things entrusted to them. Of these lovers of virgins, therefore, were begotten those who are called giants.

EUSEBIUS [260/265 – 339/340 AD] They [the giants] gave themselves wholly over to all kinds of profanity, now seducing one another, now slaying one another, now eating human flesh, and now daring to wage war with God and to undertake those battles of the giants celebrated by all; now planning to fortify earth against heaven, and in the madness of ungoverned pride to prepare an attack upon the very God of all. On account of these things, when they conducted themselves thus, the all-seeing God sent down upon them floods.

JUSTIN MARTYR [100 – 165 AD] ...God, when He made the whole world, and subjected things earthly to man, and arranged the heavenly elements for the increase of fruits and rotation of the seasons, and appointed this divine law — for these things also He evidently made for man — committed the care of men and of all things under heaven to angels whom He appointed over them. But the angels transgressed this appointment and were captivated by the love of women.

COMMODIAN [Exact lifespan unknown; flourished c. 250 AD] When God Almighty, to beautify the nature of the world, willing that the earth should be visited by angels, when they were sent down they despised His laws. Such was the beauty of women, that it turned them aside; so that, being contaminated, they could not return to heaven. Rebels from God, they uttered words against Him. Then the Highest uttered His judgment against them, and from their seed giants are said to have been born.

CLEMENT OF ROME [35 – 99 AD] ...[Angels] metamorphosed themselves... and partook of human lust, and being brought under its subjection they fell into cohabitation with women; and being involved with them, and sunk into defilement and altogether emptied of their first power, were unable to turn back to the first purity of their nature... But from their unhallowed intercourse, spurious men sprang, much greater in stature than ordinary men, whom they afterwards called giants.

TERTULLIAN [155/160 – 220 AD] We are instructed, moreover, by our sacred books how from certain angels, who fell of their own free will, there sprang a more wicked demon-brood, who were condemned of God along with the authors of their race... there are carcasses of the giants of old times; it will be obvious enough that they are not altogether decayed, for their bony frames are still extant.

SULPICIUS SEVERUS [363 – 420 AD] When by this time the human race had increased to a great multitude, certain angels, whose habitation was in heaven, were captivated by the appearance of some beautiful virgins, and cherished illicit desires after them, so much so, that falling beneath their own proper nature and origin, they left the higher regions of which they were inhabitants, and allied themselves in earthly marriages. These angels gradually spread wicked habits and corrupted the human family, and from their alliance giants are said to have sprung, for the mixture of them of beings of a different nature, as a matter of course, gave birth to monsters.

TATIAN [120 – 173 AD] …[Angels] transgressed their appointment, and were captivated by the love of women, and begat children who are those who are called demons; and besides, they afterwards subdued the human race to themselves, partly by magical writings, and partly by fears and the punishments they occasioned, and partly by teaching them to offer sacrifices, and incense, and libations, of which things they stood in need after they were enslaved by lustful passions; and among men, they sowed murders, wars, adulteries, intemperate deeds, and all wickedness.

JEROME [347 – 419/420 AD] For when the first tiller of paradise had been entangled by the serpent in his snaky coils and had been forced in consequence to migrate earthwards… afterwards sin gradually grew more and more virulent, till the ungodliness of the giants brought in its train the shipwreck of the whole world.

THE BOOK OF JUBILEES [Jewish history book believed to predate the Flood] And in the second week of the tenth jubilee Mahalalel took unto him to wife Dînâh…and she bare him a son in the third week in the sixth year, and he called his name Jared; for in his days the angels of the Lord descended on the earth, those who are named the Watchers, that they should instruct the children of men and that they should do judgment and uprightness on the earth. …[The Watchers] sinned with the daughters of men; for these had begun to unite themselves, so as to be defiled, with the daughters of men, and Enoch testified against (them) all. ...But Noah found grace before the eyes of the Lord. And against the angels whom He had sent upon the earth, He was exceedingly wroth, and He gave commandment to root them out of all their dominion. ...And after this [the time of the flood] they were bound in the depths of the earth forever, until the day of the great condemnation when judgment is executed on all those who have corrupted their ways and their works before the Lord.

Notes

Rahab

https://en.wikipedia.org/wiki/Rahab

https://www.chabad.org/library/article_cdo/aid/112075/jewish/Rahab.htm

https://biblehub.com/commentaries/matthew/1-5.htm

Salmon/Salmah

https://en.wikipedia.org/wiki/Salmon_(biblical_figure)

Salmon and Rahab

https://armstronginstitute.org/359-before-boaz-and-ruth-salmon-and-rahab

Mesopotamia

Mesopotamian Women and Their Social Roles

https://www.historyonthenet.com/mesopotamian-women-in-mesopotamian-society

What Did Mesopotamians Eat in Ancient Civilization?

https://www.historyonthenet.com/what-did-ancient-mesopotamians-eat

https://en.wikipedia.org/wiki/Ancient_Israelite_cuisine

Sacred Marriage and Sacred Prostitution in Ancient Mesopotamia

https://www.historyonthenet.com/sacred-marriage-and-sacred-prostitution-in-ancient-mesopotamia

Love and Marriage in Ancient Mesopotamia

https://www.egypttoday.com/Article/4/40169/Love-and-Marriage-in-ancient-Mesopotamia

Mesopotamian Trade Merchants

https://www.historyonthenet.com/mesopotamia-trade-and-merchants

Mesopotamian Deities

https://en.wikipedia.org/wiki/List_of_Mesopotamian_deities

Giants

The Giant Clans and the Conquest

https://drmsh.com/the-giant-clans-and-the-conquest/

City of Giants and Home of the Mighty Gibborim

https://www.ancientpages.com/2017/06/28/ancient-jericho-city-of-giants-and-home-of-the-mighty-gibborim/

The Amorites

https://www.worldhistory.org/amorite/

Jericho

Map of Ancient Jericho

https://i.pinimg.com/originals/f0/9b/f2/f09bf2fd7c56c522aef44ffe3237340b.jpg

https://www.britannica.com/place/Sweden

Ancient Jericho

https://bryanwindle.files.wordpress.com/2019/05/jericho.png

https://www.britannica.com/place/Jericho-West-Bank

https://www.worldhistory.org/article/951/early-jericho/

https://www.allaboutarchaeology.org/jericho-archaeology.htm

https://www.thearchaeologist.org/blog/ancient-jericho-the-first-walled-city-in-history

Information on Astarte

https://cosmons.com/canaanite-religion/canaanite-gods-and-goddesses/astaroth-goddess-of-love-and-beauty/

https://www.academia.edu/22703519/Goddess_Astarte

The Return of the Gods by Jonathan Cahn

https://www.christianbook.com/return-of-the-gods-jonathan-cahn/9781636411422/pd/411429

Ancient Texts

The Book of Enoch

http://www.ancienttexts.org/library/ethiopian/enoch/1watchers/watchers.htm

www.skywatchtvstore.com

The Book of Jasher

www.skywatchtvstore.com

Phoenicia

Ancient Phoenicia

https://en.wikipedia.org/wiki/Phoenicia

Phoenician Dress

https://phoenicia.org/dress.html

Phoenician Religion

https://factsanddetails.com/world/cat56/sub371/item1983.html

Ancient Sea Travel

https://www.worldhistory.org/video/2586/history-of-ancient-sea-travel-trade-burials-and-ma/

Ancient Sea Map of the Mediterranean Sea

https://webdiplomacy.net/variants/AncMed/cache/sampleMap.png

Egypt

The Great White Pyramid

https://factsanddetails.com/world/cat56/sub371/item1983.html

Amenhotep III

https://en.wikipedia.org/wiki/Amenhotep_III

Ancient Egyptian Sed Festival

https://en.wikipedia.org/wiki/Sed_festival

https://historyofegypt.net/?page_id=5262

The Egyptian Challenger

https://www.nationalgeographic.com/culture/article/pharaoh-king-punished-god#:~:text=The%20identity%20of%20Pharaoh%20in,King%20Ramses%20II%20in%20mind

Ten Plagues and the Ten Gods

https://www.stat.rice.edu/~dobelman/Dinotech/10_Eqyptian_gods_10_Plagues.pdf

Winemaking

https://en.wikipedia.org/wiki/Winemaker

Ancient Woodworking

https://www.wagnermeters.com/moisture-meters/wood-info/history-of-woodworking/

https://dendro.cornell.edu/articles/kuniholm1997b.pdf

Ancient Burial Practices in Judaism

https://www.nationalgeographic.com/culture/article/pharaoh-king-punished-god#:~:text=The%20identity%20of%20Pharaoh%20in,King%20Ramses%20II%20in%20mind.

Information on Nahshon

https://en.wikipedia.org/wiki/Nahshon

https://www.jewishencyclopedia.com/articles/11288-nahshon

https://www.chabad.org/library/article_cdo/aid/2199147/jewish/Nachshon-ben-Aminadav-The-Man-Who-Jumped-Into-the-Sea.htm

Biblical Gilgal

https://www.holylandsite.com/gilgal

https://jesusplusnothing.com/series/post/Joshua5

https://www.breakingchristiannews.com/articles/display_art.html?ID=10348

The Feasts and Festivals of Adonai

Aligning With God's Appointed Times by Rabbi Jason Sobel

https://www.fusionglobal.org/shop/aligning-with-gods-appointed-times/

Sitting at the Feet of Rabbi Jesus by Ann Spangler and Lois Tverberg

https://ourrabbijesus.com/books/sitting-at-the-feet-of-rabbi-jesus/

A Brief History of Shabbat

https://www.chabad.org/library/article_cdo/aid/261818/jewish/A-Brief-History-of-Shabbat.htm

https://www.jewishvoice.org/learn/meaning-shavuot

Ancient mosaics

https://www.mosaicartgallery.com/history-of-mosaics

All Bible quotations

www.biblegateway.com

Canaan

https://www.worldhistory.org/canaan/

The Canaanite Trade Network

https://www.researchgate.net/publication/352875529_The_Canaanite_Trade_Network_between_the_Shores_of_the_Mediterranean-Sea

Article on Ritual Sacrifice of Donkeys in Canaanite Culture

https://www.haaretz.com/archaeology/2018-05-17/ty-article-magazine/sacrificed-donkeys-in-ancient-gath-reveal-canaanite-trade-secrets/0000017f-efcc-d223-a97f-efdde2860000

Research website

https://www.academia.edu/

Kingdoms of Israel and Judah map

https://en.wikipedia.org/wiki/Kingdom_of_Judah#

https://scriptures.info/Images/tc/map3.jpg

Ancient Israelite Cuisine

https://en.wikipedia.org/wiki/Ancient_Israelite_cuisine

Boaz

https://en.wikipedia.org/wiki/Boaz

Anatolia/Turkey

https://www.britannica.com/place/Anatolia

https://www.worldhistory.org/article/1580/lost-civilisations-of-anatolia-gobekli-tepe/

https://www.everyculture.com/To-Z/Turkey.html

https://www.spectator.co.uk/article/does-an-unknown-extraordinarily-ancient-civilisation-lie-buried-under-eastern-turkey/

Mt Sinai & Jewish Weddings

Mt Sinai and Marriage

https://mycharisma.com/spiritled-living/bible-study/exodus-19-the-wedding-at-mt-sinai/

Joel Richardson Sinai to Zion

https://www.amazon.com/Sinai-Zion-Joel-Richardson/dp/1949729079

https://www.israelnationalnews.com/news/280762

Jewish Weddings

https://en.wikipedia.org/wiki/Jewish_wedding

Map of Bethlehem

https://www.mondaymorningmemo.com/wp-content/uploads/2017/12/1749_Map-of-Bethlehem_cropped.jpg

Caleb

https://www.britannica.com/biography/Caleb

https://www.chabad.org/library/article_cdo/aid/4408396/jewish/Who-Was-Caleb.htm

https://en.wikipedia.org/wiki/Caleb

The Twelve Tribes of Israel map

https://en.wikipedia.org/wiki/Twelve_Tribes_of_Israel#/media/File:12_Tribes_of_Israel_Map.svg

About the Author

Sandi K. Wilson is a devoted child of God, a wife happily married to her fellow adventurer, a loving mother of grown children, and a proud Safta (grandmother). A passionate writer and blogger, her love of words has been a lifelong companion. Sandi began with a blog, but it was her deeply personal books that carved her path: one about her father's journey with dementia, another about her grandfather's plight as a POW in WWII, and several stand-alone works exploring themes of faith, courage, and healing.

She is currently writing The House of Adonai—a visionary series of spiritual allegories—and continues to publish through her own imprint, *SKW Publishing*. Her stories invite readers into worlds marked by truth, beauty, and grace.

Sandi's website: www.skwpublishing.com
Sandi's book site: www.sandikwilson.com